DRAGON DESIRE

LISETTE ASHTON

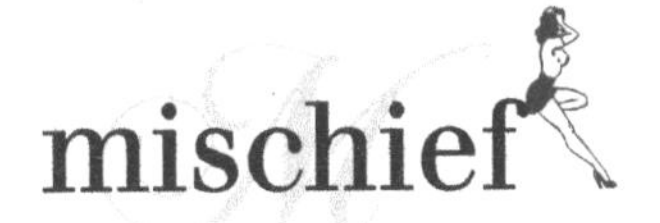

This novel is entirely a work of fiction.
The names, characters and incidents portrayed in it are the work of the author's imagination. Any resemblance to actual persons, living or dead, events or localities is entirely coincidental.

Mischief
An imprint of HarperCollins*Publishers*
77–85 Fulham Palace Road,
Hammersmith, London W6 8JB

www.mischiefbooks.com

A Paperback Original 2013

First published in Great Britain in ebook format by HarperCollins*Publishers* 2012

Lisette Ashton asserts the moral right to be identified as the author of this work

A catalogue record for this book is available from the British Library

ISBN-13: 9780007553280

Find out more about HarperCollins and the environment at
www.harpercollins.co.uk/green

Contents

Prologue

'Dragon horn!' declared Robert of Moon Valley. He said the words the way a court conjurer might whisper *voilà* before triumphantly unveiling the effects of his stage magicks. There was a broad grin across his handsome features. He brushed the fringe of sandy hair from his brow. His leer of devilish anticipation sparkled.

'Dragon horn?'

Tavia and Caitrin asked the question in unison.

Tavia and Caitrin were twin daughters to Duncan, castellan of Blackheath. The young women were famed throughout the Ridings for their complementary beauty. Although their faces were identical, Tavia's tresses were as fair as a unicorn's pelt, whilst Caitrin's locks were as dark as raven wings. Both women were of age, chaste and desired by every able man in the North Ridings.

Tavia took a wary step back toward the chamber door.

Caitrin made an eager step toward the crystal carafe. It

stood surrounded by three silver goblets on a ceremonial tray beside the four-poster bed.

'Dragon horn?' Caitrin marvelled. 'Are you serious? Where did you find it?'

'Are you tempted?' Robert asked. Casually, he toyed with the pendant that hung from a leather strap around his neck. It was a length of pitted iron, black age spots pock-marking the dull metal, the head fashioned to look like a demonic skull. The pendant was reminiscent of the sort of old and archaic key that might open a dungeon doorway.

'Dragon horn has been forbidden by the castellan,' Tavia whispered. 'There shouldn't be a drop of that stuff in the North Ridings. There certainly shouldn't be any in Blackheath.'

'Is it true what it can do?' Caitrin's eyes sparkled as she switched her gaze from Robert to the carafe. She was ignoring her sister, mesmerised by the temptation on offer. 'Is everything I've heard about dragon horn true?'

'What have you heard?'

As he spoke he lifted the crystal carafe and splashed a gill of the golden liquid into each of the three waiting goblets. He didn't need Caitrin to reiterate the legends that were associated with dragon horn. He knew all of them and had made up many more. Dragon horn was a legend amongst legends. Nevertheless, he longed to listen to her whisper all the salacious rumours about the reputed benefits of the drink. There were few things more arousing than the voice of a chaste woman talking about illicit sex.

'I've heard that the sight can melt the clothes from a maiden's bosom,' Caitrin breathed. 'I've heard that the smell can wring a woman's oil from her petticoats. I've heard the taste can fire a princess with such a wanton lust she'd happily rut with slaves and stable lads.'

'Caitrin!' Tavia gasped. 'Where have you heard such things?'

Caitrin wasn't listening to her sister. She had taken a step closer to the goblet. Her nostrils flared as she drank deep lungfuls of air with the obvious hope of inhaling the drink's forbidden aroma.

'I've heard that dragon horn can spark a fire within a woman's nether regions,' she began. She swallowed, shook her head and began again. 'I've heard that dragon horn can spark a fire within a woman's nether regions that is so strong it could melt iron. I've heard it can spark a fire so constant it makes her thighs sweat rivers.'

'I've also heard that,' Robert admitted. He smiled knowingly and said, 'I've *seen* that.'

She gave him a sideways glance. Her eyes had grown wide and the forget-me-not blue irises shone dully. 'I've heard that a taste of dragon horn can harden a healthy man's hardness and lengthen his longing.'

Robert laughed. He used the heel of one hand to rub

at his hip. 'I have also experienced that,' he agreed. 'And it is a truly formidable sight.'

Caitrin stepped closer. Her fingers stretched out toward one of the three goblets. 'I've heard that it heightens the pleasure of the flesh to a degree that makes every other pleasure seem as false and as flat as week-old beggar bread.'

'And I've heard that none of this is true,' Tavia sniffed.

Robert and Caitrin studied her in silence.

Caitrin's fingers fell away from the goblet she had been about to take.

'I've heard that these rumours are nothing more than the lies of rogues and fairy-wing traders,' Tavia said tartly. 'I've heard that the effects of dragon horn are only the self-fulfilling prophecies of idiots and the wilfully deluded.'

Caitrin looked set to respond, but Robert silenced her by raising his hand.

Instead of arguing with Tavia he nodded agreement. 'If that's the case, would you care to take a sip?'

She stepped boldly up to him and snatched a goblet from the ceremonial tray.

Caitrin gasped.

'I'll take more than a sip,' Tavia said. She swallowed the contents in one mouthful. Hurling the goblet to a corner of the room she said, 'And I'll now go and report to my father, the castellan, that you were trying to seduce his daughters with an outlawed drink.'

Robert of Moon Valley said nothing.

Caitrin reached out to grab her sister's arm but Tavia was too quick for her. She was storming toward the doorway of the tower room with a determined stride.

'Tavia,' her sister called. 'Please don't be so hasty. Please wait.'

'The castellan is not known for his leniency toward lawbreakers,' Tavia said over her shoulder. 'Branding? Imprisonment? Banishment? Hanging? Which do you think he will suggest for a man who tries to tempt his chaste daughters with the dubious promise of outlawed dragon horn?'

'Tavia,' Caitrin pleaded. 'Don't tell father. Please. For our sake. For the sake of the fiefdom and the Riding. This could ruin our reputations. It could ruin everything.'

Tavia stopped.

She stopped as though the will to leave the room had suddenly been snatched from her body. She turned slowly to study Robert and Caitrin. There was an expression on her face that Caitrin had never seen before. Tavia studied Robert with a gaze that lingered between loathing and lust.

His wry smile broadened into something made smug with secret knowledge.

'Did you enjoy your drink?'

She rushed at him.

Pushing him backward toward the padding of the

cushions on the four-poster, Tavia devoured Robert's face with kisses that looked as carnal and avaricious as anything that could be witnessed in the North Riding's bedrooms, brothels, or barnyards. She looked as though she was trying to drink the scent of sandalwood from his pores.

She tore at his clothes.

Her painted nails clawed to reach his manliness.

His dark-grey travelling tunic was rent from his shoulders exposing a broad, manly chest. Tavia straddled him as he lay on the bed. She writhed her groin against his loins. Raising her face briefly from his, tossing her head back so that her long blonde curls were no longer covering her features, she murmured, 'Take me.' There was a deep and desperate longing in her voice as she insisted, 'Take me and then take me again.'

She slid a fist around his shaft and groaned as though what she had found there was sadly pleasing. The sound of her heat-fuelled longing echoed from the walls of the tower room.

Robert pushed her to one side. Calmly, he stepped from the bed. A small and roguish smile played at the corners of his lips.

Tavia glared at him from where she lay on the tapestry-covered blankets. She had lifted her skirts to expose her woman parts. Her fingers delved into the wet flesh there and she rubbed at herself with furious determination whilst she fixed his back with a look of venomous fury.

Robert had left his torn tunic on the bed. He stepped out of his hosen and braies revealing an impressive hardness. His length swayed provocatively from between his legs. The end was swollen and ripe, like a plum tomato. He walked over to the ceremonial tray and lifted both the remaining goblets. Swigging the contents from one, he held out the final goblet for Caitrin.

'Will you be joining us, Caitrin of Blackheath?'

There was a taunting challenge in his voice.

Responding with characteristic defiance, she snatched the goblet from his hand and drank.

A week later, when morning sunrise touched the room, it found the three of them in a bed of naked flesh. They were wrapped in sex-damp sheets and ensconced in the stink of delicious satisfaction. Robert remained hard and ready for either sister, although only Caitrin was greedily stroking and sucking at his length. Her sister sat up in the bed examining the carafe.

It lay on its side.

The contents had been drained during the course of their final night together.

She lifted the crystal carafe and sniffed the neck. Her nostrils were touched by the sharp memory of alcohol. Her exposed nipples hardened. A tremor of raw need shivered through her bare flesh. Upturning the bottle she allowed a final single droplet to fall from the rim and touch the pout of her lower lip.

It was only a droplet but it was enough to make her moan with soft urgency.

'Where did this come from?' Tavia asked.

He was called Robert of Moon Valley, but she knew the barren lands of that dark shire could never yield so rich a harvest as dragon horn.

'This dragon horn,' she urged. 'Where did it come from?'

Robert shook his head. Caitrin was trying to kiss him whilst her hand worked swiftly up and down his engorged length. He clutched a clump of her black curls and guided her head back toward the thrust of his erection. Obligingly, she encircled him with her mouth. The sounds of her greedy slurping echoed wetly around the room.

'The source of the dragon horn is a secret,' Robert told Tavia.

But she noticed that his gaze had flitted toward the window.

Nestled on the horizon, across the Last Sea, she could see the lowering shape of Gatekeeper Island. The black specks of a pair of broad-winged dragons circled the temple that sat atop the island's southernmost peak. She had a small fear of dragons. It was a justifiable fear, she thought, considering the creatures had a reputation for burning and killing. But Tavia knew; if there was likely to be a source of dragon horn anywhere in any of the Ridings, it would come from Gatekeeper Island.

CHAPTER ONE

Tavia the Fair

The deadbolt slammed home with deafening force. The clang of metal sang against metal. The sound reverberated through unyielding oak doors set in solid stone walls. Tavia knew the thick silence that came afterwards was locked in the dungeon with her. She swallowed as she studied her surroundings. She struggled not to be afraid. And she doubted the sense of paying two gold pfennigs for this dubious and dangerous privilege.

Blazing torches hung from sconces on the walls. The flames splashed shadows and a glaring orange light onto the cobbled stones of the dungeon floor. Spirals of black smoke spewed upward toward the faraway roof. Sulphuric smells and unearthly stinks crept from the shadowy corners.

'This is not a waste of time.' Tavia muttered the words like a mystical chant, determined to invest them with truth. 'It was not a waste of money. It is not a waste of time.'

She had entered the dungeons against the advice of her twin, Caitrin, and without the knowledge of her father, Duncan, castellan of Blackheath. It had cost her dearly to bribe guards and key-keepers to get this far. And she wouldn't let herself believe that it could all be for nothing. She brushed a stray lock of blonde tresses from her brow and stepped nervously from one foot to the other.

She wore wooden pattens with leather straps. The heels tripped loudly against the stone floor. Drawing a deep breath she tried to decide which way she needed to walk to find the man she had come looking for. A stirring to her right made her hesitate. For an instant she feared she had woken some dangerous and malevolent creature from its slumber.

There was the growl of a man clearing his throat.

She glanced toward the sound. 'Hello?'

'Fuck off,' a voice called. 'I've got a hangover and I'm in no mood for damned visitors.'

Tavia stiffened.

In a corner of the gloomily lit dungeon she glimpsed a shadow. As her eyes became used to the contrast of fire-bright light and pitch-dark shadows she made out the shape of a figure slumped over an escritoire. He was round-shouldered, slovenly in silhouette and hunched like a predatory reptile.

'Seer?' she asked doubtfully.

He raised his head and fixed her with a sullen glower.

There was a dirty smear of beard stubbling his cheeks and jaw. Even in the black and orange of the dungeon's illumination, Tavia could see that his eyes were red from the memories of too much ale. A mop of unkempt hair, dishevelled and as dark as winter nights, fell loosely over his brow.

He picked up a pewter tankard and sniffed the contents. A sneer of disgust wrinkled his lips. Reluctance shaped his features into a frown. And yet, he drank from the tankard anyway. As Tavia watched he drained the contents.

'Seer?' she repeated. 'Is that you?'

'No. I'm not a seer. I'm a prisoner. Now fuck off.'

She was annoyed to catch herself thinking of him as handsome. She supposed it must be a remnant of the dragon horn floating through her system. There had been times since taking the dragon horn when she found herself admiring men whom she normally wouldn't have considered worthy as suitors or lovers. There had been times since taking the dragon horn when she had briefly lusted after farm hands, serfs and night soil workers. Her interest in this uncouth specimen seemed an obvious illustration of that condition. Unsettled by the moody glint in this man's eye, and appalled by her own growing need for him, she willed herself to believe that his appeal was merely an after-effect of the dragon horn. She told herself that was the only reason why her loins were now warming.

'You are Alvar, son of Erland.' Tavia stepped closer as she spoke. Her heels clipped crisply against the cobbled floor. She wished she felt as confident as she sounded. 'You were the famed seer from the Red River. You were respected counsel to Kendric of Cambrai Typus. You were –'

'I've had a change of career,' he broke in. 'I'm now the prisoner of sc tanhole dungeons. I no longer have the gift of second sight. I just have a tankard and a bucket. Now don't let the dungeon door bang your arse on your way out of here.'

Tavia glared at him.

This was not going as she had hoped, but she knew, if skill at negotiations had been easy, her own well-honed abilities to influence and manipulate would have little worth. Quashing her exasperation, refusing to let the emotion show on her features, she fixed him with a politic smile.

'What a shame,' she muttered.

She had come to him dressed in formal military surcoat over her red and gold kirtles. The surcoat was emblazoned with the silver-on-black arms of the Order of Dark Knights. The Order of Dark Knights was an elite military unit headed by the castellan of Blackheath.

Wearing the formal surcoat over her best kirtles, Tavia felt reassured by the protection that came from the symbol of silver swords crossed over a stone tower. It seemed a more imposing motif than her family heritage of three golden water-carrying maids on a crimson background.

She glimpsed the arms of the Order of Dark Knights as she reached into the folds of her skirts to remove a cloth purse. The sight gave her a surge of confidence.

'I can do this,' she whispered.

The cloth purse was heavy. The gold pieces it contained rattled together. Tavia shook the purse lightly, allowing the coins inside to chatter. There was a distinctive sound to gold on gold that she had never heard replicated by any other metals scratching together.

She saw the seer stiffen and tilt his head, as though listening.

He was clearly familiar with the sound of money.

'I had wanted to do business with a seer.'

Tavia said the words as though she was speaking to herself. She shook the purse again. The musical chink of gold on gold rang from the dungeon walls.

'But, if you no longer have the gift of second sight, Alvar, son of Erland, then I'll leave you to your tankard and your bucket. I shall say prayers to the benevolent gods that you don't confuse those two receptacles too often. And I'll wish you a good morrow.'

Turning away from him, she started toward the dungeon doorway.

It was a calculated bluff. But she knew that all successful negotiations were nothing more than calculated bluffs. And Tavia prided herself on being a mistress of successful negotiations.

She didn't hear him follow her.

He moved from his escritoire with a stealth that she would later consider chilling. She had taken three brisk steps toward the dungeon doorway when he placed his right hand on her right hip and clamped his left hand over her mouth.

Her gasp of surprise was muffled beneath his palm.

She was spun until she faced him.

The purse of coins fell heavily to the floor.

There was a clatter of gold rolling over cobbles.

Tavia's stifled squeal of surprise was lost beneath the sound of money rolling away from her on the darkened floor. Her heartbeat raced as she realised she was in the arms of a strong and powerful man. He had a gaze that made her loins melt with sultry need. The musky scent of his nearness made her yearn for him.

'Is this some sort of trick?' he whispered.

She waited until he had removed his hand from her mouth. She liked that he was holding her tight. She could feel the thrust of his rigid manliness. It pressed from his loins, through his rich obsidian tunic, toward her stomach. It struck her that he wanted her as greedily as she wanted him. She stifled that thought, knowing that throwing herself at the seer at this stage would not help with the delicate negotiations she was trying to make.

'Is this some sort of trick?' he repeated.

'You're supposed to be the seer,' she replied. 'You tell me if this is a trick.'

In the light of the raw orange flames his eyes glittered with menace. He inhaled deeply and for an instant she saw something that resembled a smile crossing his lips.

And then the expression was gone.

With a grunt of frustration he pushed her from his embrace.

Tavia stumbled and almost fell to the floor.

'Get down on your knees and pick up your gold,' he snapped. His voice sounded hurt and angry. 'Gold coins are of no use to me in this dungeon. Nothing is of any use to me in this damned dungeon; so you can take your gold coins and your nice-smelling hair and you can fuck off.'

She glared at him.

She was thankful for the poor light because it hid her blushes. He thought she had nice-smelling hair. The compliment struck her as being absurdly touching. She was grateful that someone had noticed she washed her blonde curls in a balsam of lemon and orange oils. But she wasn't sure she wanted to be touched by the seer's praise.

'I knew you weren't a real seer,' she scoffed. 'I knew you didn't have the gift of sight.'

He reached into the pocket of his tunic. When he pulled his hand free she saw he was holding a well-thumbed deck of tarot. He rolled his shoulders and shuffled the cards with one hand. For a man who looked as though he had been dragged from the depths of a grog-induced slumber, his fingers worked on the deck with surprising agility.

She stared up at him as he stood with his back to one of the torches. He was nothing more than a silhouette but she thought his shape seemed to grow as he handled the cards.

She had seen expert swordsmen demonstrate skill in the mastery of their craft and believed it was always a pleasure to watch any competent artist excelling in their field. She had watched horsemen breaking wild stallions and she had witnessed gifted sculptors carving great statues. She had seen the smiths and tailors showing off their talents in demonstrations of more commonplace skill, craft and artisan mastery. But she had never before seen a man who was so clearly in love with his own vocation as the seer was with his gift of second sight.

Alvar, son of Erland, beamed as he shuffled the cards.

He pulled one from the deck and studied it with a single cocked eyebrow.

'Your name is Tavia, twin sister to Caitrin and younger

sister of Inghean. You're the daughter of Duncan, castellan of Blackheath.'

She started to pluck the gold coins from the floor. It had not been the impressive display of second sight she had hoped to witness. 'You could have recognised me from your dealings in Blackheath. I'm known in my father's court. You might even have overheard the gaoler addressing me before I came in here.'

Alvar sniffed.

He plucked another card from the top of the deck and studied it with an unreadable gaze. 'You've recently had an experience.'

She flashed a silencing gaze in his direction.

He chuckled. It was a low and lewd sound but not entirely unpleasant. He studied the tarot card in the fluttering torch light as though it showed moving pictures. 'It seems it was a very exciting experience,' he decided. 'A pleasant experience. And it's clearly an experience you want to repeat.'

Tavia's blushes deepened.

She figured she had retrieved as many of the gold coins as she was likely to find in the dark. Drawing the strings on the purse closed she put it back into her kirtles as she stood up.

'The cards seem to tell you so much and so little,' she said primly. 'Perhaps your cards could say some things that don't sound like the cold-reading comments of a cheap court conjurer?'

Idly, he plucked another from the pack and studied it before responding. 'The cards tell me that you're willing to do a lot in return for my assistance. Is that true?'

'I have gold.'

She reached for the purse but he stopped her. The warmth of his hand on hers was surprisingly pleasing. She wanted to refuse the suggestion of pleasure that came from his touch.

'I have a life sentence to serve in this dungeon. As I've already told you, I own a tankard and a bucket. With those essentials covered, I don't have a lot of need for your gold.'

'What do you want?'

His lips settled into a businesslike frown that she wanted to kiss.

'I want three things,' he decided eventually. 'First and foremost, I want you to organise my freedom from these dungeons.'

'I can try to organise something,' she allowed. 'I can't promise success because I'm a mere maid and –'

'You *will* petition for my freedom,' he broke in. 'Your father is Duncan, castellan of Blackheath. You're one of his daughters and he is sufficiently corrupt to heed the advice of his kith and kin in matters of justice.'

He raised his hand to stop her from interrupting.

'The cards tell me you will do all that for me.'

Perplexed, she asked, 'What else do the cards tell you I'll do?'

He plucked a card from the top of the deck. It made the crisp sound of stiff paper snapping from the darkness.

'The cards tell me you're going to suck my cock.'

Tavia rolled her eyes. She had expected he would try something sexual. A part of her was almost tempted to go along with his suggestion because she did find him vaguely attractive. The heat from the dragon horn still nestled in her loins making her hungry for the taste of a man. But she had hoped the seer would try something that didn't sound like such a blatant insult to her intelligence.

'Good morrow, Alvar, son of Erland,' she said tiredly. 'Thank you for being honest with me earlier and admitting that you are no longer a seer. I'm sorry I didn't believe you.'

She turned her back on him and headed toward the dungeon doorway.

Behind her she heard the sound of him flicking another tarot card from the top of the deck.

'Do you want to hear my third condition?' he called.

'Not really.' She tossed the words back over her shoulder. 'I'm bored now.'

He sniffed. 'My third condition is not open for negotiation. I want a share in the dragon horn you're going to import.'

Tavia stopped. She turned and glared at him. 'How the hell did you know about the dragon horn?'

'Suck my dick and we'll talk about that.'

'If you were a genuine seer …' she began. She shook her head. That wasn't what she wanted to say. 'If you were able to offer me some genuine assistance …' Again, that wasn't quite right. 'If I didn't think you were an absolute charlatan,' she decided finally, 'I might consider your proposal. But –'

'How much more proof do you need that I'm a genuine seer?'

He asked the question with a forced innocence. Snapping a card from the top of the deck he glanced at the contents and then said, 'You're not wearing braies.'

She blushed. It was true. She wasn't wearing undergarments beneath her kirtles. But he could have guessed she wasn't wearing braies.

'So?'

He snapped another card from the top of the tarot.

'You had twenty-five golden pfennigs in your purse when you set off this morning. But now you've only got twenty-three. I don't know if two of them are still on the floor of this dungeon from when you dropped your purse. Or if you used the other two pfennigs to bribe your way in here. But there are now only twenty-three pfennigs in your purse.'

Tavia caught a startled breath. He was right. She had counted twenty-five golden pfennigs into her purse before leaving home that morning. The guard had insisted on two gold pfennigs in payment for opening the dungeon door. She studied the seer with renewed respect.

Was it possible that he really did have the gift of sight?

'Tell me something that only I would know,' Tavia demanded. 'Tell me something that no one else in the world but me could know.'

He pulled another card from the top of the deck.

His salacious smile glittered in the darkness. When he glanced up to grin at her she could see the sexual interest that sparkled in his gleaming eyes.

'You masturbated twice this morning. Once with a carrot.' He winked and added, 'You came hard with the carrot because it was pushed into your arsehole.'

Tavia stepped back. 'I'faith,' she gasped. She touched her brow to ward off the dangers of the evil eye.

'Now, if that's enough proof for you, you can get down on your knees and suck my cock,' he said boldly. 'It won't suck itself you know.'

She didn't hesitate.

Falling swiftly to her knees, Tavia lifted the hem of his tunic to find his braies. The linen pants, tied at the waist and hanging down to his knees, were distended at the crotch by the bulge of his excitement. She stroked the shape of him with sincere and hungry affection.

'Go on,' he urged. 'Suck it.'

She reached for the drawstring at his waist. As the braies fell to his ankles she pushed back the folds of his tunic to expose the thick length of his throbbing manhood.

A swatch of curls as dark as those on his head, covered his sac. The pale stalk of his erection protruded snake-like from the forest of his dark hairs. She traced a finger against the sweat-slick skin and sighed when she reached the swollen end of his glans. It was fat, bulbous and already dewy with arousal.

Tavia did not lay claim to any gifts of second sight but she could tell that Alvar, son of Erland, wanted her as badly as she wanted him. She stroked her thumb over the rounded end of his erection and watched him shiver with need.

'Don't just tickle it,' he mumbled. 'I've asked you to suck the damned thing.'

She moved her face close to him and allowed her long blonde tresses to caress his shaft. Positioning her head carefully she blew soft breath against the side of his length. Savouring the way he squirmed she moved closer and drew her tongue against him.

He gasped.

During the week when she had first been introduced to the pleasures of the flesh, as she languished in the highest tower of Blackheath Priory between bouts of tasting Robert's dragon horn and the hours when she watched her sister lie beneath him, Tavia had taken pains to learn how best she could satisfy the needs of a man.

Robert of Moon Valley was not a patient lover but he was precise and particular. Because they had been drinking dragon horn, an elixir noted for improving the pleasures of sex, he insisted that those pleasures they enjoyed were of an exacting standard from the beginning. He had been meticulous and instructive in every aspect of intercourse. He had gone to great lengths to school Tavia in the proper ways for a woman to use her mouth on a man's flesh, and the memory of his words now echoed in her thoughts as a reminder of how she could best please Alvar, son of Erland.

She savoured the taste of the seer's clean sweat, murmuring appreciatively as she worked her tongue from the curls at his balls up to the tip of his erection. Robert of Moon Valley had told her that a man liked to hear murmurs of appreciation from the woman lapping at his length and she felt sure that Alvar would take satisfaction from her sighs of approval. Her hands clutched at his thighs as she pressed her face closer.

It crossed her mind that she wasn't doing everything just for the pleasure of Alvar. A good deal of what she was doing was adding to the burgeoning swell of her personal satisfaction. A fat balloon of excitement swelled in her stomach. It wasn't large to the point of bursting – yet. But she knew that moment would soon come and undoubtedly make her crave further pleasures.

His hands fell to her hair.

He tugged at her long, blonde tresses.

Spikes of pain bristled through her scalp. She wanted to brush his hands away, unhappy with the flares of discomfort and not sure she wanted him trying to control her. But she did like that he was exerting some authority. She also wanted to give him a memorable bout of satisfaction, so allowed him to think he was in control.

This was sex without dragon horn.

Tavia knew that sex without dragon horn would only ever be a pale shadow of what she could hope to enjoy until she was again relishing the effects of the elixir's anise-rich flavour. And, whilst common sense told her that she had to make the experience good for Alvar in order to make it pleasurable for herself, Tavia also knew that Alvar's enjoyment of this experience was of paramount importance. If the seer was content with the way she pleasured him, he would be more likely to give her the help that came from his gift of second sight.

'Suck it,' he groaned. 'I want to feel your mouth around me.'

She didn't do as he commanded. There was a difference between making the experience pleasurable for both of them and doing everything that the seer bade.

Once his length was slathered with the wetness from her tongue, she pursed her lips and blew at him again. His erection throbbed with sullen heat. She knew his flesh would be bristling beneath the slick liquid layer of saliva she had lapped against him. As her chilly breath blew against him she knew he would be relishing the rush of warming and cooling sensations.

Briefly she wished she had been born a man, so she could experience some of the magnificent pleasure she was bestowing on the privileged and fortunate seer. Then she shut that thought from her mind, knowing that none of Alvar's pleasures would ever compare to those that she had enjoyed under the influence of dragon horn, nor those that she planned to savour in the future.

She was squatting in front of him. The hem of her kirtles was hitched up so the red and gold fabrics weren't touching the dirt of the dungeon floor. Tavia urgently pressed two fingers against the wetness between her legs.

Her flesh was warm and moist.

Her fingers slipped inside with such ease it tore a gasp of surprise from her throat. She pushed deeper, delighted by the way her velvet depths parted to accommodate the plundering fingers. The sensation of being spread and filled was so sudden and intense it left her momentarily breathless.

'Are you touching yourself?' he asked.

She moved her mouth from his length. 'Yes,' she answered truthfully. 'Why do you ask?'

She glanced up and saw he was shaking his head in disbelief.

'You're possibly the horniest wench I've ever encountered. I truly have to see what you're like when you're drinking dragon horn because I think you'd likely suck me inside out.'

'Does that mean I can rely on your fealty to my quest?' she asked.

'Suck my cock until I've finished,' he said.

The words were spat with the urgent insistence of a man on the brink of climax. His hands tightened in the blonde tresses they held. He tried to guide her face forcefully to return to his erection.

'Suck my cock and we can discuss your quest and my fealty once you've swallowed every drop of my spend.'

She continued to stare up at him, refusing to let him control how she delivered his pleasure.

'How do you know I'll swallow your spend? How do you know I won't spit your seed to the cobbled stones of the dungeon floor?'

He smiled down at her. 'I am Alvar, son of Erland,' he explained. 'I am the famed seer of the Red River. I was intimate counsel to Kendric of Cambrai Typus. I know the future.' He chuckled with a confidence so strong it was almost tangible. 'And you, Tavia of Blackheath, are going to swallow every drop of spend I squirt into your mouth.'

The fingers between her legs pressed with renewed haste. She could hear the faraway squelch of her wetness slurping greedily. As she rubbed back and forth, the blossoming eddies of delight began to sparkle in her hypersensitive nerve-endings. Her inner muscles clenched and convulsed hungrily.

'Suck me,' he insisted.

She finally placed her mouth around his end. She stretched her lips wide to encircle his glans. He was large and she found that trait to be exciting. After placing a gentle kiss on the tip of his shaft she sucked lightly against him.

'At last,' he sighed. 'Keep doing that.'

She kept one hand between her own legs whilst the other went to the base of his shaft. Holding him tight between her fingers she worked her mouth wetly back and forth along his length. All the time she tried sucking on him, maintaining a wet vacuum of pressure on his shaft. And, all the time, she could taste the flavour of his nearing climax as it filled her mouth.

'Go on,' he insisted. 'That's what I want.'

It was impossible to stifle the wet sounds of enthusiasm she was making as she used her mouth on him. She was almost spluttering with the need to giggle happily as she savoured the quickening taste of his excitement and listened to the guttural grunts of his mounting pleasure.

Her fingers rubbed swiftly against her cleft. The inner muscles of her sex were drenched with their liquid heat and the outer lips tingled with the encroaching rush of satisfaction.

'Go on,' he urged. 'Suck me faster. Suck me quicker. Swallow it all, you horny wench. Swallow it all.'

She allowed him to push against the back of her throat.

The swollen end of his length felt too large. Robert had sung the praises of any maiden willing to part-swallow a man's length. But Tavia wasn't sure she could manage the feat for Alvar. If there had been dragon horn, she knew the drink would have made her throat muscles relax enough to swallow anything that was put in her mouth.

But, without the dragon horn, she was in unfamiliar territory.

Nevertheless, because it was now important to her that the seer should be deeply satisfied by this encounter, she urged her throat to accept him and she tried to guide his end deeper into her mouth.

'Damn,' he gasped. The exclamation came out in a hoarse croak. There was honest reverence in his tone. 'You know how to pleasure a man, don't you?'

She said nothing as she pushed her face closer to him.

She was inhaling the musk of his pubic curls. Her throat ached from the pressure of his swollen glans. She fought the gag reflex that made her want to wretch his shaft from her mouth.

But, throughout the month that had passed since she first tasted dragon horn, Tavia did not think any sexual encounter had ever been more satisfying.

She kept the seer at the back of her throat and then swallowed. Her throat muscles clenched down on the bulbous end of his length. For him, she thought, the pressure must have been both exquisite and unbearable.

Alvar groaned. His hands clutched tightly at her scalp. She felt him pull her face close. And then his length was trembling with the explosion of a climax. The eruption tore itself from her throat as his length pulsed and shivered and then pulled free. A spurt of white-hot ejaculate slathered her tongue and washed the inside of her mouth. She was only just registering the taste, and the rush of cloying wetness, when his length pulsed and spurted again.

'Damn,' he croaked.

The whisper of his word was a stark contrast to the power of the ejaculate erupting from his loins.

He spurted a third time.

And a fourth.

Tavia almost choked trying to swallow all the spend he was shooting into her mouth. As soon as she had closed her throat on one thick and creamy mouthful it felt as though he had already filled her cheeks to bulging. She could taste him with every breath and knew the flavour of his climax would be with her for the rest of the day. It was a scent she would happily inhale later when she gently frotted herself to sleep.

That thought made her realise that her fingers had stopped sliding in and out of the wet crease between her legs. Rather than trying to cajole her own pleasure with subtle manipulation she realised there were three fingers jammed deep into her sex. The tips were pushed firm against the deliciously sensitive pad at the front of her innermost muscles.

Tavia squeezed her palm hard against the throbbing nub of her clitoris.

It was as much as she needed to push her body beyond the precipice of pleasure. She gasped and relished the rush of satisfaction as it rippled through her body.

And, although she had tried to maintain her balance whilst she squatted on the floor to suck the seer, an involuntary twitch of her leg muscle sent her sprawling. She cried out in protest, surprised by the way her body was trying to dump her so unceremoniously on the dungeon floor. She snatched her hand hurriedly from her sex in a bid to stop herself from falling.

Alvar caught her with one hand.

She stared at him, surprised to find him holding her wrist.

'Here,' he said, helping her to stand. 'Thank you for pleasuring me so efficiently, Tavia of Blackheath.'

He raised her wrist to his lips and kissed her hand.

It was the hand she had just used to finger herself to climax. His kiss lingered on the wet knuckles. His eyes studied her as his lips continued to caress the oily flesh of her fingers. Slowly, once she was safely standing up, he lowered himself on one knee. At no point did he ever let his lips leave her hand.

'I pledge my fealty to Tavia of Blackheath and her

quest for the dragon horn,' he declared. 'Is that what you wanted to hear?'

She allowed him to continue kissing her knuckles, excited by the way he seemed to be lapping the flavour of her sex from her fingers.

'Your pledge of fealty will do for the moment,' she allowed. 'Although I'd appreciate it if you could also tell me how I shall find the source of the dragon horn.'

'Petition for my release,' he insisted. 'Once I'm free from these dungeons then you can put me on the birlinn that the castellan will have waiting in the west harbour. That vessel will transport us both to the source of the dragon horn. But I won't say any more until you've petitioned for my release.'

He climbed up from his knee and kissed her on the lips.

His tongue explored her mouth and she knew he was tasting the remnants of his own ejaculate from her kiss. She was not surprised to feel a stiffness return to his loins as their tongues intertwined and he drank his own flavour. She wondered if he was more excited by the passion of their kiss or his narcissistic delight in tasting himself. It was a cruel and uncharitable thought, she supposed, but that did not mean it was any less accurate.

'Will we find the source of the dragon horn?' she demanded. 'Is it really within our power? How long will it take? And will we be able to get dragon horn into the North Ridings without upsetting my father the castellan?'

Alvar, son of Erland, patted Tavia gently on the rear. He bent down and pulled up his braies, cinching the drawstring tight around his waist.

'Go and petition for my release,' he told her. 'Once I'm a free man I'll give you all the answers you want.' His smile was broad with lewd meaning as he added, 'I'll give you all the answers you want, and anything else you desire.'

She said nothing.

Although she knew he was a seer, and bound to tell the truth by virtue of his vocation, Tavia was suddenly struck by the worry that it might be unwise to place all her trust in Alvar, son of Erland.

CHAPTER TWO

Caitrin the Dark

Caitrin stole into the mage's private offices with the stealth of a noble Greek hero on a bold and daring quest. She was Jason retrieving the Golden Fleece from Colchis; she was Odysseus plundering the harbour of the Laestrygonian's island; she was Theseus venturing into the labyrinth at Crete. Caitrin quivered with the excitement of what she might achieve.

She had slipped past the mead-asleep guard at the base of the stairs and tiptoed up the stone steps of the tower. She had kept to the shadows of the unsconced stairwell, wary that her errand would be hard to explain if she met the wrong pair of eyes. Softly, she whispered to the gods that protected Blackheath with a prayer that her actions would be fruitful but unnoticed.

And it was as easy as sunset.

The lock on the thick oak door was no trouble. She

used the pin from the brooch on the breast of her kirtles to force the tumblers into an easy acquiescence. The brooch showed three maids carrying water: gold on an enamelled crimson background.

The tumblers clicked noisily as she worked them into submission.

Accompanied by the sigh of the age-old hinge as it complained about the door's movement, Caitrin crept cautiously into the mage's lair.

It was a room she had visited many times before, but never alone. The air was sweetened by scents of cinnamon and spent candles. A brass spyglass stood in one window. She saw a crystal ball, an astrological chart and the paraphernalia of divination tools cluttering a central counter. Wooden shelves lined the walls. All of them were filled to the brink of catastrophe with jars, books and ancient scrolls.

Her heartbeat quickened.

Not for the first time that month, she was touched by the thrill of knowing she was engaged in a forbidden act. The blood rushed more quickly through her veins. A heated longing surged in her loins. The sultry wetness of need blossomed in her sex and its insistence forced her to hold her breath. But now was not the time to suffer arousal, she told herself. Now was not the time to be distracted by the siren call of her constant sexual excitement.

For this moment she had to remain focused.

There was enough twilight lingering in the sky to keep the room well-lit. She guessed that the windows in the east and west walls kept the tower room bright from dawn until dusk. Through the east window she could see the oncoming night sky as sable as the cloaks worn by the castellan's Order of Dark Knights. The tower room's formidable height allowed her to see the glow and flicker of torches lighting cottage windows up to the fiefdom's walls and beyond. If there had been a glimpse of Jack-o'-Lantern or Jenny-Burnt-Tale in the Howling Forest to the east of the fiefdom, Caitrin knew she would have seen both of those spectres from this vantage point.

The west window stared out to the silvered waves that rippled on the Last Sea. The day's sinking sun sizzled into the horizon beyond. She could see the silhouette masts and sails of knörr, cogs and hulc idling in the harbour. She could see a faraway crew were working on furling the sail of a large birlinn that dominated the port this evening. The west window showed the taverns and trading square of Blackheath's commercial streets. But it was the distant harbour with the glittering seas and the lazily pitching and yawing boats where her gaze lingered.

The sky through this window was a blaze of brilliant yellows, fading up through a spectrum of darkening peaches and lowering reds. Caitrin was struck by a sudden and stinging certainty that her destiny lay in the direction of the harbour.

The idea caused a prickle of icy foreboding to tickle down her spine.

Shaking her head, knowing there was no time to be wasted admiring the view from the mage's offices and speculating on the uncertainties of tomorrow, Caitrin hurried to the shelves on the north wall and studied the jars that were kept there.

A faraway noise made her hesitate.

It was a heavy clatter that sounded like boots on stone steps.

She swallowed down the rising taste of panic and told herself that the guard had not woken and he was not making a patrol of the rooms under his charge. Even if such a catastrophic situation was occurring, Caitrin knew the guard would not enter the mage's offices. It was only her dread of discovery that was causing her to tremble with apprehension.

Inwardly she cursed the fact that her body was becoming excited by the idea of being caught. Her stiffening nipples pressed tight against the cotton of her red and gold kirtles. The muscles deep within her sex tingled through a greedy desire for satisfaction. She supposed the responses were all residual effects of the dragon horn that lingered in her blood. But rationalising those responses did not soften the urgency of her needs.

Ignoring the threat of faraway sounds, convinced they were nothing more than echoes from her imagination, she stepped up to the shelves and considered the rows upon rows of stoppered glass jars.

The jars gleamed in the dusk light as though they had all been recently polished. Caitrin could see the contents in each one. Some contained murky liquids, moving ominously of their own volition. Others were filled with disconcerting items such as eyeballs, tongues or locks of hair. All of them were labelled on white card written with the painstaking precision of the mage's exact hand. The labels, Caitrin noted, were in the same order in which she'd been taught her letters as a girl.

That would make things easier, she supposed. She traced her finger along the shelves in search of the cards beginning with the letter D.

Demon Claws. Diamond Milk. Dodo Feathers.

Dog Hairs were stored next to Duck Feet.

From what she recalled of her letters, dragon horn should have sat between those two jars. But there was no jar labelled dragon horn. There wasn't even an empty space where a jar should have been.

'Fie,' she muttered.

She turned to the H section of the jars and her hopes were briefly raised. There was a section dedicated solely to animal horn.

Horn: Buffalo.

Horn: Chameleon.

Horn: Griffin.

'Fie!'

If there had been a jar labelled 'Horn: Dragon' Caitrin knew it would have sat between Chameleon and Griffin. She stamped her foot angrily on the floor, annoyed that she had risked so much in stealing into the mage's office and all without achieving any gain.

'Fie! Fie! Fie!'

'Quite the foul-mouthed little trespasser, aren't you?'

Caitrin glanced toward the sound of the voice.

She hadn't seen the door open and she hadn't seen the mage enter the room. Now she realised that Nihal stood blocking the doorway. There was no way to escape. She clutched one small hand over her mouth to contain the squeal of surprise that wanted to escape.

'Who are you and what are you doing in my offices?'

'I'm sorry, Nihal,' Caitrin began. 'I was trespassing. Please forgive –'

'You're not sorry yet.' Nihal's voice rang from the stone walls of the tower. The words were not shouted but there was no denying the authority with which they were spoken. 'You're not sorry yet. But you will be sorry if you don't tell me who you are and what you're doing here.'

The mage looked resplendent in a crimson cowled robe tied at the waist with a ceremonial gold cord. Youngest of the castellan's household wizards, a migrant from the southernmost borders of the North Ridings, Nihal was a mage with a deserved reputation as the most powerful master of magicks in the whole of Blackheath. Nihal cast spells to end the cold cruelty of the long winter nights. Nihal made the first flowers bloom in spring. And, Caitrin had heard it said, Nihal could draw the truth from reluctant lips as effortlessly as the farm maids drew milk from the cows.

Goosebumps prickled her flesh.

Her nipples stiffened.

'Nihal,' she whispered. 'It's me, Caitrin. Don't you recognise me?'

'A shape-changer would likely visit my offices in Caitrin's form,' Nihal growled. 'It's known I have a tenderness for the castellan's dark-haired daughter.'

She touched a hand to her coal-black tresses.

'You have a tenderness for me?'

Caitrin could not stop the smile from sitting on her lips. She had never realised Nihal had a tenderness for her. The thought was warming and made her suddenly yearn for the mage. Her heartbeat quickened.

'You should have said something,' she began. 'Perhaps you and I –'

'Stand up straight,' the mage barked.

Her body reacted instantaneously to the command. She stood stiff, as though her backbone had been replaced by a pikestaff. The idea that Nihal was controlling her actions and movements inspired a thrill of helpless excitement.

Standing rigid, Caitrin felt as though it was only her eyes that could move.

Her gaze scoured the room for some hope of salvation.

She studied Nihal and tried to silently beg for leniency.

It was impossible to see the wizard's face. The hood of the ceremonial cowl was drawn forward to throw shadows over the mage's features. In the dwindling light of the offices, Caitrin caught only the occasional flash of bright almond eyes and dazzling teeth fixed into a cruel smile. It was a combination she found unsettling and yet deeply and darkly attractive.

'You do look like Caitrin, the castellan's daughter,' Nihal admitted. 'So you're either her, or you're a very skilled shape-changer. I'm curious to discover which.'

'I am her,' Caitrin insisted. 'Why would a shape-changer visit your offices?'

A wand appeared in the mage's hand. It was a fifteen-inch length of bitternut hickory, as thick as Caitrin's thumb and tipped with a silver cap. The silver tip glowed a dull cerise, although Caitrin wasn't sure if it was a reflection from the settling sun, the nearness of the mage's robes or some magical power lighting the wand.

She swallowed thickly.

The sight of the wand stirred a slick and fluid warmth in her loins.

'By the power of all the magicks I command,' Nihal's voice boomed from the walls. The brightness in the offices briefly intensified.

Caitrin couldn't imagine where the extra light came from.

'By the power of all the magicks I command,' Nihal repeated, 'you will tell me now your true identity.'

'I'm Caitrin, youngest of the castellan's three daughters,' Caitrin admitted. 'I'm Caitrin, twin to Tavia and younger sister of Inghean. Don't you recognise me, Nihal? I'm Caitrin.'

Something in the stoop of the mage's shoulders suggested Nihal was not yet convinced. 'I don't believe you're a shape-changer,' Nihal allowed. The mage began to circle her. 'Yet I still have my doubts. You seem different from the Caitrin who last visited my offices. Why would that be?'

Caitrin blushed.

Only able to move her eyes, she lowered her gaze.

She was a different person from the Caitrin who had previously visited Nihal's offices and she knew why she was different. Before, she had been a girl who knew nothing of men, the pleasures of the flesh or the significant wonders of dragon horn. Now, she was a woman with a woman's knowledge of such forbidden secrets.

But the idea of admitting as much to Nihal was unthinkable.

'Please don't force me to tell you the truth,' she begged. She was going to say that she would explain things in her own way and in her own time. She was going to add that the truth was unladylike, unflattering and unbecoming.

But Nihal did not allow her to say the words.

The mage thrashed the wand through the air.

Caitrin had thought she saw a cerise glow originally. This time she was certain she saw a flash of coloured light. Its aftermath fizzled in the air behind the tip of the wand. And, whilst that would have been impressive to behold – a private display of fireworks and pyrotechnics from the castellan's most powerful mage – she was more startled by the fact that her kirtle disappeared with the gesture.

Caitrin gasped.

Her crimson and gold brooch fell to the floor where it tinkled loudly in the silence of the offices.

Again Nihal thrashed the wand through the air.

This time her undershirt disappeared. Caitrin shrieked as the clothes were torn away by invisible hands.

Thrash.

Another flash of dark, pink light.

Her chemise, breast girdle and braies disappeared in the same instant.

One moment she had stood before the wizard in her underclothes. She had been inexplicably erect and standing as still and motionless as a child playing gargoyles. And in the next moment she was stripped bare and touched by the chill of the room's coolness against her naked flesh.

She gasped.

Her eyes opened wide in astonishment. She glanced down at herself and saw that her bare body was completely uncovered. Her breasts, well-rounded and firm, were revealed to the mage. The secrets of her sex, the dark curls shorn into the same fashions that Robert had said were in vogue amongst revered courtiers and courtesans from the palaces of the Southern Kingdoms, were exposed to Nihal.

The mage took a step back.

'Caitrin,' Nihal murmured with approval. 'It seems you've matured into a comely young woman.'

Caitrin wanted to wrap protective hands over her body and cover herself from the mage's gaze. But her arms stayed firmly by her sides. When she did make a concerted effort to cover herself she was appalled to find that her hands would not move as she willed them. Through the power of some dark magicks, Nihal had an absolute control over her.

The muscles inside her sex rippled hungrily at the idea. Her nipples stiffened as though they had been teased by the mage's long and slender fingertips.

'Why have you stripped my clothes away?'

She tried to say the words without revealing her excitement. As panic strained her nerves she began to wonder if Nihal might hear the sexual need colouring her voice. She wasn't sure if that was something she desperately wanted or if it was something she heartily feared.

'I have to make sure you are who you said you were,' Nihal explained. 'If Gethin ap Cadwallon is a potential threat to this fiefdom he could send spies to my offices disguised as someone above suspicion. The man could even be a dark mage capable of such shape-shifting himself –'

'Getting at codswallop?'

She didn't know what the words meant. The name sounded vaguely like the title of one of the landed gentry discussed in her father's politics, but it was not a name to which she'd ever paid any attention. Her brow wrinkled with the effort of trying to understand the conversation.

'Gethin ap Cadwallon,' Nihal corrected. 'And if you really are Caitrin it's a name you'd do well to remember. Gethin ap Cadwallon is High Laird of the West Ridings.' Nihal pronounced the visitor's name with an emphasis that was somewhere between lofty importance and cool contempt. 'The lairds of the West Ridings want to forge an allegiance with Blackheath and there will be mutual benefits in regular trade links between our two regions. But, obviously, Duncan is alert to the danger that Cadwallon may have an ulterior motive. There's a fear that Gethin may want to seize control of Gatekeeper Island. And I have to be constantly vigilant about the threat of dark mages. But all the parties believe a betrothal –'

'Does this laird look like me?' Caitrin broke in impatiently.

'No,' Nihal admitted. The mage seemed nonplussed by the interruption. 'Gethin is a swarthy wretch. He's contemptible, according to all the accounts I've heard. But it's said he employs shape-changers for spies. And, as I said before, your shape would be perfect for this errand because it's commonly known I have a long-held tenderness for you.'

Again those words made her smile.

'It wasn't commonly known to me,' she murmured.

Her frown returned deeper when she realised there was a fault to the logic of Nihal's interrogation. 'But you've undressed me,' she pointed out. 'You had no idea what I look like naked, so seeing me without clothes wouldn't prove one way or another that I'm me and not a shape-changer.'

The mage shrugged. 'True enough. But I've always wanted to see you naked and this seemed like the ideal opportunity.'

Before Caitrin's blushes could deepen, the mage's wand touched her three times. The first time the silver tip graced the thrust of her right nipple. Caitrin caught her breath and tried to decide whether the silver cap on the bitternut wand was as chilly as winter ice, or possessed the searing burn of a smith's forge. She couldn't properly decide whether she was being stung by an extreme of heat or cold. But her body responded with the knowledge that she was enjoying an extreme of some description. She sucked breath and savoured the ripples of pleasure that eddied from her breast to her centre.

The same thrill of excitement rushed through her core as the wand brushed her left nipple. This time she was unable to contain the groan of arousal. She released a heartfelt, throaty purr and regarded Nihal with an expression of undisguised lust.

With the third touch, a soft caress of the silver cap against the lips of her sex, Caitrin realised her body was scaling the heights of ecstasy. She bit her lower lip and stared at the shadow in the centre of the cowl where the mage's face should have sat. Of all the desires she had harboured since first taking dragon horn, she could not recall a desperate need stronger than the longing she now held for Nihal.

'Why are you here, Caitrin?' the mage asked. 'I command an honest answer. Why are you here?'

'I was looking for dragon horn.'

'Dragon horn!'

Nihal's exclamation was shrill with surprise and outrage. Whatever special connection had been growing between them was rent asunder before the words had finished bouncing from the stone walls of the offices.

'What the hell would you want with dragon horn, Caitrin? You shouldn't even know about dragon horn. You certainly won't find any here. These are respectable offices.'

'Dragon horn is very nice,' Caitrin confided.

'Nice? You've tried it?' Nihal took a wary step backward. The crimson shoulders inside the robe stiffened with indignation. 'You mean you're no longer chaste?'

Caitrin giggled. 'I've been chaste and I've been caught. That's not a problem, is it?'

'You're no longer a virgin?'

Caitrin frowned. 'The stories of your superior intelligence weren't an exaggeration, were they? There's not a lot slips past the keen observational skills of Nihal the legendary mage from the southernmost –'

'Fuck!' Nihal roared. 'Fuck! Fuck! Fuck!'

If she had been able to control her physical responses, Caitrin would have flinched from the ferocity of the exclamation. Instead she could only stand naked and motionless and tolerate the mage's fury.

'No!' Nihal shrieked. 'This can't be happening. Not again.'

The mage suddenly stepped close. One hand encircled Caitrin's waist. The weight of the velvet robe was a forceful and erotic caress. She caught the fragrant scent of sandalwood and incense that always lingered on the mage's flesh. It was a sultry combination that now made her inner muscles clench with greedy haste.

A hand pressed between her legs.

The thrill of excitement blossomed between her thighs. The rush of wanton need turned her loins to a fluid heat. From the shadows within the cowled hood she caught a glimpse of the mage's features. There was a suggestion of high cheekbones, almond eyes and ripe, kissable lips.

Strong inquisitive fingers stroked against her labia.

The desire to be penetrated was sudden and avaricious.

She parted her thighs and grinned as not one but two fingers slipped into the smouldering confines of her wetness. In the stillness of the moment she could hear the soft dewy squelch of the penetration. She imagined she could hear her inner muscles suckling lightly against the cool fingertips that nestled in her warmth. The mage's touch slipped into her with such ease she murmured, 'Why don't you glide a third in there?'

'Fuck!' Nihal exclaimed.

The mage tore the fingers from her sex. The exclamation and the action were so pained and unexpected Caitrin stepped back in surprise. With a twinge of sadness she realised that the spell that had been holding her in place was now spent.

Broken.

'What's wrong?' Caitrin asked.

'You've lost your innocence,' Nihal snapped sharply. The mage stepped to the left and then the right. It was the dance of someone harried, perplexed and uncertain.

'The castellan will be outraged. Heads are going to roll for this.' With a shrill cry of despair, Nihal added, 'It'll probably be my head that rolls for this. Why do you keep doing this, Cait? Fuck! Fuck! Fuck!'

'Why is my innocence the concern of my father?'

Nihal glared at her. 'Didn't you hear what I was saying before? The thane is going to offer your hand to Gethin ap Cadwallon this evening.'

It was a revelation to Caitrin. She was sure that wasn't something that had been discussed before. She stared at Nihal in disbelief. 'He's going to offer my hand?' She couldn't keep the shock from her voice. 'He's going to offer me up for betrothal? To a man with a name I can't pronounce?'

'It's not just you,' Nihal allowed. 'Gethin will be allowed to choose between you and your sister.'

'And that's supposed to make it better?'

'I thought you knew.'

Caitrin clutched at the mage. 'You have to help me,' she begged. 'You have to do something to stop this.'

'I don't have time,' Nihal complained. 'I'm supposed to be casting protection spells around the whole of Blackheath. I'm supposed to scrutinise Gethin ap Cadwallon with my own magicks to make sure he's not a dark mage and I've got to –'

'You have to do something to stop this,' Caitrin insisted.

The mage thought for a moment. 'I can get your virginity back for you.'

'What?'

'I can get your virginity back. I have a spell.' The mage pushed her away and rushed to the south wall to rummage through the books on the shelves. 'I have a grimoire from the Orient,' Nihal mumbled. 'It's on one of these shelves. I've done this for you before.'

'Why would I want my virginity back?'

Pulling volumes from the shelves, the mage spoke without looking back. 'If your father marries you to Gethin, and Gethin discovers you're not a maid, it could prove catastrophic for the fiefdom. It could prove catastrophic for the whole of the North Ridings. Gethin will see it as an insult.'

'That's ridiculous.'

Nihal shrugged. 'I don't make the rules for this sorry excuse for a society. I have enough difficulty following the magicks.' With a sigh of relief Nihal pulled a large leather-bound tome from a high shelf and said, 'Here. This is the grimoire. This is the book that holds the spell I need.'

'You don't have to –' Caitrin got no further.

Nihal swiped the bitternut wand in her direction. Further words refused to pass her lips.

'If I don't restore your virginity there'll be war,' the mage grumbled. 'Imagine if someone discovered that you'd been naked in my offices this evening. Imagine if someone learnt that I'd had my fingers inside you.'

Imagine if you were to do it again, Caitrin thought dreamily.

She wouldn't let the idea take hold of her thoughts. She couldn't even produce the words to tell Nihal that no one would learn of what had happened in the offices from her lips. She could only stand silent and watch as the mage pulled necessary ingredients from the stoppered jars on the walls.

'Sit here,' Nihal barked, clearing clutter from the central counter in the middle of the chamber.

Caitrin found herself sitting on one of the mage's high counters. She hadn't even been aware that her body had been moving in response to the mage's instructions.

'Part your thighs. Drink this.'

A flagon of honeyed wine was thrust into her hand. She sniffed it doubtfully.

'What's this?'

'Wine.'

'What does it do?'

'It will get you drunk.' Nihal was busying collecting ingredients for the spell. 'Now drink the damned stuff and stop pestering me with stupid questions. Isn't it enough that I've got to mess around to try and remedy all the problems that you've already caused?'

She could hear the irritation in the mage's tone and

wished Nihal's upset didn't sting. She liked the mage and hadn't wanted to cause problems. She watched as Nihal alternated between reading from the large leather-bound grimoire and then rushing to find necessary ingredients from the shelves before adding them to a granite mortar.

Warily, she sipped the honeyed wine.

It was a heady elixir of sweetened grapes. From the first taste she knew it would be dangerous to sip any more. It threatened to dissolve her inhibitions and wash away all sense of propriety. Immediately she raised the flagon to her mouth and took another swallow. Her tongue traced softly over the remnants of the taste that lingered against her lips.

With a flourish, Nihal added a final ingredient to the mortar and then began to pound the mix with a pestle. Caitrin studied the mage's stiff shoulders, sensing the urgency in each movement, and wondering why the mage would go to such lengths just to protect her reputation. She would have asked the question if she could have seen the mage's face. But, even when Nihal turned to anoint her with the mix, Caitrin could only see shadows that concealed the depths of the hooded crimson cowl.

'*Sahasrara*,' Nihal intoned.

A splash of chilly oil touched the top of Caitrin's head and she struggled not to shiver. The word sounded deliciously strange and foreign and she wanted to give herself to the echoes of excitement it seemed to suggest.

'*Anja*,' Nihal said, daubing another wet splash between Caitrin's brows.

The movement made her close her eyes. In that moment she saw a world coloured only by a rush of rich royal purple.

'*Vishudda*,' the mage added, touching oily fingertips against the rise of Caitrin's throat.

The caress was soft and subtle and disturbingly exciting. The sheen of viscous wetness that made the fingers slippery was how she expected Nihal's sexual caress to feel. Her nipples had been stiff before. Now they ached with the need to be teased and suckled by the mage's hungry mouth. As much as Caitrin wanted to purge that idea from her thoughts, she couldn't stop herself from imagining Nihal's mouth suckling against her bared breasts. The idea made her sigh with need.

'*Anahata*,' Nihal whispered.

Anahata, Caitrin agreed, not knowing what the word might mean.

Fingers pressed at her sternum. Although there was nothing acutely sexual about the caress, Caitrin knew that the mage's touch could have gone to either of her breasts. She held her breath wondering whether or not the mage would be so bold as to touch her in the way she desired. If she had been allowed the chance to speak she would have begged to have the fat tips of her nipples squeezed.

'*Manipura*,' Nihal said, sliding his fingers downward.

Caitrin trembled.

The mage's fingertips inched through the neatly shorn curls above her sex and delved toward the moist lips of her labia. She drew a slow shuddering breath.

'*Swadhisthana*,' Nihal grunted.

Fingers touched the sensitive flesh between her thighs.

Caitrin groaned.

The fingers slipped inside. They were still oily from the salve that had been used to anoint her head, brow, throat and breast. The mage's fingers pushed her wide and stretched her lightly. It was a thrilling moment and Caitrin wondered if the mage shared her excitement from the intimate contact.

When a thumb touched the nub of her clitoris, she drew jagged breaths of amazement. The rush of pleasure soared inside her body.

'*Muladhara*,' Nihal said eventually.

One oily fingertip slipped against the super-sensitive sliver of skin between the edge of her sex lips and the ring of her anus.

Caitrin held her breath, sure that her body was resting on the precipice of an orgasm. Slippery fingers remained between her thighs, teasing the lips of her sex and cajoling ripples of pleasure through her loins. Unable to stop herself, she whimpered as the need for satisfaction grew closer. Once the sounds had fallen from her lips, and she realised Nihal was allowing her to use her voice, Caitrin struggled to speak in the most conversational tone that her body could manage.

'Is that it?' she asked. 'Is that the spell cast? Am I virgin again?'

Nihal silenced the question with a kiss. A soft and silky tongue slipped between her lips. A passionate mouth pressed urgently against hers. Strong hands held the back of her head, as though there was a risk that she might pull away.

Caitrin gave herself to the experience.

Her need for satisfaction became an irresistible impulse.

Slowly the mage's kisses moved downwards, paying homage to each of the previously named and anointed chakras.

Caitrin shivered with every kiss and caress.

Nihal has a tenderness for me, Caitrin thought wistfully. It was a thought that made her smile. She wondered why the mage had never said anything about this tenderness before, and then realised that it was probably because the daughter of Blackheath's esteemed castellan would not have been permitted to fraternise with a mage. What would be the point of voicing the existence of such affection when it could never amount to anything?

And before she could even bring herself to contemplate a response to that rhetorical question, she realised the mage's hooded cowl was between her legs. The caress of the velvet fabric pressed against the soft, milky smoothness of her inner thighs. The mage was mumbling something in a whispered Latin whilst strong hands pushed her knees apart. Then the slick caress of a tongue slipped against the warm flesh of her sex.

Caitrin groaned.

The mage's mouth moved over her labia. Fingertips teased at the sensitive lips but it was the warmth of the tongue gliding smoothly back and forth that made her want to scream with mounting excitement.

Nihal trilled the tip of a deft tongue against the thrust of Caitrin's clitoris. The tiny bead of flesh was already pulsing with the need for a surge of release. The attention of the mage's tongue set Caitrin close to exploding with raw desire.

'Is this a necessary part of the spell?' she asked.

Nihal's head tilted back.

Caitrin caught a glimpse of kind eyes shining apologetically.

'I needed to taste you before I sealed you up for Gethin,' Nihal explained. 'I needed to ...'

Caitrin shook her head. 'No need to explain,' she said softly. 'Just carry on doing that for me.' She arched her back so the mage could have easier access. 'Just carry on,' she repeated. 'And, if the day comes when I must have this stranger as my betrothed, I can always close my eyes and pretend that it's you and not him between my legs.'

The pleasure resumed.

Nihal attacked her sex with a ferocity that left Caitrin breathless. The fingers that had been holding her knees apart were now teasing the musk-oily lips of her sex. Nihal's flat, smooth tongue slipped against her with the ease of a polished glass sphere gliding over oiled skin.

A rush of delicious responses trembled through Caitrin's sex, blossoming into small explosions in each of the areas where Nihal had touched. She remembered the mystical quality of each word that had been murmured: *muladhara, swadhisthana, manipura, anahata, vishudda, anja, sahasrara.*

It came to her that the words were flashing through her thoughts in reverse order to the way that Nihal had said them. And then, as the remainder of the words flooded through her mind, she realised she didn't care what order the words came in.

All she cared about was the blistering rush of satisfaction. All she cared for was the pleasure pouring out of Nihal's mouth and into the eager wetness of her hole.

Her climax struck with a force more powerful than she had enjoyed whilst quaffing dragon horn with Robert. It came in repeated bolts of satisfaction that hit her again and again as a cavalcade of multiple, magnificent thrills of pleasure. She found herself clutching the sides of the mage's hood, urging Nihal to continue tonguing her depths and willing her body to suffer further waves of delicious and divine pleasure.

Eventually, after a glorious age of golden bliss, Caitrin realised the mage had stopped tonguing at her sex. The light had been bleached from the room and her desire for gratification had been replaced by a tranquillity of serene satisfaction.

Drowsiness held her in a lover's embrace.

'Is it done?' Caitrin asked.

Nihal nodded. 'Yes. Once again, I've restored your virginity.'

Caitrin was puzzled by the comment.

The words 'once again' suggested they had gone through this interaction before, although she couldn't recall when she and Nihal had previously done something so intimate. She knew she wasn't the brightest of the daughters of Blackheath, but she figured even someone with her limited capacity for remembering details would recall something as memorable as having a mage restore her virginity.

She opened her mouth to ask the question and a flood of memories came rushing back.

Nihal frowning with disapproval.

Nihal performing the restoration ceremony.

Nihal concluding the ceremony with a memory incantation.

She trembled, saddened by the idea that the mage would force her to forget the pleasure they had just shared.

The offices were now held in shadow. Glancing out through the west window she could see that the sun had finally set beyond the edge of the Last Sea. Braziers and torches burnt in the taverns and whorehouses around the port. The silhouettes of lewd revellers began to break out into the streets as a large covered wagon was drawn down the main road leading toward Blackheath.

'You have to promise me that you'll give up your quest for dragon horn.'

'Give up the quest?' Caitrin laughed, surprised by the ridiculousness of the suggestion. 'Never.'

Nihal's shoulders stiffened. One trembling hand raised the bitternut hickory wand. The silver tip glowed dully. 'Don't say never, Caitrin. Reconsider your decision before I have to do something we'll both regret.'

Caitrin pressed her mouth close to the mage.

'Don't make me forget what we just shared,' she begged.

Nihal stiffened as though stung by the suggestion.

'Don't make me forget what we just shared,' Caitrin repeated. 'And don't make me forget my quest for dragon horn. It's important to me. If you knew what dragon horn was like I'm sure it would be important to you.'

'But, Cait,' the mage began. 'It's such a dangerous substance.'

Caitrin thought she liked having her name shortened by the mage. It made her feel as though there was something developing between them.

'You've never tried dragon horn,' she whispered. 'And until you've tried it you can't judge me for wanting to experience it again.'

'But, Cait –' the mage started.

Caitrin silenced the interruption with a kiss. She allowed the moment to linger as their tongues twisted and twined together inside the battleground of their joined mouths.

'I'll make you a promise, Nihal,' she decided. 'I'll continue my quest to find dragon horn. And I will find it. And once I've got a secure supply, I'm going to bring some back here so that you and I can share it together.'

'But, Cait –' the mage began again.

Caitrin shook her head and continued. 'If, once you've tried it, you still think I should give up my quest, then I'll consider your point of view.'

There was a long silence from within the shadows of Nihal's hooded cowl. Eventually the mage said, 'You're determined to do this, aren't you?'

'More than you can know.'

'In that case,' the mage sounded sad but determined, 'I'll do what I can to help you find dragon horn.'

Caitrin brightened, shocked to discover she now had an ally in her quest.

'You should join your father at the banquet hall this evening,' the mage went on. 'I believe the castellan is greeting Gethin ap Cadwallon and it would serve you well to meet the High Laird of the West Ridings.'

'I wish I could stay here with you.'

The mage's head moved from side to side inside the cowled hood. The bitternut hickory wand was suddenly flashing bright light into the room. And Caitrin realised the clothes had returned to her body. She also realised that there was a ring now sitting on the middle finger of her left hand. It was a band of gold emblazoned with a shimmering eye of moonstone that looked like the pearl-white stone they called a mage's eye.

Caitrin examined the ring and then glanced into the shadows covering Nihal's face. Again, she said, 'I wish I could stay here with you.'

'If you ever need me,' said Nihal softly, 'all you have to do is call my name.' The mage spoke with a soft and earnest conviction that could only be the truth. 'If you ever need me, simply take yourself to the peak of a climax, close your eyes and then whisper my name. If you do that, I'll be with you.'

'I want more than that,' Caitrin sighed. 'I want to stay here with you.'

'Go to the banquet hall, Cait,' Nihal whispered. 'My magicks aren't strong enough to grant all your wishes.'

CHAPTER THREE

Owain of the West Ridings

Owain had a momentary insight into the figure that he presented. He was tall and broad and conventionally handsome. The linen tunic he had worn for travelling was a plain green that hugged the muscles of his powerful chest. With fresh hosen on his legs, and a sword dangling idly from his left hip, he supposed he looked like a debonair and attractive stranger.

Not that the redhead by his side was there because of his appearance, he thought glumly. She would have stood eagerly outside the cage if he had been a hunchback dwarf dressed in motley and burdened by pox scars.

She wasn't there for him.

She was there to see what was hidden inside the cage behind the flag.

Not that the flag was hiding much, he reflected. The flag showed a red dragon, six foot tall, standing on a white background above a green base. The dragon on the flag was as red as the brightest sun rubies. It was as red as the most heartfelt desire. It was as red as the dragon hidden beneath the flag concealed inside the cage.

On the journey up to Blackheath, Owain had told Laird Gethin ap Cadwallon that using the flag to cover this cage was like hiding the whole of the West Riding's coffers beneath a flag decorated with golden coins, sapphire purses and diamond-encrusted ingots.

But, not for the first time, Gethin had ignored Owain's observations.

'Are you sure you want to see this?' Owain asked the redhead.

She was a pretty young maid who had taken the time to help him guide the wheeled cage into a covered store-room beside Blackheath's stables. The earthy smell of horses filled the air around them. There were no torches or sconces inside the stables but there was sufficient moonlight for Owain to appreciate the young woman's milk-skinned beauty and the shine of daring that danced in her emerald eyes. He had seen that her hair was the russet colour of an autumn sunset. He had also seen the leather band on her heart finger but he was doing his best to brush that latter consideration from his thoughts.

All men, he knew, were able to brush that sort of consideration from their thoughts.

The redhead giggled and pressed close to him.

His nostrils flared as he caught the sweet scent of her nearness. She wore a perfume that reminded him of the exotic aroma of the flowers from the kingdom's most forbidden gardens. The bouquet was rich and heady and intoxicating.

His need for her hardened.

'I've seen dragons before,' she admitted.

There was a musical lilt to her voice. He didn't know if it was a typical accent for someone from the North Ridings, or a dialect peculiar to Blackheath, but from her it sounded different and enchanting. His yearning for her grew stronger.

'I can see Gatekeeper Island through my spyglass when I stand in the highest offices of the watchtowers,' she told him.

She nodded back over her shoulder, as though gesturing toward the main buildings of Blackheath Priory. He glanced at the silhouettes of towers standing black against the midnight-blue sky, blocking the stars from shining down. This was his first visit to Blackheath and it looked as though the entire fiefdom was made up of too many dark towers.

'I can see the dragons circling the temple through my spyglass,' she explained. 'But I've never seen a dragon up close. I've never *touched* one.'

She stressed the penultimate word: *touched*.

He stiffened. She had a warm body and was pressed

lithely against him. The well-rounded swell of her thinly covered breasts brushed against the brawny muscles of his bicep. Her small hands, delicate and cool, touched him with deliberate urgency. Her nearness inspired a healthy hardness to spring between his thighs and strain against his hosen. He cautioned himself against being tempted by her before knowing more about who she was.

He cautioned himself to remember Carys.

Owain had suffered for being imprudent in the past. He did not believe himself to be a man who often made the same mistake twice. Whilst he was trying to tell himself to proceed with caution he continued wilfully not thinking about the leather band on the third finger of her left hand.

'You need to be careful around dragons,' he whispered.

He found himself murmuring the words into her ear. There was something about her height and shape that made him yearn to share the sentiment in an intimate fashion. He didn't know if it was the vibrant colour of her hair, the whey-like milkiness of her complexion or if it was simply an effect of working so closely with dragons.

'Dragons breathe fire. Those dragons that are out there with foul tempers can cause harm and devastation to anyone who earns their ire. It's something you need to remember whenever you're handling these beasts.'

She nodded attentively.

'But the very nearness of dragons has an effect on us

humans.' His voice dropped a notch lower, so that he was sure she was straining to hear him. 'It's an effect that we can't control,' he murmured.

'And what effect might that be?'

She returned his whisper with lips so close he could have kissed her without moving his head. Her breath was sweet with the memory of summer fruits and evening wine. Her emerald eyes shone for him with a reflection of the sparkling moonlight.

'Is it an effect similar to dragon horn?' she asked.

He pulled away from her with a stiff abruptness. Whatever passion had been blossoming between them was instantly rent apart.

'Dragon horn is a stupid myth,' he grunted. His hand fell to the sword on his hip. With a deliberate effort he moved his fingers away from the pommel. 'Dragon horn is a lie put about by charlatans and bastards and those who know less than a headless cockerel. Dragon horn is nothing but –'

'I didn't mean –' she faltered.

Needing to do something with his hands, he gripped the flag and tore it away from the cage. 'Dragon horn is a story put about by those who've never seen a dragon and don't realise that dragons don't even have horns.'

The flag fell to the floor in a noiseless rumple.

He realised that the redhead had stopped listening to him as he prattled on about the inefficacy of dragon horn and its part of the lore of unsubstantiated myths. She was staring into the cage. Her eyes had been wide before. Now they were as large as a berserker's battle shield. Her mouth had fallen into a broad O of silent amazement. She stood motionless as she stared into the cage.

Owain wasn't really surprised.

Y Ddraig Goch was an impressive sight. Standing on all fours the dragon would have been an imposing six foot tall. From the tip of her snout to the spike at the end of her tail, she was closer to double that length. The dragon was as scarlet as blood-red dreams. She regarded Owain and the redhead with unblinking onyx eyes. A forked tongue slipped from between her crimson lips.

'He's beautiful,' the redhead muttered. 'He's truly beautiful.'

'She,' Owain corrected. He reached through the bars of the cage and patted the dragon on the top of its spiny head.

Despite the moment's irritation that had woken in him at the mention of dragon horn, he found himself warming to the redhead.

She smiled for the dragon. Her expression bore the sort of affection that suggested she was a genuine animal lover who possessed a sincere kindness of spirit.

'Drusilla is a female dragon,' he explained with patience. 'She's one of the last of her kind from the West Ridings.'

'Drusilla the dragon?' The redhead smiled sourly.

Owain shrugged. 'She was named by a former princess of the West Ridings,' he admitted. 'And the girl was only three at the time.'

The redhead seemed to allow this with a nod of her head. Her gaze had never left Drusilla. Cautiously, she took a faltering step toward the bars of the cage. She had one arm extended and a doubtful expression on her lips. She hesitated and then turned to stare at Owain with a submissive expression.

Despite the darkness surrounding them he could see the dark green flecks in her pupils. It was a colour that reminded him of Carys's eyes.

'May I pet her?'

'Gently. Of course,' he said. 'But remember what I said before. An irate dragon could burn you alive.'

She nodded and began to slip her arm through the bars.

He placed a hand on her shoulder and said, 'Remember also that dragons inspire an uncontrollable passion in us humans. Touching dragons makes it impossible to ignore those passions once they're stirred.'

She nodded and hesitated for a moment longer. Then she pushed her hand through the bars.

Drusilla was one of the friendliest dragons that had fallen under the charge of Owain's husbandry. She was affectionate to strangers. She was careful around all those animals that she wasn't expected to eat. In truth, the only person Drusilla had never taken to liking was High Laird of the West Ridings, Gethin ap Cadwallon. In his presence *Y Ddraig Goch* would snarl and hiss, then catch breath as though preparing to sear his worthless hide with a flurry of flames from her nostrils.

Drusilla purred softly as the redhead stroked her cheek.

'Aren't you a pretty girl? Aren't you a lovely, crimson girl?' the redhead cooed. A forked tongue slipped against her wrist and she giggled. 'It tickles,' the redhead laughed.

Her gaze turned to Owain. There was a moment when he could see the unbidden desires shining behind her eyes. The longing inspired by the dragon's nearness had clearly begun to stir in her nether regions and he knew her pulse would be racing and her loins would now ache with the bitter pain of unsated lust. Her cheeks flushed to the same colour as the dragon's leathered wings and the redhead looked away and busied herself with petting Drusilla and allowing the creature to stroke its forked tongue against her wrist.

He patiently allowed her to continue.

He had seen the signs before and knew how the game would develop.

The redhead would be fighting the arousal that grew within her. She was still not convinced that her contact with the dragon was causing her to become driven by a need for him. As she tried to disguise her responses, she would busy herself by petting the dragon which would only serve to exacerbate her arousal. Eventually her need for him would outweigh whatever practical considerations were making her arousal such a source of embarrassment. And when she did submit to him, her acquiescence would be far more noble than any conquest won by a charlatan peddling dragon horn.

As long as he could continue to overlook the fact that there was a leather wedding band on her heart finger, Owain knew he would enjoy rutting with the redhead in any one of the hay-filled stalls.

'I didn't mean to upset you with my ignorant comment about dragon horn.'

She didn't look at him as she said the words. Instead they were spoken over her shoulder as she continued to pet Drusilla. The dragon continued to purr as she caressed its cheek and wings.

'You weren't to know,' he assured her. He was thankful for the darkness of the stalls. It stopped her from seeing the solemnity of his features. 'I once had a bad experience because of someone spinning lies about dragon horn,' he explained. 'I suppose I overreact whenever it's mentioned nowadays.'

He looked up to see she had stopped petting the dragon.

Silently, she had moved to stand by his side. She stared up at him, her emerald eyes sparkling softly. Her chest seemed to rise and fall with a quickened pace. His gaze fell to the heave of her breasts. The thrust of her nipples jutted sharp against the light cotton of her kirtles.

Unable to stop himself, Owain licked his lips.

'Do you like what you see, sire?' she asked coyly.

The red and gold kirtles were laced with ribbon at the breast. She reached for the dangling thread of one ribbon and teased it so the binding began to unravel.

'Would sire like to see more?'

The coquettish lilt to her voice was thoroughly endearing.

Owain dearly wanted to show decency and propriety. He wanted to mention the fact that she wore a leather band on her heart finger and was therefore either married or betrothed to another. But, whilst he wanted to act like a gallant knight or chivalrous suitor, his actions were dictated by the needs of his loins.

'I'd like to do a lot more than see,' he told her.

He pulled her into his embrace, snaking one arm around her waist so that she was brought close to him. He lowered his face to her lips and then they were kissing with a passion that was as ferocious and fulfilling as he had expected.

Her tongue explored his mouth. She curled one leg around his hip, pressing the centre of her sex against her thigh. A sob of raw desire whimpered from her throat as she ground herself against him. Her hands pushed at his chest, fumbling to remove his tunic and gain access to his bare flesh.

With a moan of desperation she wrenched her mouth from his.

'Take me,' she pleaded.

He couldn't hide his smile.

'If you insist.' He lowered his face to the unfastened décolletage of her kirtles and pressed his nose between her breasts. Drinking in the dusky scent of her nearness he moved his mouth over one orb and suckled against the stiff, throbbing tip of her nipple.

She groaned.

He stiffened at the sound and cast a wary glance toward the doorway. When he realised that no one had been alerted by the cry of her pleasure he allowed himself to relax and enjoy the experience and stop worrying that she might have a husband or fiancé lurking in the shadows ready to accuse her of being adulterous or challenge him for being a swiver.

When the redhead groaned again, Owain savoured the sound.

He resisted the urge to buck his loins against her.

Working with dragons fuelled him with a constant arousal but he was loathe to surrender himself so quickly to such a base response. Holding her in one arm, teasing the shape of her exposed breast with one hand as he suckled against the hard and unyielding tip of the other, Owain revelled in her heightened responses to his teasing.

She was breathless and trembling and desperate for his cock.

'Take me,' she begged. 'I'm so wet for you now.'

She grabbed at his tunic with her left hand. It was the same hand that bore the leather band on her heart finger.

'I'm *so* wet,' she insisted.

He refused to think about the fact that she was in a relationship with someone else. Instead he caught her nipple between his front teeth and pressed the tiniest nibble against her exposed flesh.

'Yes!' she breathed. 'Oh! You can do that all season. Yes!'

He could hear the tears of need being squeezed from her voice. He would have carried on alternating his kisses from one breast and then onto the other if she hadn't managed to slip her fingers beneath his tunic.

The sensation of her cool hand against his warm flesh was too much to resist.

Her fingers stroked downwards, pushing beyond the drawstring waist that fastened his hosen. He knew she was reaching for the pulsing hardness at the centre of his loins.

And then she had a fist encircled around him.

'My goodness,' she exclaimed. 'I see you're smuggling a longsword in your pants.'

She squeezed her grip around him and he shivered.

'I trust you know how to handle such a weapon,' she teased.

'I think you're handling it just fine for me,' he grinned.

It wasn't the first time he had enjoyed such banter. Lifting her in his arms, comforted that she didn't remove her fingers from their hold around his shaft, he carried the redhead to one of the hay-filled stalls. They lay down slowly together, their bodies buoyed by a mattress of prickly hay.

As he moved his head back toward her breasts, anxious to suckle again against her stiff nipple, she pulled herself away.

He frowned, concerned that he had done something to dampen her ardour.

'Please don't tease me,' she insisted. 'I want you now. I need to feel you inside me.' The hand around his erection gripped tight as she added, 'I need to feel you inside me right now.'

He laughed and nodded.

The nearness of dragons had that affect. Aside from the pleasure of working with the beasts themselves, it was one of the main benefits of being responsible for the husbandry of the dragons. Every man or woman who petted a dragon was filled by the immediate urge to rut.

He pushed the redhead's legs apart and knelt between them.

She shifted the hem of her kirtles upwards and lay back for him.

In better light he would have been able to appraise the

sight she revealed. He would have been able to admire her moonlight-pale thighs and the sight of her exposed sex. He could imagine that the curls around her labia would be as rich and vibrant a red as the russet-red curls at her head.

But the light in the stalls transformed every sight into shadows and shapes and every colour was simply saturated in darkness. He could make out pale skin touched by shards of moonlight, and dark curls that glistened sharply with dewy wetness at their centre.

Then he realised the urgency of her need matched the strength of his own arousal and he tried to understand why he was wasting time admiring the woman when he could be rutting with her and satisfying both their appetites.

The redhead tugged at his erection, urging him toward her.

As eager to be inside her as she was to accept him, Owain made no attempt to deny what she wanted. She fumbled to release his shaft from his hosen and then she was guiding him toward her sex. Her left hand was cool against the super-heated ferocity of his hardness. He was gratified to note that she held her fingers so he couldn't feel the unwelcome weight of that wedding band on her heart finger.

She had been right to describe herself as wet.

The slippery secrets of her sex were oily around his

length as she rubbed the swollen head of his erection back and forth against her nether lips. It was a languid motion that had him torn between wanting to push into her and desperate to revel at the hand of her masterful taunting.

'Do you want me?' she asked.

'You know I want you.'

'Say it.'

'I want you.'

Her fingers squeezed around him. She held him over the moist centre of her sex, her dewy lips lightly kissing the end of his length. 'Say it as though you mean it,' she insisted.

'I want you,' he repeated. He wasn't sure how else he could say the words without sounding stupid.

'Louder,' she demanded.

'I WANT YOU!'

At the same moment he cried out, she bucked her hips forward. There was one moment when it felt as though she was squeezing hard around him with a grip that was unbearably tight and painful. Then his length was filling her and her warm, sultry wetness sheathed his hardness as he pushed all the way into her moist and welcoming confines.

They cried out together.

It took Owain a tremendous effort not to release his climax into her with that first thrust. She was tight. She was simultaneously slippery and heated and he thought it was like having his erection caressed by the perfect embrace of an angel. His chest was pressed against her exposed breasts. Her lips were at his neck, whispering encouragement and telling him that his size was massive and impressive and unbearable and divine. And he wanted to savour the pleasure of simply allowing his length to pulse and thrust and pump into the haven of her dark confines.

But, more than that selfish impulse to simply take what he could from the experience, he wanted to make the rutting pleasurable for the woman beneath him.

Resisting the urge to give in to his climax he savoured the pleasure of having her appreciation made manifest in the words she poured into his ear. Resisting the urge to give in to his climax, Owain rode himself slowly back and forth and in and out of her wetness.

The redhead groaned.

It was a throaty moan of approval. It was a sound borne from absolute bliss.

He quickened his pace, relishing the sultry friction of her muscles clutching at him as he ploughed in and out. He maintained the same languid pace and discovered that she was raising and lowering her pelvis in an adopted rhythm that perfectly matched his.

Each time he pushed himself into her wetness, the redhead urged her hips upwards to meet the thrust of his penetration. She stroked at his nipples, pinching them lightly with the tips of her gaily painted nails. In retaliation, he trapped the buds of her nipples between the calloused knuckles of his fists.

As she raised one leg to encircle him, he found himself shifting a leg to get closer to her.

The change in position allowed him to slide deeper into her sex.

The fresh sensations had them both sighing in unison.

'You've done this before,' she laughed softly. Her words were carried by breathless grunts of approval. 'You must be a guildsman in this art. Is that your profession, sire? Do they call you the Owain the fucker?'

He smiled at the idea of being known as Owain the fucker. The smile hardened to an expression of self-reproach when he realised he didn't know her name. He had either never bothered learning what she was called, or, if she had told him her name, he had forgotten it in the urgent desire to get between her legs. It was not the first time he had ended up rutting with a woman whose name he did not know. But knowing that he had fallen into this habit repeatedly did not make Owain feel better about himself.

'I'm not a guildsman between a woman's thighs,' he grumbled apologetically. 'I just happen to be a gifted amateur.'

She reached behind him and clutched at his backside. 'I'd say you were a *very* gifted amateur,' she conceded.

Pulling him deep into herself she rubbed her hips vigorously up and down until they were both gasping with the choking need for release.

When the thrill of his climax finally struck, Owain knew the release was only coming in defence against the rush of satisfaction that she was enjoying.

The redhead pressed and squeezed at his length with a furious grip from the inner muscles of her sex. Her fingernails raked at his backside as she clutched him in her embrace. Her body convulsed with paroxysms of animalistic satisfaction.

And Owain groaned as the pleasure was wrenched from his body.

His erection throbbed as it pumped his thick seed into her. Each pulse was powerful and driven by a vigorous force. The muscles at the base of his shaft clenched hard and tight with each spasm of his ejaculation. The force of the climax was so powerful it was almost painful.

Spent, Owain and the redhead collapsed together on the hay.

They lay side by side, basking in the aftermath of pure satisfaction that was being expelled from their bodies by exhausted sighs.

Behind them, from the confines of her cage, Drusilla purred with soft approval.

Owain could hear other sounds beyond the walls of the stable where they lay.

He could hear the conversations of those untroubled by the care of dragons, the falseness of circumstantial fealty or the need for vengeance. He could hear the sounds of guards in chain mail marching noisily around the castellum and he figured he was listening to the powerful presence of the castellan's dark knights.

The castellan's Order of Dark Knights were the heavily armed protectors of Blackheath. Their presence was imposing and, Owain knew, the dark knights of Blackheath were one of two reasons why High Laird Gethin ap Cadwallon was approaching this mission with diplomacy and tact rather than his usual application of brute force and ignorance. The other reason, Owain believed, had something to do with a mage in the castellan's employ.

The redhead nuzzled against Owain's chest. She placed a gentle kiss against his nipple and absently suckled against him. The familiarity was instantaneously warming and comforting. It was also wholly disheartening because she wasn't Carys.

Even though the sex he had just enjoyed had been superlative, the redhead had not been Carys. The experience had been great for him. It had clearly been good for the redhead. At the back of his mind he suspected what he had just enjoyed would be galling for the man who had placed the ring on the redhead's finger. But that wasn't something he would think about. It was enough to acknowledge, even though the experience had been satisfying for the participants, it had not been an experience he was sharing with Carys.

He pulled himself away from the redhead's kisses.

She didn't seem to notice that his mood had swung toward impatience.

'Are all the men in the West Ridings as well-equipped as you?' she asked.

'I haven't lain with all of them,' he said. 'Are all the maids in Blackheath as welcoming as you?'

She considered the question and then nodded. 'Yes, we are. Especially, it seems, once we've been able to stroke a dragon.'

He considered pulling on his hosen and trying to find where his sword and tunic had been discarded. A sliver of moonlight glanced against her bare breasts. Despite the suggestion of melancholy he had suffered a moment earlier, the need to experience the woman by his side again struck him with sudden and unexpected force.

'Would you like to stroke my dragon again?' he asked coyly.

She reached for his spent shaft. Her fingers slid against the slippery meld of her juices and his own spent climax as she teased him back to erection.

'I'd rather stroke this until it was ready to fill me again,' she said earnestly.

And that was all it took.

This time, when he entered her, she seemed to accept the pleasure with less surprise and more satisfaction. This time, when he pushed deep into her sex, she managed to meet his gaze in the darkness and study his face as he rode back and forth.

'You do know I'm married, don't you?'

He had tried not to think about the fact that it was her left hand that guided him into her sex. He had tried to stop himself from dwelling on the fact that she had caressed his length with the same hand that bore the leather band on her heart finger.

'I'd noticed your ring,' he admitted. 'But I'd figured it wasn't troubling you.'

'My husband is a captain in the Order of the Dark Knights,' she explained. 'He spends many months on foreign shores. Currently he's away leading the Blackheath Cavalry to quell an uprising on the Silver Sands. I know he spends many nights with other women. He knows I spend many nights with other men.'

Owain didn't know what to say.

He thought it safest to say nothing. Her words weren't exactly souring his arousal. But they were adding nothing to it either. He figured that as long as she spoke about the arrangement she had with her husband he could prolong both their pleasures.

'We have a relationship where we try not to embarrass each other,' she explained. 'I take visitors to Blackheath between my legs when the mood strikes me. He takes foreign women when the mood strikes him. As long as neither of us does something as embarrassing as being publicly exposed as a swiver, it's a relationship that we both find convenient and satisfying.'

'And is there a reason why you're telling me this?'

'So that you know there is nothing more between us, just sex.'

He nodded. As he continued to ride in and out of her, he said, 'Not that I could tell anyone about you, or what we've done. I don't even know your name.'

She gripped him tight with her inner muscles.

He came close to climaxing in response. She giggled as she saw the frown of concentrated consternation that wrinkled his brow.

'You've got no need to know my name either,' she laughed. 'I can call you Owain the fucker and you can call me the apprentice to your longsword.'

He laughed at that and found himself gliding into her with increased passion. She wasn't Carys. But she was pleasurable company and skilled in the art of sex.

This time, when they hurried toward their respective climaxes, he was struck by the stronger focus they each seemed to have on ensuring that the other was properly sated.

His length teetered on the brink of explosion for an age. She sighed and moaned and clutched at him with brittle ferocity. Her inner muscles convulsed wetly around him as she shivered to the point of explosion. And then they were holding each other tight as the ripples of blistering satisfaction bound them together.

'Owain the fucker,' she muttered. 'If I wasn't a married woman I'd be tempted to properly bond my apprenticeship to your longsword.'

'And I'd be tempted –'

He got no further. The door burst open with a clatter.

'Dirt and dragon dung! Is this where you're hiding?'

Drusilla hissed. A flash of slick yellow flame spat from her nostrils.

Owain stiffened, momentarily fearing that he was about to encounter the absent husband the redhead had mentioned. A fight with a captain from the Order of Dark Knights sounded like more of a challenge than he would be able to handle after exhausting himself in her accommodating depths.

He calmed himself immediately.

He knew his fears should have been banished by Drusilla's hissing. There was only one man in all the Ridings that inspired her to hiss with such vitriolic anger. But the shock of the moment didn't allow him to think so quickly.

The man who had entered the room carried a blazing torch.

Shadows and light danced against the horsehair walls of the stalls.

He was a stocky figure with dark shaggy hair and a swarthy complexion.

'High Laird Gethin ap Cadwallon,' Owain muttered. He tried to make saying the laird's name sound like an apology. He stood up, naked and opened his hands in a gesture of contrition. 'I was just showing this maid –'

'I can see what you were showing her,' Gethin grumbled. He cast a dour glance in the direction of Owain's exposed penis. 'Cover yourself up, take a shower, and put on court clothes ready for the banquet. I have a task for you.'

'A task?' Owain repeated dumbly. 'What task?'

Gethin walked over to the redhead and considered her naked body with a cruel and acquisitive expression. He flashed a smile that was met with stony indifference.

'The damned castellan will want me to kiss his arse and bribe him to Sunday and back before he'll grant permission for us to visit Gatekeeper Island,' Gethin told Owain. 'I really don't have the patience to kowtow to the puffed-up little arsehole that stands between me and the success of my ambition, so you're going to pretend to be me at tonight's banquet.'

'You want me to pretend to be you?' Owain frowned. 'Does that mean you're going to pretend to be me?'

'Why the fuck would I do that?' asked Gethin with genuine incredulity. 'You're not important enough to merit the pretence. What would I say to people? I'm

Owain. I fuck local trollops and mop up dragon sc tan. Give over. No one would be interested in your identity in the first place.'

Owain clenched his teeth tight together. 'Doesn't the castellan of Blackheath already know what Laird Gethin ap Cadwallon looks like?'

'Hardly,' Gethin sneered. 'The bumbling old sc tan's got two daughters and, from what I hear, he has difficulty remembering which one is which. The idea that he'd know what I'm supposed to look like is not even a remote possibility.'

'As a matter of fact,' the redhead said, standing up, 'the castellan of Blackheath has three daughters.'

Gethin regarded her with a wary scepticism.

The redhead covered her breasts with her red and gold kirtles and defiantly met his gaze. 'The castellan has twin daughters of Tavia the fair and Caitrin the dark. He also has a daughter older than those two twins. The third daughter is the one with fiery red hair. Her name is Inghean the red. Inghean of Blackheath.'

The redhead walked toward Gethin with one hand extended. Her smile was acid as she said, 'I'm sure my father, the castellan, will also be very pleased to hear that you were trying to deceive him.'

Gethin's frown was foreboding as he took her hand and raised it courteously to his lips. His fingers held her tight. 'Go to the banquet hall, Owain,' Gethin barked. 'Go to the banquet hall and do as I instructed. Tell that stupid old fool of a castellan that you're Gethin ap Cadwallon. I'll deal with this problem you've created here.'

'Don't hurt her,' Owain warned.

'Are you trying to give me instructions?' hissed Gethin. He held Inghean's hand but studied Owain with a challenge in his steely glare. 'Are you telling me what to do?'

'No,' Owain said stiffly. 'I'm giving you a direct command. If you want me to pretend that I'm you, you'll promise me now that you won't hurt her.' His voice rose as he added, 'You'll promise me on the honour of the Cadwallon name.'

The moment hung between them.

Gethin glowered.

Owain kept his features composed, as though they had been carved from granite. Inghean cast her wide-eyed gaze from one man to the other.

'Very well,' Gethin allowed stiffly.

He did not look happy about the agreement but that gave Owain some reassurance. If Gethin had looked happy, Owain would not have trusted the man's honesty or integrity to abide by the condition. If Gethin had looked happy it would have meant the man had worked out a way to break the promise Owain had just extracted.

'I'll pledge now that this woman won't be harmed whilst she's in my charge.' Gethin was no longer holding the redhead's fingers. His hand was now wrapped firmly around her wrist. His serious gaze met Owain's as he said, 'But I'll warn you now: one of these days, your obsession with showing gallantry to every woman you fuck will land you in trouble.'

CHAPTER FOUR

Inghean the Stupid

Inghean walked reluctantly by Gethin's side as his entourage marched toward Blackheath's grand banquet hall.

Inwardly she cursed herself for the stupid notion that had led her to keep her identity secret as she greeted the visitors earlier in the evening. Her father had explained that High Laird Gethin ap Cadwallon was bringing a red dragon to Blackheath and he had asked her to escort the bearers of the rare cargo to a safe building within the walls of Blackheath. Inghean had obeyed her father's instruction. But she had been overcome by a childlike desire to see the creature before anyone else and had gone to meet the visitors without a welcoming honour guard. When she first encountered Cadwallon and his entourage, Inghean had pretended she was a local maid enamoured by the company of strangers. And now she was paying the price for what she had thought was a harmless deception.

She watched Owain enter the banquet hall before her and knew he would easily pass for a visiting laird. He was no longer Owain the fucker. He looked regal and resplendent in dark breeches and a green and white surcoat emblazoned with the motif of *Y Ddraig Goch*. Admiring him from behind, her arousal more than a little stirred by the sight of his comely rear, she willed herself not to blame Owain for her predicament. He had been gallant enough to warn Gethin not to harm her. Whilst she believed he could have done more to protect her from the laird's wrath, she was touched by the chivalry he had shown.

She tried to rationalise the reasons why she had rutted with him but embarrassment kept stopping her from thinking about the experience. Admittedly, he was not the first man she had taken from outside her marriage bed. But usually she took such lovers after months of consideration and days of introspection. The urge to rut with Owain had been instantaneous and her surrender to him had been equally swift. Admittedly he was attractive but she didn't think he was so attractive as to make her forget her usual devotion to common sense.

She thought it likely that the whole experience had been influenced by the dragon's nearness. There had been some presence in the stables that had stirred an animal need in her loins. Inghean was more willing to believe it was the dragon that had inspired her arousal rather than a genuine longing for Owain. But, whatever the cause, she had to admit the lusty need still smouldered.

Inghean shook her head and wrenched her gaze from the sight of his rear. She refused to acknowledge that a part of her body still wanted him and she slowed her step to keep her distance from him.

'Keep by my side, my lovely.'

She scowled at Gethin ap Cadwallon's term of endearment.

He was an arrogant and contemptible wretch, a swarthy, shaggy-haired reprobate with a hidden agenda. And she had already decided that his motives toward Blackheath were potentially hostile.

His claim to be visiting the castellan in the name of diplomacy was clearly nothing more than a calculated ruse. However, as long as she was forced to be by his side, Inghean had no way of warning anyone that he was a potential threat.

She tried to tug away from him.

Gethin pulled her close and whispered in her ear. His words were low, but spat loud enough to be heard over the pageantry of trumpets that heralded their approach toward the grand banquet hall. She could smell the memory of pomegranate wine on his breath. It was a fragrance that was sourly reminiscent of Owain's lust-fuelled kisses.

'How many times do I have to tell you this, Inghean

of Blackheath? If you leave my side this evening, if you give away my deception or send one word of warning that reaches the castellan, I'll expose you as a common adulteress.'

She stiffened. It was a low threat and it struck its mark as effortlessly as a well-drawn arrow from a longbow.

'If you play along with my ruse,' he went on, 'I shall say nothing and I shall keep the tawdry secret that you're a slattern. Then, when I leave Blackheath tomorrow morning and head for Gatekeeper Island, your questionable honour won't be tarnished by words from my mouth.'

Her cheeks turned crimson but she said nothing.

She could cope with rumours about her lack of honour. She was tempted to tell him as much and defy his insidious threats. But Inghean knew it was not only her honour that would suffer from Gethin's gossip. Her husband would suffer if such rumours began to circulate.

As though reading her thoughts, Gethin asked, 'How is Captain Clement of the Blackheath Cavalry? He's stationed overseas at the moment, isn't he? Am I right in thinking he's quelling an uprising in the Silver Sands? That's the work of a very brave knight.'

She did not miss the subtle revelation that he had already discovered the name, rank and regiment of her husband. Her hands curled into fists. She squeezed them so tight she could feel the fingernails pushing against the soft bed of flesh in her palms. She kept her jaw clenched into a rigid silence rather than respond.

'As long as you remain obedient to my instructions, word that the captain's wife is a slut won't reach his regiment from my lips.' Gethin smiled greasily and added, 'You have that promise on my reputation as a laird and on my honour as a Cadwallon, my lovely.'

She wanted to slap his face. Instead, she remained stiff and contained her anger. If Gethin had only been threatening her and her honour, she would have sacrificed her reputation to the vagaries of his whisperings. But he was threatening her husband, Captain Clement. If talk about her indiscretions reached the ranks of the Blackheath Cavalry it could mean the captain was shamed or embarrassed or called on to fight duels to protect her honour. It was not a situation she wanted her husband to suffer.

'The honour of a Cadwallon?' she snorted. 'I hear that's as rare as fairy farts.'

'Is it as rare as the chasteness of a Blackheath woman?'

She was about to round on him, ready to rant against the insult and slap a hand across his face.

He grabbed her wrist and pushed her against a wall.

Oblivious to the confrontation between Gethin and Inghean, Owain and his modest entourage of Cadwallon knights continued to enter the hall. The clomp of their boots was echoed by the rattle of chain mail and armour clunking after each step like pursuant ghosts. The fanfare of welcoming trumpets continued to herald their arrival.

And Inghean realised she was trapped alone with Gethin outside the doorway.

Stars sprinkled the velvety black depths of the sky above. She could see the dark silhouettes of helmed guards manning the battlements. A yellow light glowed from the highest window of the mage's tower. Maidservants and stewards scuttled hurriedly through the shadows. She figured everyone she could see was too busy or too far away to heed the predicament of the castellan's most addled daughter: Inghean the stupid.

Her back was pressed against the stone wall of the grand banquet hall.

Gethin pushed himself forcefully against her.

He was big, broad and powerful. His smile leered dangerously close.

'I promised Owain I wouldn't hurt you,' Gethin muttered. 'But the truth is, with what I have in mind right now, I'd have no intention of hurting you.' He pressed a kiss against her throat. 'The truth is: I'd make every moment wholly pleasurable, my lovely.'

His lips were velvet caresses against the sensitive flesh of her neck. She could have been enchanted to the point of surrender by each debilitating kiss. With a massive effort she yanked her face and neck from his reach.

'The truth,' she snapped, wrinkling her nostrils as she sneered. 'Like Gethin ap Cadwallon would know the meaning of the truth.'

He pressed himself hard against her.

He already held one wrist in a cruelly tight grip.

She had no way of pushing away from him. He slipped a knee between her legs and forced her to spread her thighs. She could feel the strong muscle beneath his hosen-clad leg pressing at the soft flesh of her sex. His kisses moved from her throat and started to slip downwards to her exposed décolletage.

'Stop,' she demanded. The word came out on an eddy of urgent breath. 'Don't do this,' she insisted. Even to her own ears the cries sounded like the lusty laments of a maiden urging her suitor to continue. Her nipples were as stiff as they had been whilst she rutted with Owain. The heat between her thighs was fluid and as molten as the coals in any smithy's forge. The inner muscles of her sex seemed to clench and convulse as though they yearned to have him penetrate her depths.

'Please,' she whispered. As an afterthought she added, 'Please stop.'

'You really are a debauched little wench, aren't you?' he murmured.

She wanted to pull away but his kisses were warm and exciting and it was only natural to push herself against him.

His upper thigh pressed through her kirtles against her crotch. The weight was deliciously heavy. She could feel the lips of her sex, acting against her will, trying to kiss at him as he forced himself against her. As their bodies heaved together she could feel the rigid length of his shaft straining to touch her flesh.

His manhood was not as long as Owain's but she figured his girth was slightly thicker. She also thought he would be large enough to satisfy the need that now throbbed insistently inside her loins. It was a thought she denied as soon as it came into her mind. But she was already imagining how it would feel to circle his thickness with her fingers and guide him toward her centre.

'Stop kissing me,' she breathed. 'I'm a married woman.'

He pressed his mouth over hers. His tongue slipped between her lips as his arms worked their way round his body. One hand found the small of her back. The other hand caught a buttock and clutched it tight.

Eventually he tore his lips from hers and gasped, 'You might be married. But you don't want me to stop.'

Loathing herself, Inghean responded to the kiss with hungry enthusiasm. She pushed herself against him and relished the sensation of his tongue's slippery entry between her lips. Her bosom heaved forward so that her nipples were crushed against his manly chest. The inner muscles of her sex pulsed with a greedy hunger that left her weak and desperate to feel him inside her.

Knowing her actions were beyond being irresponsible, she urged herself to resist him. With a demonstration of willpower she had not known she commanded, Inghean straightened her back against the wall and finally found the strength to push Gethin away.

'No,' she said firmly. 'You're a contemptible wretch.'

He stepped back and wiped her kisses from his lips with the back of his hand. He appraised her from beneath heavily-lidded eyes. One hand adjusted the swollen bulge at the front of his breeches. Inghean refused to accept that the size was appealing.

'Yes, my lovely,' Gethin admitted. 'I'm a contemptible wretch. But I'm a contemptible wretch that you want, aren't I?'

She refused to answer. She turned away from him and prepared to flounce into the grand banquet hall.

Gethin was fast.

His strong fingers clutched her bare bicep before she could storm away from him. He pulled her to his side and, with a flash of his hateful smile, he forced her to fall into step beside him.

Together, they entered the grand banquet hall in Owain's wake.

The cavalcade of trumpets continued to blister to the highest rafters of the roof. The noise was so loud it roused a flutter of nesting rock doves that had settled in the eaves. The birds flapped and circled excitedly above the tallow candles that blazed from the iron chandeliers overhead.

In addition to the heralding fanfare the hall was made noisy with the chatter from the castellan's guests and other members of the Blackheath gentry. Officers from the Order of Dark Knights, all dressed in the formal surcoat of silver on black, and bearing the arms of crossed swords over a castle tower, gathered noisily around a beer barrel near the blazing fireplace. Low maidens from the docks caroused around the knights and tried to lure them with giggles and suggestive banter.

At the head of the banquet table Inghean saw Tavia the fair kiss their father on the cheek and then rush excitedly away. Inghean's gaze followed her blonde sister as she hurried to one shadowy corner of the hall beside a concealed entrance.

There were three key-keepers there, identifiable by their uniform leather jerkins and the heavy ring of keys each wore on their hips. Two of the key-keepers held the shoulders of a man with a sack over his head. He was dressed in dirty black tatters, clutching a deck of oversized playing cards, and Inghean suspected he had been dragged up from the dungeons.

A criminal gambler, Inghean guessed. She sighed.

She watched her sister rush to the tallest of the key-keepers. Tavia was constantly glancing back to her father as though confirming the details of some illicit arrangement.

Eventually the two key-keepers holding the hooded man pushed him away.

He fell into Tavia's arms, clutching uncertainly at her for support. As the pair held one another Inghean saw the glint of longing flair in her sister's eyes. And, before the man could have the hood removed from his head, Tavia was escorting him from the banquet hall with an embarrassing and unseemly haste.

Curse of the Blackheath women, Inghean thought. *Always falling for the wrong man.* She considered warning her sister about becoming involved with a man who was obviously in trouble with the authorities. Then she realised she was physically in no position to warn anyone whilst she was in the company of Gethin ap Cadwallon. Given the way she had ended up in this situation, and the things she was prepared to do with Gethin ap Cadwallon, even though she knew the man was a dangerous threat to Blackheath, Inghean supposed she could not honestly claim any moral high ground to warn her sister about the dangers of getting involved with the wrong man.

But she wouldn't let her thoughts follow that depressing downward spiral.

Gethin placed his lips close to the lobe of her ear.

She anticipated the feather-light weight of his mouth against the soft flesh of her neck. When, instead of kissing her, he whispered into her ear, she was almost crushed by the wave of disappointment.

'Keep my secrets,' Gethin warned. 'If you keep my secrets for the duration of these festivities, I shall let you ride me later this evening as a reward.'

'Do you really think I want that?' she sniffed.

He placed a hand against her rear. It was a hateful contact because Inghean believed that Gethin might be able to feel the greedy and wanton heat radiating from her body. In a bid to distance herself from the sensations he inspired, and to wrench her thoughts from their obsession with her hateful captor, Inghean tried to concentrate on the other details within the hall.

Caitrin the dark sat morosely at the banquet table.

Her pretty features were spoilt by a sombre frown. She toyed with a ring that sat on the middle finger of her left hand. Inghean couldn't recall seeing the jewellery before. From her position at the other end of the room she thought it looked like a band of gold set with a moonstone or a mage's eye.

Most likely it had been a gift from a suitor.

More man problems, Inghean guessed. When she saw that Caitrin was staring gloomily toward the head of the table, where the castellan was surrounded by the sable-cloaked Commander of the Dark Knights, the crimson-cowled mage and the Sheriff of the Howling Forest, Inghean figured her sister was besotted with one or the other of the castellan's advisors.

The curse of the Blackheath women, she thought with

bitter dismay. We should all wear motley and be called on to tell our stories for the mirth and merriment of everyone in court. For those warped enough to laugh at such folly, it would be far more entertainment than anything presented by the court's professional fools.

Mercifully, the fanfare came to an end.

There was, Inghean thought wearily, only so much trumpet music a person could hear of an evening. She thought the only way she could have enjoyed greater relief than hearing the fanfare taper to a memory was if Laird Gethin ap Cadwallon finally deigned to take his clammy hand from her backside.

But that, she acknowledged, wouldn't give her the relief she honestly craved.

Owain approached the head of the banquet table.

The castellan stood up to greet him.

The castellan's mage made an elaborate ceremony of sprinkling Owain with droplets of chrism before wafting a censer near him. Frowning, the mage eventually nodded a degree of reluctant approval.

Owain fell to one knee and bowed his head with a dutiful respect that seemed majestic and heartfelt. 'Castellan,' Owain said. He cast a sly glance at Gethin and then returned his gaze to the elderly man at the head of the banquet table. 'I am Gethin ap Cadwallon, High Laird of the West Ridings. Thank you for welcoming me to Blackheath.'

'It's a pleasure to have you visiting our realm,' the castellan said politely. The hall fell dutifully silent as everyone listened to his speech of welcome. 'We are seldom blessed with the company of our respected brethren from the West Ridings,' the castellan went on.

'Arse-kissing,' Gethin muttered darkly.

Inghean realised he was talking to her. She frowned, wishing he could see that it was not acceptable to ridicule the castellan and the Blackheath traditions in such a brusque manner. Gethin seemed neither to notice her discomfort nor care about its effects. Admittedly, no one else could hear Gethin's words. Yet Inghean was uncomfortable with the lack of respect he was showing.

'This is the sort of crap that I despise,' Gethin told Inghean in a low voice. 'Why can't he just welcome us with a cold beer and a warm woman and the promise of some decent pies?'

'Perhaps it's because,' Inghean began stiffly, 'unlike the West Ridings, Blackheath is built on civilised traditions.'

Gethin chuckled darkly. 'For now, I'm sure it is.'

Inghean did not like the smile that played on his lips as he said those words.

'I have organised a modest banquet to mark your arrival,' the castellan told Owain. He gestured toward the three grandly laden banquet tables that lined the halls.

Scowling at the fare that decorated the tables, Gethin

said, 'Modest is the right word. I've seen more meat on the skeletons in Hangman's Cove.'

It was, Inghean thought, a harsh and unfair criticism. There were turkeys, pheasant and chicken. The poultry was basted in fruits and still fresh enough from the cooking fires to smell richly appetising. Tankards of ale, flagons of mead, and goblets of honeyed wine stood at every place setting. Inghean thought it looked like a grand and sumptuous feast but, clearly, Gethin ap Cadwallon was used to more prestigious banquets.

'We are humbled by your generosity,' Owain told the castellan.

'More arse-kissing,' Gethin grumbled. He yawned.

Owain said, 'We hope we can honour Blackheath with the gift that we bring.'

'Gift?'

The castellan sounded as though he didn't know the meaning of the word. He certainly did not look like a man who had sent his daughter to Blackheath's gates to welcome the visitors and to help Owain guide the dragon and its cage into the barn by the stables. For a brief instant Inghean sympathised with Gethin's disapproval of the artifice of court diplomacy.

Gethin whispered at her ear. 'Tell me true, my lovely: don't you find this sort of pretence and fakery to be irritating?'

They were far enough from the castellan so that their

lowered voices were not going to be overheard. But Inghean still found it unsettling that her father was being derided by someone as patently unworthy as the High Laird of the West Ridings.

'I only find it irritating when I have to endure polite conversations and listen to the whining of a spoilt ingrate at the same time,' she sniffed.

He frowned.

The expression was replaced by a tight smile.

'Dirt and dragon dung!' he exclaimed in soft wonder. 'You really do want me, don't you? You want to rut with me.'

'Piss off,' she snorted indignantly.

'I couldn't tell whilst we were outside,' he admitted. 'I thought you were genuinely brushing me off. But you really do want me, don't you? You want to rut with me.'

'I'd rather rut with farm hands.'

The hand on her arm pressed hard. He pulled her closer. 'You do. I can tell. You want me.'

She tried to pull away from him. She wanted to deny that he stirred an arousal in her loins. But his hold on her arm was too strong. And, as much as she didn't want to admit it, there was something appealing in his self-assured and arrogant confidence.

Physically he was not unattractive.

Even though his personality was repulsive she found she wanted to know how he would perform as a lover.

A man who was so filled with self-importance and self-possession had to be capable of something devilishly good in the bed chamber. But she was reluctant to admit that much to herself and she was certainly not going to share the thought with Gethin.

'Take me out of here now,' he muttered, 'and I'll let you ride me.'

She stiffened and tried again to pull away from him.

'Take me out of here now,' he said softly, 'and I'll let you ride me the way you so clearly want to ride me.'

'No,' she insisted.

He continued as though she hadn't spoken. 'We're not in the main entourage,' he urged. 'No one will notice us leaving.'

Her cheeks flushed crimson. His suggestion was base and low. Most infuriatingly, his words stirred a dark and sultry need in her loins. It was the same dark temptation that he had inspired outside. It was the same dark temptation that had filled her just before she rutted with Owain in the stables beside the dragon's cage. Against her better judgement, Inghean could feel herself coming to a decision.

'We mustn't,' she hissed.

'You want to, my lovely. I want to. What's stopping us?'

He shifted his hold on her arm. She guessed he had moved so he could get closer to her. The hand that had touched her rear before now clutched tightly at one buttock through the fabric of her kirtles. His fingers slipped from the meaty flesh of her rump and slid against the crease between her cheeks.

The reluctant desire she had for him blossomed into a low and hateful need. In that instant she decided she would submit to the dictates of her libido. She would let him have her, simply because she was desperate to have him. Whatever consequences befell her afterwards would simply be consequences that she had to accept.

Slyly, Inghean slipped her arm around Gethin's waist. With half an ear, she listened to what was happening at the head of the hall as she surreptitiously escorted the High Laird of the West Ridings away toward the doorway.

Owain, still pretending to be Gethin, remained kneeling on the floor at the head of the banquet table.

'I've brought you the gift of *Y Ddraig Goch,* the red dragon,' Owain told the castellan. 'The species numbers grow thin in the West Ridings. Before their Bedgeridkind expire altogether, I wanted to see one of these fine creatures in the charge of the dragonmeister at Gatekeeper Island.'

A smattering of polite applause greeted Owain's speech.

'*Y Ddraig Goch* is a generous gift,' the castellan allowed. 'It is a gift which, I know, the dragonmeister at Gatekeeper Island will be happy to receive. In return, I would like to suggest that we strengthen the allegiance between Blackheath and the West Ridings. I propose, if you agree to the suggestion, Laird Gethin ...'

Inghean had stopped listening.

She was hurrying out of the hall with Gethin. She intended leading him toward the stable, near *Y Ddraig Goch*. It had proved a comfortable location whilst she rutted with Owain. If that shelter didn't prove sufficiently discreet for Gethin's tastes, she could take him to her bed chambers or –

Gethin pulled on her arm.

He pushed her against the wall where they had kissed before entering the grand banquet hall. Before she could mutter a word of protest his body was pressed heavily against hers. The thrust of his arousal pushed through his breeches against her belly. His masterful hands held her wrists so she couldn't struggle. His mouth enveloped hers as he explored her lips with a kiss.

'Not here,' she grunted. 'Someone will see.'

'There's no one here to see.'

She considered this response, convinced it was a lie, but tempted by the idea of having him as soon as possible. The majority of the castellan's guards were inside the grand banquet hall. Typically, all the low maids from Blackheath's docks had followed them.

Inghean knew the maidservants and stewards would now be bustling behind the scenes to make sure there were provisions for everyone at the banquet tables. Those who had been working hard to prepare the welcome would doubtless be asleep by now. She didn't think there would be anyone else in Blackheath awake and so bored they were examining the shadows for glimpses of rutting couples.

Which all suggested she was safe to do what she wanted with Gethin. And he was safe to do what he wanted with her.

She tore one hand free from Gethin's grasp and reached for his loins.

He was rigid beneath her fingertips.

She tugged the belt away from the waist of his breeches and then unfastened the braies at his hips. The fabric fell to his ankles.

'Horny wench,' he grunted.

'You're not complaining, are you?'

She hoisted her kirtles, exposing her sex for him. The night's air felt cool against her bare buttocks and exposed thighs. A chilly breeze tickled against the slippery heat that glistened on her labia. The gritty pressure of the wall against her backside was an unfamiliar sensation. But it was the warm length of Gethin's erection where she focused her attention. His shaft was fat and heavy in her hand. She guided it to the broiling wetness between her thighs.

'No teasing, my lovely?' Gethin sounded surprised. 'Maids in the West Ridings usually prefer their men to spend an evening kissing at their nether lips or nuzzling at their privates.'

'You're not in the West Ridings now,' Inghean reminded him.

And with those words she slipped his length into her sex.

They both drew startled gasps, as though shocked by the powerful sensations that the intimacy produced. Her inner muscles were skewered by his long, hard length. He pushed into her with such swift force she was left momentarily breathless as her body became used to the swollen pleasure of his penetration.

His shaft was fat and rigid and long enough to fill her. He was blessed with a heat that almost matched the smouldering sear of her wetness. The rush of pleasure that ran through her was nearly climactic.

She sighed.

And then he was sliding out.

The cool dry night around them only served to emphasise the warm and sultry heat of their union. She could hear the animal slurp of her sex. Her nether lips guzzled on his shaft as he ploughed into her with a force that was almost brutal.

She rocked her hips back and forth, trying to match his pace. He was using her with such a swift determination she knew she couldn't hope to keep up with him. Breathless from the exertion of trying, and desperate to bask in the satisfaction she knew he could provide, Inghean placed her arms over Gethin's shoulders.

He paused from his vigorous pounding, and seemed

to sense what she wanted from him. His hands went to her buttocks.

Inghean lifted one leg and then the other. She circled her calves over his hips, crossing her ankles behind his back, whilst Gethin supported her weight with his strong hands. It meant that she felt as though she was resting solely on the support of the thick erection that filled her, but Inghean did not see that as a bad thing. Given the ferocity of her need for satisfaction, she did not think she could ask for a better way to be ridden.

With powerful and athletic thrusts, Gethin began to ride her with more vigour.

She groaned.

It was a position that made her feel as though her sex had never been so open or so exposed or so full. Each penetration was a glossy and thrilling fulfilment of every satisfaction she had ever desired.

She clutched tight against him: her arms over his shoulders; her hands clutched behind his back; her breasts pressed to his manly chest. She savoured the rush of satisfaction as it came hurtling through her body. It was wrong to be with a man who was not her husband, she knew that much. But she also knew that she and her husband had discussed an arrangement before his regiment left for the Silver Sands.

Whilst pledged troths and vows of unfailing fidelity worked for some couples, she knew that the passionate libido she shared with Captain Clement would be strained rather than hardened by such unnecessary tempering. They had come to a compromise that allowed him to enjoy his time spent on foreign shores whilst she was free to do things with men like Owain and Gethin.

Gethin's fingers tightened against her rear.

He pushed forcefully into her, the end of his length pressing deep inside her centre. She stiffened against the first threat of satisfaction that now promised to spill through her body.

The only saddening thing about the pleasure she was enjoying with Gethin was the knowledge that he was obviously an enemy toward Blackheath. He was threatening her with exposure as an adulteress; he was hiding his identity from the castellan; and for all his skills as a lover there was something devious about the man that she simply didn't trust.

His fingernails clawed at her backside.

His pace quickened as his length slipped furiously in and out of her sex. The ripples of pleasure grew quicker and stronger and sweeter in their flavour.

'Great Gods of the West Ridings!' he gasped.

She croaked her own exclamation of pleasure for him, delighted that the shock of satisfaction was coming in such a rich and heady explosion. His length pulsed repeatedly inside her sex whilst her inner muscles clenched and convulsed around his thickness.

As the soaring pleasure flooded through her body, Inghean had an epiphany. Her thoughts were suddenly so clear she knew exactly what needed to be done.

She couldn't simply let him continue to deceive her father: that was unthinkable. But she couldn't force a confrontation either.

She would continue to pretend to be cowed by Gethin. For the sake of her own reputation, and to save her husband from embarrassment, she would remain silent whilst the High Laird of the West Ridings was in Blackheath.

Then, once he and his party had continued on toward Gatekeeper Island, she could tell the castellan that Gethin was a liar. With the truth exposed, her father could then have his mage contact the dragonmeister of Gatekeeper Island who would refuse to allow the visitors to land on the island.

She wasn't sure what would happen then, but she thought that the plan of action might be enough to save her own reputation and to make sure Gethin didn't get to execute whatever wicked schemes he might be plotting.

'Most enjoyable,' Gethin allowed, slipping his spent length from her.

Inghean barely heard him. Her worries that she might be endangering Blackheath were now behind her. She could enjoy the remainder of the evening without fear that her actions would bring about irreversible consequences. She leant against Gethin and kissed him lightly in gratitude. Now that she was no longer worrying about the folly of rutting with the laird, she wondered if they would be able to share a bedchamber for the remainder of his stay in Blackheath. If he didn't want to share her bedchamber she supposed she could open the invitation to Owain. For some reason, that prospect struck her as being even more exciting.

Those warming thoughts continued to stir syrupy excitement in her loins as she brushed down her kirtles and waited for Gethin to fasten his braies and breeches. Once he was properly dressed she allowed him to gallantly escort her into the grand banquet hall.

'Inghean,' the castellan called.

She glanced anxiously up at him, wondering if he had caught some notion of the indiscretion she had just enjoyed with Gethin ap Cadwallon. Her cheeks flushed at the idea of having her father berate her for her licentious behaviour.

'Inghean,' the castellan pronounced loudly. 'I was wondering where you'd gone. I was about to send men searching for you.'

He tilted his head. His smile was trusting and patient.

She thought he did not deserve to have his trust disabused by the likes of Gethin ap Cadwallon and Owain the fucker. She supposed he did not deserve to have his trust disabused by his daughter either, but that was a consideration she knew she could dwell on at a later date.

'I was …' she floundered.

There was no way to artfully hide the truth. Instead, she realised it was best to gloss over the episode and hope he didn't press any further questions. 'I was outside.'

The castellan shook his head, as though uninterested in her explanation. 'You missed the exciting developments, daughter.'

Inghean noticed that Owain was glaring at Gethin with an expression that looked like impotent fury. He wore the narrowed brows of a man who had been forced to make a choice larger than his calling. He wore the frown of a man who now feared he had made the wrong decision. Inghean wondered what they had missed.

'Gethin ap Cadwallon,' the castellan patted Owain on the shoulder as he spoke to Inghean, 'High Laird of the West Ridings, has kindly brought us the gift of a red dragon.'

'I'm aware of this, father,' Inghean said patiently.

'The beast will join the Bedgerid of dragons in the catacombs on Gatekeeper Island. High Laird Gethin and his entourage will sail with *Y Ddraig Goch* for the island tomorrow morning.'

Owain mouthed an apology to Gethin.

Gethin tilted his jaw, seeming unclear as to why this news merited an apology.

'This is very exciting, father,' Inghean told the castellan. 'I've seen the red dragon and she is truly beautiful. I don't doubt the dragonmeister at Gatekeeper Island will be thrilled by the addition to the catacombs. But why did this news mean you needed me?'

The castellan held Owain's shoulder with a paternal tenderness. 'To show that we're grateful for his generosity, and to help strengthen ties between Blackheath and the West Ridings, I have offered Laird Gethin the hand of either Caitrin or Tavia.'

'Marriage?' Gethin snapped.

Inghean didn't need to glance at him to know that he wore the same expression of horror that twisted her insides into knots. The idea of either of her sisters being betrothed to Gethin ap Cadwallon was appalling. To add to the confusion, her father thought Owain was Gethin. The whole situation was becoming as confused as a fool's farce. She made to step forward, ready to expose the High Laird of the West Ridings as a liar and to admit her own involvement in the deceit.

Gethin grabbed her wrist and forced her to stay by his side.

'Stay silent, my lovely.'

She steadied herself with a deep breath and realised there would be time to expose him once Gethin had left Blackheath and she was safely alone with her father.

'The high laird has kindly accepted the invitation to marriage,' the castellan explained. 'But he's asked if he can get better acquainted with Caitrin and Tavia over the next few days, so he can ensure the marriage is the happiest one possible.'

'Dirt and dragon dung!' Gethin spat. He was glowering at Owain with unrestrained fury.

'That's unexpected news,' Inghean said with forced cheer. 'But how does it affect me, father?'

'The high laird will be getting acquainted with them on the journey to Gatekeeper Island,' the castellan explained. 'As a matter of propriety, and since your husband is currently quelling the uprising in the land of the Silver Sands, I want you to accompany the party to Gatekeeper Island and act as chaperone to Tavia and Caitrin.'

Inghean considered this for a moment before nodding reluctant consent. She didn't know whether she was more appalled by the idea of her sisters being pledged to Cadwallon, or the prospect of sea travel. She wanted to speak. She wanted to say so much. But she knew, if she opened her mouth, the only words likely to come out would be, 'Dirt and dragon dung!'

CHAPTER FIVE

Tavia the Curious

Caitrin and Tavia sat on the aft deck of the birlinn as it ploughed its way stolidly through the waters of the Last Sea. Sapphire and azure horizons stretched in all directions and the seas and the skies blended together. White-topped waves rippled the dark surface. An occasional dolphin leapt from the waters whilst black-legged kittiwakes honked at them from the cloudless blue overhead.

Ahead loomed Gatekeeper Island.

It was a lush and verdant outcrop blossoming from the sea. Still too far away for them to make out anything other than its greenery and the temple towers, the skies above Gatekeeper Island were circled by the dark flying shadows of faraway dragons.

Neither Caitrin nor Tavia bothered to study the creatures. Tavia had always been unnerved by the creatures and she knew there would be plenty of time to enjoy the dragons at closer proximity once the birlinn had landed. Tavia also knew now was not the time to waste peering at faraway dragons. Now, she thought determinedly, was the time to discuss those important matters that needed to be addressed with her sister.

The birlinn was a broad-sailed vessel, commissioned by the castellan, to take them from Blackheath to Gatekeeper Island. It provided fairly comfortable accommodation. It helped that the seas were smooth and unruffled, and that the winds were with them. But Tavia did not think all the comfort in the world would make it easy to endure the company of her sister and the conversation they needed to have before they reached their destination.

'I won't stand in the way of true romance,' Caitrin said easily. 'You can have Muscles, if you want him. I don't want him, or his companion Dragon Dung.'

Tavia gritted her teeth.

Caitrin had a habit of giving nicknames to everyone she encountered. *Muscles* and *Dragon Dung* were the nicknames she had given to the High Laird of the West Ridings and his travelling companion – a man who constantly exclaimed with the words: 'Dirt and dragon dung!'

There had been other nicknames that Caitrin tried, and Tavia was sure there would be others that she'd invent before the journey to Gatekeeper Island was ended. But the childishness of the name-calling did not lend any sense of seriousness to the discussion on potential marriage partners.

'You're too generous, dear sister,' Tavia replied with forced ease. 'But I wouldn't want to deprive you of such a regal specimen of a husband. You should have him.'

'I couldn't. You have him.'

'Don't be selfless. I'm thinking of you.'

'And I'm thinking he would be better suited for you.'

Tavia frowned. She produced a bota of fire wine from the pockets on her hip, snatched a swallow, and then passed the drink to Caitrin.

Caitrin chugged the fire wine with surprising enthusiasm.

As was the family custom, they were dressed in matching outfits. Rather than wearing the traditional red-on-gold colours of Blackheath women they were adorned in the subtly different garb of gold-on-red, hidden and muted by the sable travelling furs. The little winds that filled the sail were strong enough to tousle Tavia's blonde locks. She could feel herself shrinking into her furs. It took an effort of willpower not to glance toward the horizon, because the approach of Gatekeeper Island suggested an end to their journey.

Tavia believed that the important decisions would all be made on Gatekeeper Island. That was where she believed High Laird Gethin ap Cadwallon would make a choice between marrying her or her sister.

A sense of dark foreboding told Tavia that she would not like his decision.

'Marriage issues aside,' she said stiffly, 'I trust we can reach a more acceptable agreement with regards to finding dragon horn.'

Caitrin scowled at her. 'Whatever we find, I vow now that I'll share it evenly and fairly with you. You know that, fair sister.'

Tavia nodded. 'At least we can agree on that much.' She sighed then said, 'But, whilst it's easy to agree about the dragon horn, it seems neither of us wants to be married to High Laird Lackwit himself.'

'He's preferable to that oily servant that Inghean's been fawning over,' Caitrin admitted. 'But the muscle-bound clodhopper does nothing for me. He's from the West Ridings. He smells of uncleaned stables. And I think he might have been dropped on his head as a child.'

Tavia nodded reluctant agreement. 'But, since one of us will be expected to take him as a husband, shouldn't we decide now which one of us it should be?'

'I've already decided,' Caitrin said quickly. 'And it's not me.'

'That's not fair.'

Caitrin shook her head. 'I've got designs on someone else.'

'Who?'

'That would be telling. But what's your excuse? Why can't you have him?'

'The same reason as you,' Tavia admitted. 'My heart belongs to another.'

'If it's just your heart, I'm sure Laird Git-face Coldwilly can work around that. I suspect that your heart is the last of your body's organs that he'd be worried about.'

Tavia sighed and took another swallow of fire wine. 'You really are an impossible bitch, Caitrin. Can't we discuss this like civilised adults?'

'Why am I being branded an impossible bitch? Because I don't want to marry a man who you find repugnant? Grow up, Tavia. You're being just as impossible.'

She gestured for Tavia to share her bota of fire wine but Tavia refused to pass the skin over. 'If we can't come to a decision between us, then Laird Git-face will make the decision for us. I really think we should talk this through and try to reach an equitable agreement.'

Caitrin thrust a finger inside her left nostril. It made her pretty features look grossly unappealing. She left the finger there as she glared defiantly at Tavia. 'I think we should just let Laird Git-face make the decision. If he doesn't want me by the end of this voyage I shall learn to console myself to the disappointment.'

Not trusting herself to say anything else, feeling as though she was ready to scream with outrage, Tavia turned away and flounced below the deck.

Out of the sunlight the world beneath the deck seemed impossibly dark.

It took a moment for her eyes to adjust to the lightlessness. In that time she could hear the amplified sounds of the sea splashing against the oak planks of the birlinn's keel. She could hear the sounds of the iron nails and the birlinn's ribs straining to hold together. They were not the most reassuring of noises, but she supposed they were common enough sounds for any vessel crossing the Last Sea.

Heading toward the bow, lurching from side to side in rhythm with the birlinn's pitch and yaw, she wondered if she dared find the dragon stored in the ship's hold. The creature was called Drusilla and, even to someone with a mild fear of dragons, Tavia had to concede she was attractive and affable and a compelling curiosity. Finding her and petting her, she thought, might help to counter the ridiculous fear she harboured.

Ideally Tavia would have hoped to encounter Alvar of Erland.

On her instructions, officers from the Order of Dark Knights had bundled him aboard the birlinn after the castellan had agreed to his release from the dungeons. It was the wish Alvar had expressed when she first met him, before Tavia had known there would be a birlinn waiting in the harbour to take a party across the Last Sea and onto Gatekeeper Island. But because Alvar was a stowaway aboard the ship, and trying to avoid discovery, she thought it unlikely she would find him.

She stopped on hearing raised voices from the darkness ahead.

'Get to the aft deck and pay court to those two sisters.'

'Pay court? Why?'

From her limited knowledge of the birlinn's geography, it sounded to Tavia as though the voices were coming from the captain's quarters. She couldn't decide whether she should eavesdrop and find out more, or return the way she had come to avoid the embarrassment of overhearing what was being said. As she was trying to come to a decision the voices continued their heated exchange.

'Dirt and dragon dung! Isn't it enough that I've told you to do it?'

'It just strikes me as pointless. You have no intention of marrying either woman. And if you did, I don't think you'd want me to have *paid court* to either maid before you could get in there.'

'We haven't yet landed at Gatekeeper Island. You'll do as I've told you and keep up this pretence until we're safely harboured at our destination. Do you understand?'

'I understand perfectly. I understand that you've forgotten our arrangement. I'm not here as your bloody servant. I have my own reasons for going to Gatekeeper Island and it was never so that I could pretend to be you, or follow your stupid instructions.'

The final exclamation was followed by the sound of a slamming door.

A hand rested on Tavia's shoulder. Softly spoken words were whispered in her ear. 'They've been arguing like that all morning. It's playing merry hell with my hangover. Who the hell are these damned people?'

She turned and saw Alvar's bearded face looming at her from the darkness. Unable to resist the impulse she took him in her embrace and kissed him.

He seemed momentarily surprised.

And then he melted into her arms.

His hands were instantly behind her, pulling her against him, and she realised she was being held by a man who desired her company. That, she thought bitterly, was far more appealing than the idea of being offered to a nobleman as though she was being swapped in exchange for the present of a dragon.

'I wish I could have spent time with you last night,' she whispered. 'I'm so sorry I wasn't able.'

'You got me out of that dungeon,' Alvar told her. 'You have no need to apologise for anything.'

He pressed kisses against her cheeks. His lips were warm. Each time they connected with her skin her senses were lit by small fires of anticipation. Every one of those fires seemed to nestle in her loins and build into something larger. But it wasn't just his kisses.

His hands also seemed to be working more magicks than she could expect to see from all of Blackheath's mages during the height of the summer magicks ceremonies. Those were the ceremonies when mystical fireworks erupted and exploded to the pleasure and satisfaction of everyone watching. Those were the ceremonies when the night sky was brought to life with the shapes of shadow-monsters looming from the clouds. And none of those magicks had ever affected her as powerfully as the caresses she was enjoying from Alvar's hands.

Her cheeks blushed as she thought of the pleasures she could enjoy with Alvar. In the darkness below decks she didn't think he noticed her embarrassment.

Somehow, and she didn't have time to think how, Alvar had managed to open the furs that she wore to protect herself from the cold winds that blew across the Last Sea. His fingers had ingratiated themselves underneath the furs, and slipped between her gold overdress and her red travelling chemise.

There was an urgency in the way that he scrabbled to reach her skin.

His blatant desire for her made Tavia anxious to enjoy his touch. She yearned for the heady frisson of bare and needy flesh writhing against bare and needy flesh. And she knew, if she asked him, Alvar would give her far more than the simple frisson of bare and needy flesh writhing against her body.

He would likely be willing to give her a lot more.

'Where can we go?' she asked.

'I was bunking in the feed store,' Alvar said. 'I have a blanket there.'

'You make it sound so tempting.'

She laughed at her own attempt to be facetious, aware that the invitation to be alone with him did sound absurdly irresistible. Tavia couldn't work out why she found Alvar to be so attractive but it was true that the idea of spending an hour on a blanket with him in the feed store was preferable to the prospect of lounging on the upper decks with her obdurate sister, or being forced to suffer the insufferable company of the High Laird of the West Ridings or his conceited travelling companion.

She thought of telling Alvar as much and then decided he didn't need anything else helping to exacerbate his overdeveloped high self-opinion.

He held her hand. His fingers intertwined with hers. He hurried her along the shadowy corridors of the underdeck as though he knew where he was going. She supposed, as he'd had a night to familiarise himself with the layout, it was to be expected that he knew his way around the birlinn. But it was still reassuring to think that he was now taking the lead for them.

'We'll have to be quiet,' Alvar whispered.

'Why?'

'Sound travels too well aboard this damned boat,' he grumbled. 'You heard those two idiots arguing as though they were standing right next to us, didn't you?'

She nodded. Sound did seem to travel too well beneath the decks of the birlinn.

'We need to keep that in mind,' Alvar explained. 'When we start rutting in the feed store, as soon as I have you screaming with pleasure, we'll be surrounded by sailors, slaves and a captain. Your cries will be so lusty they will all likely think I've taken to murdering you. It will be a sure way to expose the fact that I'm a stowaway here.'

'*When we start rutting*?' Tavia tried to sound surprised as she repeated his words. 'You're being very presumptuous, aren't you?'

He stopped.

She continued running and bumped into him.

For the first time she noticed he was carrying a sword. The scabbard hung from his hip and nudged her leg as she ran into him. A glance down showed her it was a shortened weapon. Tavia suspected it was a riding sword and she guessed it was possibly stolen, won or bought from one of the Order of Dark Knights.

It never occurred to her that he might have come by the sword legitimately.

The idea of Alvar possessing a sword made him seem suddenly darker and more dangerous. Her heartbeat raced and she couldn't explain why that knowledge should be so exciting. But, knowing he was armed, and knowing that he now had the ability to threaten her and demand she satisfy his every whim, Tavia found herself needing him with an even greater urgency.

He captured her in his arms and held her close. His mouth moved to hers and she was almost smothered by the kiss he gave. The sword hung forgotten from his hip. Then his fingers slipped down to the open front of her overdress and went to the breast of her scarlet chemise.

The nipples he found were hard buttons of raw desire. When he caressed them through the wool of her chemise she had to bite her lower lip to stifle a cry of desire. Sparkles of bright white longing crackled through the tips of her breasts and scorched her with the greedy need for satisfaction. His hand dropped, his knuckles slid softly over her belly, and she was touched by the thrilling idea that he was about to caress her sex.

She closed her eyes and held her breath.

The moment lingered indefinitely.

When she opened her eyes she saw Alvar was studying her with a smug smile of superiority on his lips.

'No,' he said eventually. 'I don't think I was being presumptuous. You're desperate to rut with me. And I know damned well I'm going to have you screaming with satisfaction.' He paused for a moment before adding, 'Unless I maybe try gagging you whilst we're together? Perhaps that might stop you from screaming loud enough to alert the whole crew?'

She clasped a hand over her mouth, excited by the idea

of him controlling her in such a way. In that moment she knew she would do whatever he asked of her.

He gripped her wrist and, again, they were hurrying off into the darkness. She caught the smell of livestock, an earthy animal stink that was simultaneously repellent and reassuring. She feared for a moment that he might be taking her to the dragon and the idea made the muscles of her stomach tighten with momentary dread. Then she caught the dusty smell of grain and knew they were nearing the birlinn's feed store where Alvar had bedded for the night.

Her heartbeat quickened.

As her pulse raced she realised she was about to enjoy the pleasure of bedding with the seer. The idea inspired a heightened thrill of arousal. Her need for him bristled in her loins like a live thing trying to make its presence known. Excitement flourished in the pit of her stomach. She grew warm and wet and pulsed with swelling need.

It was dark. The slatted planks from the deck above were the ceiling to the birlinn's feed store. Bars of light came through in diagonal slants, each one catching the dancing motes of dust that lingered in the air. But there weren't enough bars of light to properly illuminate the room.

She knew her eyes would eventually get used to the darkness but, at first, she could only rely on the input from her other senses. She drank in the appetising smell of grain and the heady aroma of Alvar's nearness. She listened to the stifled silence of the room and the hasty breath of his anticipation. And she savoured the sensation of his strong, masculine hands as they took command of her body.

He eased her to the floor.

She heard the sound of him discarding his sword. The weapon landed atop a mound of feed and the noise was reduced to a whisper. In the darkness, she felt him guiding her toward a blanket and realised it was supported on a surprisingly comfortable mattress of grain. He pressed himself on top of her, positioning himself between her legs, and began to slip kisses against her cheeks and throat.

Maddeningly, a question occurred to her. It was a question that she knew she should have asked when they first met. The knowledge of that oversight was too important for her to let it go past for one further moment.

She pushed his kisses away as she sat up.

'What's the matter?' he asked.

She could hear from his tone that he was perplexed.

'Why were you in the dungeons?'

Alvar gave a soft snort of laughter. 'Seriously? You're asking that now?'

'I'm asking that now,' she agreed. 'But it doesn't sound like I'm getting an answer. Why were you in the dungeons, Alvar, son of Erland? Why were you in a cell awaiting a visit from the hangman? What the hell had you done to merit the death penalty?'

He looked away from her. 'I cheated at cards.'

'I didn't know that was a crime that resulted in the death penalty.'

'I happened to be playing cards with a magistrate, two commanders from the Order of Dark Knights and a senior key-keeper from the dungeons.' He smiled sourly and said, 'Working together, those four managed to expedite the judicial process and increase its effectiveness. I'm only thankful the hangman wasn't at our card table that evening, otherwise I would have been swinging from my neck by the time you first came looking for me.'

His fingers, ever inquisitive, were pushing through her furs and finding their way again to the warm flesh of her breast. When his thumb rubbed firmly over the stiffness of one nipple, Tavia held her breath and wanted to lie back. Her need for him had grown to an insistent demand.

But she needed more answers before they did anything else. She wasn't sure she was hearing the entire truth.

'Why were you cheating at cards?' she asked

'To get money.' The words were whispered as a kiss just below her ear.

'Can't you get money with your powers as a seer?'

'I could,' he admitted. 'But I can get more money from cheating at cards. And it gives me a chance to exploit the greedy. That's always quite satisfying.'

The quietness of his voice was a reminder that they were alone in the dusty room. His words had dropped to a whisper that she had to strain to hear. She lowered her voice to the same cautious tone, fearful that they might be overheard. For some reason that she couldn't understand the whispering added to the heightened sense of intimacy.

'Do you really find it satisfying to exploit the greedy?' she asked.

He chuckled and she understood there were other ways of interpreting her question. His lips returned to the side of her neck. The bristle of his beard scratched at her skin. The abrasive caress was a perfect balance between discomfort and euphoria. His hands found their way inside her furs and she savoured the sensation of skin-on-skin caresses. She was caught in his embrace as he pressed himself close and kissed her. And she found, even though she didn't fully believe it was true, she was ready to accept his explanation that he had been sentenced to death for cheating at cards.

Eager to experience him as fully as she could, Tavia reached for the thrusting bulge at the front of his hosen. She tugged him free from his braies and held his length in the palm of her hand.

In the darkness she could feel that he was thick, warm and throbbing. The sticky perspiration that lacquered his shaft was an oily sheen on her fingertips. She savoured the sensation of having him in her hand for a moment. Whilst she needed to guide him to the centre of her sex, she wanted to relish the pleasure of simply holding his most sensitive part.

'You're a tease,' he murmured.

'And you wouldn't want me any other way,' she returned.

Then his hands were working on her clothes in the darkness and he was hoisting up her overdress and her kirtles so that her bare sex was exposed.

His hands smoothed up her legs toward the tops of her thighs. His fingertips reached the sensitive crease of flesh where her hip met her leg. As his inquisitive touch stroked toward the lips of her broiling sex, Tavia groaned with encouragement.

She pressed a hand over her mouth to muffle the sound.

'Should we really be doing this?' he asked.

Her heart had been racing before. Now it hammered with desperation at the idea that he might leave her untouched, unsatisfied, and unfulfilled.

'Don't you want me?' she asked.

He chuckled. She could feel the vibrations of his mirth echoing through the throbbing length of flesh that filled her palm. He placed a beard-prickly kiss against her throat and his long hair caressed her cheek as he shook his head.

'Of course I want you,' he told her. 'I was just wondering if we should hold off until we reach Gatekeeper Island

and we're able to get hold of the dragon horn that's waiting there.'

She squeezed his erection tight.

The pulse beneath her fingertips seemed to beat with renewed passion.

'We can do this now. We can do it again when we've got a supply of dragon horn. Maybe we can compare the two experiences. Maybe we'll decide never to do it again without dragon horn,' she said brightly. Her tone became firm as she added, 'But I know that you're not leaving this room until you've rutted with me like you promised. I know you're not leaving this feed hold until you've had me wanting to scream with unabashed pleasure.'

'Very well,' he allowed. 'But I hope you're ready for how good this is going to be. I'm a proficient lover. I could have been knighted for my services to wenches throughout the West Ridings of Erland.'

And, whilst she wanted to baulk at his arrogance, Tavia couldn't help but expect that the experience of being with him would be truly superlative.

Alvar knelt between her parted thighs.

She eased the rounded end of his length against her sex and stroked him against her wetness. It was possible to feel the tremor of anticipation that tingled from him. As the weight of his shaft pressed against her, she held her breath and squeezed down, to make the pleasure of his penetration seem more thrilling.

As he pushed into her, Tavia whimpered.

His mouth was over her face.

They shared a rich and passionate kiss where their tongues intertwined as they fully explored one another.

Then his length was slipping into her. He filled her. He urged echoes of raw satisfaction to throb to each and every nerve-ending.

'Alvar, son of Erland,' she breathed.

'Keep practising that name,' he encouraged. The words came on grunts of growing passion. 'Keep practising my name because you'll be screaming it in a moment.'

She wanted to berate him for being conceited, but she couldn't help feeling he might be right. She yearned to scream his name when he took her to the height of orgasm. And she suspected that any pleasure bestowed by Alvar would be a damned powerful pleasure.

Her ankles slipped behind his back and she linked them together. The wooden heels of her pattens knocked lightly together. When she squeezed the muscles of her thighs she was rewarded to find the pressure of his broad hips sitting firmly between them.

Straining to urge him deeper into her hole, Tavia bucked her pelvis upward to meet Alvar. In an act of forceful retaliation, he pushed himself fully into her sex.

Her nipples shimmered with echoes of pleasure. Her sex was full to the point of bursting. She knew, when the height of her climax struck, it was going to be a euphoric and all-consuming orgasm.

His hands fell to her buttocks. He caressed her cheeks with open palms that seemed to bask in the pleasure of such intimate contact. She could feel him raising her as he pushed back and forth into the heart of her sex. His length seemed to expand and grow more solid.

Tavia braced herself for the overflow of joy that she knew was coming.

The hands at her buttocks gripped tightly.

He began to ride back and forth with increased ferocity. She was starting to make shapes from the shadows and could see the concentration furrowing his brow as he rode her with determined swiftness.

The pleasure stole quickly upon her.

She was aware that shards of raw enjoyment were trickling through her body and heightening her responses. She arched her back and tried to buck her hips toward him as he plunged ever-deeper into her sex.

'Faster,' she insisted. She spat the words from between clenched teeth. 'Faster and deeper. Satisfy me, Alvar of Erland. Satisfy me.'

'Greedy bitch,' he muttered.

But he did as she asked and rode himself into her with renewed and furious passion. Tavia gripped at him so hard she was thankful he still wore his doublet. If not for the protection of his obsidian-black clothes she feared that her nails would have raked the flesh from his back. Her thighs pressed more forcefully against him and the rush of climactic satisfaction began to hurtle through her body.

Tavia opened her mouth to scream with gratitude as the rush of elation flooded through her centre.

Alvar placed his hand over her mouth.

Her eyes opened wide as she understood he was stifling the scream that she so desperately wanted to release. The knowledge that he was controlling her body and silencing her cries only added to the thrill of satisfaction that hurtled from her loins.

When his thick shaft pulsed inside, juddering and swelling and daubing her with its heated wetness, she savoured another rush of satisfaction as his spend gushed into her most intimate parts.

With a weary sigh, she finally released her grip on his shoulders and hips, pulled herself away and moaned with satisfied dismay.

'I'll be damned,' Alvar gasped. He sounded weak and breathless. 'If I'm this good without dragon horn,' he marvelled, 'I'm going to be amazing when I've swallowed a skinful.' He pulled her back into his embrace and hugged her tight. 'We'll suffer so much pleasure together we're going to stop the hands of time.'

Tavia wanted to pull away from him but the pleasure of his sated mood was infectious. 'If your cock was as imposing as your self-opinion you'd be able to pleasure every nymph in the Howling Forest,' she said with sour good humour.

She could see that Alvar was seriously considering this. He pressed close to her in a comfortable embrace and seemed to nod agreement. 'I don't need dragon horn for that,' he decided. 'I think I could pleasure every nymph in the Howling Forest with my abilities as they are.' He gave her a sly wink and said, 'Should we play that as a game before this ship lands on Gatekeeper Island? I'll pretend I'm a wandering wizard and you can be a woodland nymph?'

His hands brushed against the too-too-sensitive skin near her sex.

She didn't know whether to beg him to continue or to push him away with a complaint that he was too demanding and that her body needed time to recover. The fear that he might never return if she pushed him away was all that it took to stay her hand.

Tactfully, she moved his fingers from their exploration of her intimate folds and raised them to her lips. After placing light kisses against the tip of each one she raised her gaze to meet his.

The light in the store room hadn't changed but her eyes were now used to the unrelenting darkness. She could see the swarthy smile glittering from beneath his dark and bushy beard.

'Tell me my future, Alvar of Erland. Tell me what will become of me.'

Alvar held her tight in his embrace. 'Your future is easy for me to tell,' he said. 'You're about to go between my legs and suck my cock. I predict that you will spit, and then suck me hard again so I can –'

She punched him on the arm.

'Tell me my future,' she insisted. 'The choice between my sister and me has been pledged to a visiting laird. Tell me which of us he'll choose.'

Alvar fumbled in the darkness for something. Tavia wondered what he was trying to get until she heard the snap of a card from the tarot.

She could see the deck of cards in his hand. The cards looked like a part of his fist – a natural extension of his body.

'Curious,' he muttered.

A frown wrinkled his brow. He reached into another pocket of his discarded jacket and produced a fat ball of thread.

'Give this to your sister,' he said. 'She'll remember her mythology lessons from the books she read as a child. She'll have heard stories about Ariadne, Theseus and the Minotaur. She'll need this to secure the dragon horn you seek.'

Tavia accepted the twine, not sure how a ball of string could possibly help to secure dragon horn, but not doubting Alvar's word. He was a famed seer and due to his foresight he had already got them travelling halfway across the Last Sea towards Gatekeeper Island. She had no reason to doubt him or his abilities.

'What can you tell me about my future?' she insisted. 'I just told you, Caitrin and I have been pledged to a visiting laird. Which of us will he choose? Can the cards tell you that?'

Alvar glanced at the card he had just uncovered and said, 'This visiting laird will not choose you.'

She wanted to sigh with relief. Knowing that would not be a fair way of thinking about her sister she asked, 'Does that mean he'll pick Caitrin?'

Alvar turned over another card. In the bars of light that touched his face from the decking above she could see he was frowning.

'No,' he said. 'This laird won't pick her either.'

Tavia shook her head. 'That makes no sense. Won't the castellan of Blackheath see it as an enormous insult if the offer of a marriage contract is refused?'

'Who is this laird?' Alvar asked, turning a card.

'It's Gethin ap Cadwallon, High Laird of the West Ridings.'

She noticed that the card Alvar had turned over bore the skeletal figure of death. Alvar's frown was clouded with ferocity.

'Gethin ap Cadwallon? That bastard is here? On this

boat?' He was standing up, pulling up his hosen and snatching the riding sword from where he had discarded it before they lay together. 'Gethin ap Cadwallon? That bastard is here? How could I have missed my opportunity?'

'Do you know him?' Tavia asked. 'Who is he? How do you know him?'

Alvar pushed past her. She stood up and saw he was headed for the rope ladder that led to the aft deck.

'Alvar,' she called. 'Where are you going? Who is he? Do you know him?'

Alvar of Erland paused briefly. He fixed her with a scowl that was darkened by the shadows from below the decks. 'I don't just know him,' Alvar growled flatly. 'I've vowed to kill the damned bastard.'

CHAPTER SIX

The Mage's Eye

Nihal sat alone in the highest tower at Blackheath. A spyglass stood on the window ledge, pointing out toward the Last Sea. The spyglass was trained in the direction of the birlinn as it ploughed through the waters toward Gatekeeper Island.

But Nihal faced the opposite direction. He sat alone at the tower room's centre desk, staring through a veil of tears into the cloudy mists and shapes that lurked inside a crystal ball.

'Don't do this, Cait,' the mage whispered. 'Please don't do this.'

Nihal touched the polished glass, as though the crystal ball allowed two-way communication with Caitrin through the mage's eye ring she now wore. But the ring and the crystal ball were not so sophisticated. The magicks enchanting the two devices only allowed Nihal to see what was happening in Cait's world. All that Nihal could do was remember the phrase that she had whispered when they were last together: '*If the day comes when I must have this stranger as my betrothed, I can always close my eyes and pretend that it's you and not him between my legs.*'

Another tear trickled down the mage's cheek.

'Please, Cait,' Nihal murmured. 'Please don't.'

'Caitrin of Blackheath? Caitrin the dark?'

She glanced up to see the man with long hair and the broad muscular chest standing over her. She hesitated for a moment, on the verge of calling him 'Muscles'. Remembering that was the private nickname she had given him, she corrected herself before causing any embarrassment. 'High Laird Gethin ap Cadwallon,' she said with forced politeness. 'It's a pleasure to see you.'

Caitrin had noticed, whenever she addressed Muscles by his full name and title, the man always looked around as though he was expecting someone else to be standing behind him. It was an unusual trait, she supposed, and she was annoyed to admit that it was somewhat endearing. Once again, on this occasion, when she greeted him by his full name and title, Muscles glanced over his shoulder and then smiled bashfully as he turned back to study her.

'Caitrin of Blackheath,' he began. 'I see you're alone.'

'There's not much escapes the finely honed observation

skills of a man from the West Ridings,' Caitrin agreed. Conscious that her sarcasm was seldom appreciated she added, 'I managed to annoy Tavia and she's gone below decks to studiously ignore me from down there. I haven't seen Inghean since this birlinn left port.'

'Your elder sister is in the captain's suite,' Muscles explained. Uninvited he took a seat next to her at the table. 'I think Inghean's having difficulty finding her sea legs.'

'They're likely just beneath her sea arse,' Caitrin grinned.

She was concerned that her sister was neglecting her duties as chaperone aboard the birlinn but she supposed seasickness was an acceptable excuse. And, whilst Inghean's absence meant that there was no one looking out for her honour aboard the ship, Caitrin figured her honour had survived long enough without Inghean's diligent efforts. Admittedly, her honour had needed resuscitating and resurrecting a couple of times, thanks to the help of Nihal's magicks. But it was currently intact and she supposed that was as much as anyone could ever want from honour. It was, she conceded, probably more than most people managed to get from their honour.

She studied the man sat beside her for a moment, trying to make a decision.

He was, she admitted, conventionally handsome. Because it was such a cruel title, she inwardly conceded that the nickname of Laird Git-face Cold-willy would have been more appropriate for the man's companion – *Dragon Dung* – the one with whom Inghean had seemed briefly and inexplicably besotted back in Blackheath. Caitrin supposed Muscles was a fairly descriptive name given this man's broad chest, bulging biceps and infuriatingly attractive figure.

But she didn't want to find him attractive.

She would have been happier to think about Nihal and remain faithful to the idea of one day being betrothed to the most powerful mage in the whole of Blackheath. Nihal, Caitrin now realised, had been repeatedly coming to her assistance. Nihal had been consistently helping to retrieve her easily mislaid virtue. Nihal had been tactful enough to banish the memories of those moments from her thoughts so she didn't feel indebted or burdened by shame or guilt.

But, now she knew how much Nihal had been helping her, Caitrin wanted to properly thank the mage. Her affection for Nihal remained a secret but she realised it was a secret she had come close to sharing with her sister.

And, now Caitrin was sure that Nihal was the one she truly desired, she didn't want her fickle libido being swayed by the temptation that was presented by the muscular specimen of manliness sitting beside her.

'I'm glad I found you alone up here,' Muscles said quietly. His voice was strong and the West Ridings accent gave it a timbre that was unusual and exciting. 'I've been looking forward to talking with you and getting to know you better.'

Unbidden, a snake of arousal slithered in the pit of her stomach.

She tried to resist the idea of considering Muscles as a lover but there was an irresistible appeal to rutting with someone so handsome and clearly capable. If his naked body was as imposing as the desirable figure he cut in a tunic and hosen, she suspected she might climax from simply looking at his unclothed form.

Idly, she toyed with the ring on her finger.

Common sense told her that the mage would have no way of knowing what she was up to whilst she was aboard the birlinn and headed toward Gatekeeper Island. There was even a chance Nihal might have forgotten about her by the time she returned to Blackheath, although Caitrin acknowledged that was extremely unlikely.

She considered herself to be fairly unforgettable.

But, whether or not the mage was thinking about her, Caitrin had to admit that her need for sexual satisfaction was between her legs on the birlinn, whilst Nihal was in a high tower back in Blackheath. It was a pragmatic perspective that helped her come to an immediate decision.

'I don't suppose you have a skin of wine on you, do you?' Caitrin asked.

She had seen the bota hanging at his hip. When he shrugged an apology, and said that he was only carrying pomegranate fire wine, she tried to contain her smile.

'That's a shame,' she said. 'But I'll take a taste of your fire wine, if I may. It might help warm me against these chill sea winds.'

Muscles was nothing if not gallant. He pulled the cork stopper from his bota and passed it to her. Caitrin took a long and satisfying swallow and realised the pomegranate fire wine he carried was even stronger than the drink she had shared with her sister earlier. She swallowed and felt the taste scald her throat and simmer in her stomach. Her veins seemed suddenly charged with a heated energy that was thrilling, throbbing and powerful. 'Good stuff,' she said, struggling not to cough as the drink took her breath away. 'Thank you.'

'If it helps warm you,' Muscles said, retrieving the bota. 'Then I'm happy to be of assistance.'

'I can think of something else that might help warm me.' She gave the words a lewd inflection and studied him with a raised eyebrow. Her smile was sly and suggestive. She tugged at the front of her open furs, exposing the gold of her kirtles, the scarlet of her chemise, and the alluring valley of her cleavage. If she hadn't thought it would look outrageously obvious, Caitrin would have licked her lips as she gave him her most winsome smile.

'Excuse me?' Muscles asked warily.

'I've thought of something we could do to banish the chill of this crossing,' she explained. She shivered theatrically, as though saying the words had made her realise that the winds across the Last Sea were surprisingly cold. 'Would you like me to explain what I think we could do?'

His mouth worked soundlessly for a moment.

It was almost amusing, she thought, to see him hovering between discomfort and desire. She wished that the sight of a man torn between his conscience and his lust didn't always fill her loins with such devastating hunger. But it seemed the sight of a man torn between desire and duty had always been as potent an aphrodisiac as the pleasures of dragon horn.

The only lover she had never seen studying her with such conflicting reactions was Nihal, and she figured that was because the mage's features were invariably hidden by the hooded crimson cowl of a Blackheath mage. Even allowing for that consideration, Caitrin thought Nihal would have more self-possession than she was shown by these other suitors.

She shook her head to dismiss Nihal from her thoughts. Now was not the time when she wanted to be thinking about the mage of Blackheath.

Muscles took a swallow from the bota. Caitrin gestured for him to share the drink and he happily passed it across the table. It still tasted hot and left a flavour of danger in her mouth but Caitrin wasn't sure those were such bad things. She was headed toward an island of dragons and could end up being married to a stranger from a foreign land. The taste of danger already seemed like a familiar flavour on her lips.

'I'd love to hear some of your suggestions for ways in which I could warm you,' he said. He was trying to sound casual but Caitrin had noticed that his gaze fell to the front of her chemise.

Absently, she reached for the V-shaped neckline of her kirtles and pulled it lower to expose more cleavage. 'I was thinking we could participate in some shared bodily warmth.' She lowered her voice to a husky drawl to deliver the words. 'I've heard that shared bodily warmth is quite an effective way of raising body temperatures.'

'Shared bodily warmth?' His gaze flitted briefly up from her chest and met her eyes. His tone was gently mocking. 'Are you flirting with me, Caitrin of Blackheath?'

'I'm hoping to do more than flirt with you,' Caitrin admitted.

'I hadn't thought you even liked me.'

She shrugged. She had told Tavia that she had no interest in marrying the man and she supposed that opinion still stood true. But she reasoned it would make sense to find out if she was passing up the opportunity of being wedded to a tremendous lover, or if she was escaping the prospect of eternal matrimonial misery.

'By the time we return to Blackheath you'll either be

my betrothed or my brother-in-law,' she reminded him. 'Don't you think we should get to know one another properly before we're limited by those roles?'

If he had been closer she would have chased a lazy finger against the front of his surcoat. He wore the green and white colours of Cadwallon emblazoned with the bright red motif of *Y Ddraig Goch*. His brow was furrowed with an expression of frank disbelief and she could tell that he didn't know what to make of her intimated suggestion.

After a moment's consideration he asked, 'What if I end up being your brother-in-law? Won't it be embarrassing if we've been rutting?'

She reached across the table and took his hand. His fingers were long and strong. She could imagine them taking a commanding hold of her body. She could easily imagine those fingers pinching and plucking at her nipples or slipping into the slippery velvety warmth of her sex. The idea made her tremble and she felt sure that he knew she was not shivering from the cold.

She held his hand and used the fingers of her other hand to trace lines and shapes against the sensitive flesh of his inner wrist. She could see him stiffen in his chair and watched his nostrils flare with a gesture of suppressed and contained approval.

'It might be embarrassing,' she admitted. 'Or it might be enlightening. It could be us who end up together.

Or you might marry Tavia and discover that you enjoy spending nights pleasuring me instead of my sister. I'm sure there could be countless other erotic possibilities. And I'm also sure, if we simply talk about them and do nothing, each one will pass us by before we've reached Gatekeeper Island.'

Again, she could see that delightful conflict on his face where he was torn between discomfort and desire. He looked set to ask another question and she sensed it would be the one that led to them finally rutting together.

Her heartbeat quickened and the tingling between her thighs grew more intense.

An untidy bearded figure lurched onto the aft deck. He was a scruffy stranger dressed in dark tatters and brandishing an unsheathed sword. His eyes glinted with sultry menace.

Acting as though he had been placed on the aft deck to protect her, Muscles snatched his wrist from Caitrin's hand and stepped up to face the stranger.

'Who the hell are you?' Muscles demanded.

The stranger glowered at him.

'I've met every crewman, sailor and slave aboard this birlinn,' Muscles explained, 'and I've not seen you before. Are you a stowaway?'

'Aye, I'm a stowaway,' the bearded man proclaimed. 'And I'm looking for Gethin ap Cadwallon.' He brandished his stubby sword. 'Where is the damned bastard?'

Whilst the stubby sword did not look like the most effective weapon Caitrin had ever seen, she figured the man looked like he would be able to use it well enough. It wasn't so much the suggestion of skill in his stance. It was more the glint in his eyes which belied an obvious intention to cause harm. She was thankful that Muscles stood between her and the bearded stranger.

'Who are you?' demanded Muscles.

The bearded man shook his head. 'I've got the bare sword. I ask the questions. Where's Cadwallon?'

'This is High Laird Gethin ap Cadwallon,' Caitrin declared boldly. 'Now answer his question, you impertinent stowaway. Who are you?'

The scruffy man laughed. It was an expression that was made ugly with obvious contempt. 'No. He's not Cadwallon. Cadwallon is shorter and skinnier. Cadwallon has dark hair and he's forever shouting out that stupid fucking exclamation about –'

'Dirt and dragon dung!'

The cry cut through the stranger's words.

The exclamation came from behind him.

Confused, no longer sure who was High Laird of the West Ridings, Caitrin saw the man she had nicknamed *Dragon Dung* standing next to the birlinn's mainsail. He had one hand above his eyes, shading his face from the overhead sun. His features were twisted into a sneer of surprise and outrage.

'Alvar of Erland? What in the name of blazes are you doing here, Alvar?'

Caitrin frowned, not sure what was going on nor why this felt so important.

'Didn't I pay two magistrates to have you swinging by the neck?' asked the man by the mainsail. 'What's to become of a world where a bribed magistrate can't be trusted?'

Alvar whirled on him. His stubby riding sword was raised. 'Cadwallon!'

Dragon Dung's eyes widened when he saw the sword being so expertly wielded. He reached quickly to his own hip. Caitrin could see, from the way the man's fingers scrabbled frantically at his unadorned hosen, he had only just realised he was unarmed.

A frown of obvious dread coloured his features.

'*Sc tan!*'

'Did you ask me what I'm doing here?' the bearded stranger cooed. He advanced slowly toward the mainsail, adopting the *Pflug* stance of a practised swordsman. The stubby riding sword projected from his hip angled upwards.

It looked, Caitrin thought, like a huge and thrusting penis jutting from his loins.

'I'll tell you what I'm doing here,' the scruffy stranger called. 'I've come to claim my revenge. I've come to take your life.'

Caitrin's heartbeat quickened. She clutched at Muscles. 'Shouldn't we help?'

Muscles seemed to consider this after a shrug. 'Which one should we help? One of them clearly doesn't need my help and the other one doesn't deserve it.'

Before Caitrin could respond, Dragon Dung had started to run. He feinted to the right and then headed left. The bearded stranger was equally fast and followed in his wake. His sword was raised to the *Ochs* position with the pommel by his brow.

Dragon Dung threw himself at one of the hatchways that led to the underdecks. He disappeared as though he had never been aboard the birlinn. The bearded stowaway hurried after him, screaming as though he was a charging berserker with his sword held *Oberhut*.

And then he too disappeared through a hatchway to the underdecks.

Caitrin turned to Muscles. 'What the hell happened there?'

He shrugged. 'Onboard entertainment?'

She fixed him with a solemn expression, struggling not to be amused by his wry humour. 'What the hell happened there?' she repeated.

'I don't bloody know.'

'You're not Gethin ap Cadwallon, are you?'

He shook his head. 'No. That was High Laird Gethin ap Cadwallon who just got chased below deck.'

She took a step back. 'Then, who are you? And what should I call you?'

'My name's Owain. I'm the dragon handler.'

Caitrin considered this and then nodded. His being the dragon handler explained the smell of animals that lingered on his flesh. But that was about all that Owain's admission explained. She stepped close to him and put her arms around his waist. 'Hold me, Owain the dragon handler,' she insisted. 'Give me another mouthful of fire wine from your bota, and then help me find one of those other ways to get warm that we were discussing before.'

She could sense his hesitation, even though he was passing her the skin. 'Are you sure this is what you want us to do?'

'I have no intention of being betrothed to him,' she said, nodding toward the hatchway where High Laird Gethin ap Cadwallon had disappeared. 'And I assume he would have no interesting in being betrothed to a woman who has been dishonoured by someone as lowly as his dragon handler.'

Owain regarded her with obvious respect, as though he was surprised by the way she had so accurately assessed Gethin's shallow levels of respect. 'That's a fairly safe assumption,' he conceded. 'Gethin would look on you as unworthy if he thought you'd been with me.'

'Then take me,' she insisted.

She pressed against him, savouring the way her breasts

could be squashed against his broad chest. Her nipples were already hard and stiff and tingling with the thrill of the pressure as she pushed herself into his embrace. 'Take me and make me unworthy and make me forget about this cold wind and these sword fights and all the complications of high lairds and low dragon handlers and unwanted marriage contracts.'

'But what about your honour?'

She thought of the easy and delightful way that Nihal had re-established her honour in the tower. The idea of having to endure that pleasure again was enough to send a shiver of anticipation bristling down her spine to nestle in her sex. It was, she thought wistfully, almost worth losing her honour again, just for the pleasure of having Nihal return it to her with such a satisfying sexual ceremony. She pressed a kiss against Owain's firm and manly jaw and said, 'Just take my honour, dragon handler. I'll worry about getting it back.'

Those words were all it took to encourage him to return her kisses. He lifted her and then placed her so she sat with her buttocks on the edge of the aft deck's coarse wooden table. Then he stood between her parted thighs.

She supposed it would have been warmer if they had found some space in the shelter of the underdecks, or if they had decided to make use of one of the rooms in the captain's suite. But that would have meant moving from the deck and Caitrin did not want to do anything that could potentially jeopardise the mood of avaricious need she had for this man.

'*Owain*,' she thought quietly. '*His name is Owain. He's not Muscles. And he's not High Laird Gethin ap Cadwallon. He's Owain the dragon handler.*'

His name was repeated in her thoughts as Owain unfastened her furs and then began to pluck at the ties securing her kirtles. The wind blew harder against the sails, ruffling her black tresses as she arched her back and spread her thighs for him.

She allowed him to unfasten her braies, savouring the sensation of his cool fingers toying with the laces that secured the underwear around her waist. It was an intimate sensation that made her realise they were close to having sex.

The heat in her loins grew moist. The muscles inside her dark confines rippled with expectation. A thrill of raw excitement tumbled through her wetness as he slipped the braies down her waist, hips, legs and then past her ankles and over her leather-strapped wooden pattens.

Caitrin drew a steadying breath.

The Last Sea's winds touched her cleft. The caress of the breeze threatened to cool her molten heat but she could feel her eagerness growing more wanton with each teasing whisper of the wind.

She reached eagerly into his hosen. With an expert hand she found his hardness and extricated the length. He was thick, long and hard. Holding his shaft in her fingers she knew she was touching a vital and essential part of him. She also knew this was the part that would fill her and satisfy her and push her to the brink of a cataclysmic orgasm.

He drew a startled breath as she pulled him closer.

'Have you ever been with a man before?' he asked.

'I think I've been with several,' she said honestly. 'Although I'm still a virgin.'

He frowned. 'That's not possible.'

'Of course it's possible,' she assured him. 'I come from Blackheath.'

She laughed and stroked the end of his length against her sex. The caress was subtle and impossibly light, yet it radiated a glowing promise of satisfaction through her body. Urging him to rest the shaft against her sex lips, she anticipated the initial thrust when her virginity would be taken again.

She wondered how many previous times she had savoured that thrill.

It occurred to her, if she concentrated, she might be able to remember each instance. The revisitation to those memories felt so close she believed she would only need to close her eyes and she would be able to return to the first, second and third times that her innocence had been taken. But Caitrin resisted the urge to wallow in those memories, preferring to relish the experience that was about to be visited between her thighs.

She supposed the pleasure of the moment would never fail to improve on each occasion as long as she took the time to properly instruct her lovers how to deliver her pleasure. Sensing that this man did not need such instruction, she figured that this experience would be even more satisfying than the previous ones. Nevertheless, she placed a hand on his hip, stopping him from trying to slide into her.

'Play with my tits,' she said calmly. 'I want to be properly wet before you slide into me.'

Obediently, he reached for her breasts.

Then he stopped himself.

'You're very commanding, aren't you?'

'I'm Caitrin of Blackheath,' she reminded him. 'I'm highborn and I have every right to be commanding, dragon handler.'

She could see that the words stung him as a reminder of their different social status and she inwardly cursed herself for being so careless with her words. Words were not like virginity, she thought bitterly. Words could not be recovered once they had been carelessly spent on someone.

'I'm only commanding when I'm with someone too stupid to pleasure me properly,' she said quickly. 'Now play with my tits. Don't make me tell you twice.'

He was chuckling as he opened her yellow-gold kirtles and began to fondle her exposed breasts. She could see that her flesh was milky white against his sun-kissed hands. The nipples were flushed and hard and the colour of new-ripe strawberries. His fingers, as she had hoped, were the ideal strength and length for tweaking and plucking at those strawberries. He teased one breast with his fingertips whilst he bowed his head to the other and suckled against her. The richness of the experience began to grow and she realised he was going to swiftly take her to the rush of a satisfying orgasm.

She rolled her hips and pressed the lips of her sex more firmly against his end. He felt large and swollen and ready for her. But she was pleased to note that he made no attempt to push inside her. He continued teasing and suckling at her nipples, seeming content to let his length rest against the prize of her hole, whilst he focused on her excitement.

She was pleased to note that he seemed adept as a lover.

He had found the perfect balance between nibbling too sharply against her breasts and teasing with too much subtlety. His lips and teeth and fingertips all seemed attuned to her specific sensitivity. Her body responded to him as though she had been restoring all her virginities just for this moment.

She shut that thought from her mind.

Owain was not the man she wanted. She wanted Nihal.

He pulled her closer, one hand going to the small of her back whilst his mouth remained pressed over the tip of one nipple. She could smell the earthy appeal of his perspiration, the memory of pomegranate wine on his skin, and the searing scent of the fire wine they had been drinking. More importantly, she could feel the broad and strong warmth of his hands on the small of her back.

Unable to resist her need for him she pushed her sex against him.

In the same moment Muscles pushed into her.

'*Owain*,' she reminded herself. '*His name is Owain. He's not Muscles. And he's not High Laird Gethin ap Cadwallon. He's Owain the dragon handler.*'

'Owain,' she breathed, as his length filled her.

His name came out as a sigh of appreciation. He silenced her with a kiss as his shaft slipped past the resistance of her virginity. Then he was plundering deep into the tightness of her sex.

They both chugged sighs of ecstasy and Caitrin thought the wind was whipping more ferociously around their heads, as though the gods of the Last Sea were urging them to enjoy a crescendo of debilitating pleasure.

'Slowly,' she told Owain. 'Don't ride me too swiftly.'

'Stop giving me instructions,' he said, pushing hard into her. There was a smile in each of the kisses he delivered when he said, 'I've ridden more women than you have.'

'And I've been present at the loss of my maidenhead more times than you,' Caitrin gasped. She panted the words, each syllable forced out by his thickness sliding into her sex. 'Don't ride me too swiftly.'

'Have you been this demanding each time you've lost your virginity?'

His mouth had fallen to her breast. He was nipping at the tip of her nipple as he asked the question. She wrenched a fistful of hair and snapped his face up so it was opposite hers. 'I've discovered,' she said stiffly, 'that my pleasure increases every time I let my lover know exactly how I want to be satisfied.'

He laughed and brushed her fingers from his hair.

'And I've discovered, if a woman starts to give me commands in the bedroom, then she's only been used to lying with shadows of men who don't properly take her virginity.'

Before Caitrin could respond he had plunged forward again. This time it felt as though he had slipped deeper. She didn't know how but it felt as though his shaft had grown thicker. The waves of pleasure rippled through her with a pulsing swell of satisfaction that was stronger than anything she had previously known.

Her heartbeat raced.

The tingling sensation of raw pleasure began to swell in her loins.

She stared at Owain with open-mouthed amazement. And he plunged into her again. This time she heard herself squeal with delight.

He pushed swiftly but not hurriedly into her sex. The hands at the small of her back made sure she was brought forward to meet the thrust of each penetration. His length remained hard and deliciously rigid. With her attention focused on the pleasures occurring in the depths of her sex, Caitrin could have sworn that his erection was growing fatter and more satisfying with each and every plunge forward.

And then the climax struck her.

She clutched at him with a combination of surprise, amazement and absolute satisfaction. The explosion that burst from her loins was a rush of every sated need she had ever harboured. It was a delicious release of pure and powerful ecstasy that left her weak and trembling and bewildered.

Her climax came in the same moment as Owain's ejaculation.

His length thickened and spurted. The muscle erupted inside her. The rush of increased heat and wetness made her groan with the fury of her body's heightened satisfaction. She had thought she knew the extremes of pleasure when she had been drinking dragon horn and rutting with Robert of Moon Valley, but those pleasures were nothing compared to these extremes.

He pulled himself slowly from her.

She realised, during the throes of their passion, he had managed to remove her furs and kirtles. It remained cool aboard the aft deck of the birlinn as the winds from the Last Sea brushed her sex-sweated flesh. But Caitrin was content to bask in the aftermath of their shared satisfaction rather than racing to dress again.

Owain laid her down on the table and placed a gentle kiss on the tip of one tingling nipple.

It was almost too much pleasure.

Caitrin thought of telling him as much and then decided she could cope with a pleasure that was almost too much. She simply wanted to lie beneath the endless blue skies, broken only by the shadows of black-legged kittiwakes, as she savoured the delicious experiences he had visited on her body.

The clash of steel against steel rang through the air.

Caitrin looked toward the noise.

She saw movement.

Modesty forced her to cover her nakedness with her furs. Glancing toward the metallic ringing noise, she saw that the stowaway had caught up with the man he wanted to kill. The pair were in the midst of a harsh and menacing sword fight and it was obvious who would be the winner.

High Laird Gethin ap Cadwallon was no match for the stranger.

Even though the sword he had found since she last saw him was longer and heavier, his skill with the weapon was inferior to that being demonstrated by the bearded stowaway. More importantly, he was only driven to defend himself with a need to protect his own life. It seemed obvious that the stranger was compelled by a much more powerful motive.

Lunge-thrust-attack.

Lunge-thrust-attack.

Gethin parried and ducked and stepped backward to avoid the cut and slice of the stowaway's stubby sword. Each time he retreated the stowaway lunged at him again, as though this time would be the moment when he finally won the duel.

Lunge-thrust-attack.

Lunge-thrust-attack.

A slice of crimson daubed one of Gethin's cheeks, as though he had already been bloodied by the fight. Caitrin suspected, if things continued to go against him, he would soon be suffering far worse injuries than a mere scratch to his face.

'Help me, Owain,' Gethin bellowed. 'Help me, you fucker.'

Owain rolled his eyes.

Caitrin placed a hand on his bare shoulder. 'Are you going to help him?'

He shrugged. 'I don't really want to. Gethin's a contemptible wretch.'

Caitrin considered this. She still had no explanation as to why the High Laird of the West Ridings had been pretending to be a dragon handler, whilst his dragon handler was pretending to be the high laird. She had to admit that a part of her did think there was something patently untrustworthy about Gethin ap Cadwallon. But she felt it would be wrong to let this fight end without trying to get the two duelling men to address their differences amicably.

'Gethin might be contemptible,' she agreed. 'But you don't know this other man, do you?'

'No,' Owain admitted. 'Although I suspect he's probably got a very good reason for wanting the High Laird of the West Ridings dead. Most people who know Gethin want him dead for one reason or another.'

The clash of steel on steel came closer.

Every time the song of metal sounded across the deck, Caitrin flinched for fear that she was about to hear the noise followed by a mortal scream.

She saw her sister climbing out from one of the hatchways.

Tavia's eyes opened wide with horror when she saw the sword fight that was taking place across the deck. She looked as though she was going to try and run to intervene. The man with the dark beard fixed her with a stony glare that left Tavia unmoving.

'Please,' Caitrin begged Owain. 'If you're able to do something to stop a death from happening here would you please stop those two from trying to kill one another?'

Owain rolled his eyes. Reluctantly he pulled away from her.

'Do you really want that?' he asked.

'I really want that,' she assured him.

He nodded. He seemed unmindful of his nudity. He walked absently across the deck with his exposed length swaying large and daunting between his legs. Caitrin noticed that his shaft glistened with the wetness from their shared moments together. And she saw that her own sister was studying Owain's impressive physique and making no attempt to disguise her interest in him.

Owain walked past Gethin and then stepped past the stowaway as the pair duelled their way across the aft deck. When it looked like he would completely bypass the pair without making any move to intervene, he stepped between them.

A flash of fury crossed the stowaway's brow.

Gethin fell backwards. He landed heavily on his rump. The longsword he had been using fell from his fingers.

The stowaway reached for Owain's arm, ready to push him aside.

Owain slammed an uppercut into his face.

It was a powerful blow and lifted the man from his feet. The stowaway dropped to the floor like a sack of discarded grain. The sword skittered from his fingers and slid across the deck. The stowaway remained unconscious and unmoving, his face staring blindly up to a sky filled with screeching black-legged kittiwakes.

'Who the hell is this one, Gethin?' Owain asked tiredly.

'That's Alvar of Erland.' Gethin staggered to his feet, retrieving his longsword from where it had fallen. His hands were shaking as he raised the weapon above his head. 'Although, he's about to become food for the gurnets of the Last Sea.'

'No!'

Tavia rushed from the hatchway, she looked determined to stop any harm from befalling the bearded man. Her arms were outstretched and her wooden pattens clomped heavily on the deck.

'No. Don't you dare hurt him! Don't you dare!'

Too shocked to find words, Caitrin clapped a hand over her mouth.

Gethin had raised his sword and she could see he was going to kill the stowaway as he lay defeated and unconscious on the floor. It was an action that stank of dishonour. Tavia was screaming for the High Laird of the West Ridings to stay his hand. Caitrin was about to shriek out for Gethin to put his sword down and stop being a coward.

Owain acted before she could splutter the words.

He wrenched the sword from Gethin's hand and threw it across the deck. In the same swift movement he punched the High Laird of the West Ridings hard in the nose.

Gethin went down heavily.

He raised a warning finger that trembled with incredulity. 'You'll pay for this, Owain the dragon handler,' Gethin growled.

Alvar of Erland was pulling himself from the deck. He staggered to his feet and seemed to focus blearily on Gethin. Gethin stumbled to get his feet beneath him.

Owain sighed. 'Likely I will bloody pay for this,' he said sharply. And, as the shadow of Gatekeeper Island loomed closer on the horizon, he strolled forward to try and intervene and prevent Gethin and Alvar from killing one another.

As she watched him take masterful control of the two men, Caitrin realised she had never wanted a man more.

Nihal threw a sheet of dark silk over the crystal ball.

The images immediately disappeared.

Cait was in trouble. There was an escaped convict aboard the birlinn. There was also a brutal thug knocking everyone unconscious. And it appeared that Laird Gethin ap Cadwallon had been deceiving the castellan by pretending to be someone else. There was something about that deception that did not sit well in Nihal's mind. The mage rushed to the bookshelf on the south wall.

There would not be time to launch another vessel to follow the birlinn. And there was no way to secretly convey a message about the approaching danger to the dragonmeister on Gatekeeper Island. However, from what Nihal recalled of the old stories of Blackheath, there was a secret passageway that led beneath the Last Sea to the shores of Gatekeeper Island.

Remember what I told you, Cait, Nihal thought grimly. *Remember the power I gave you.* A part of the mage's mind was listening in the hope that perhaps she had remembered the spell that was hers: *If you ever need me, simply take yourself to the peak of a climax, close your eyes and then whisper my name. If you do that, I'll be with you.*

But Nihal felt sure that Cait was in no position to use that particular spell.

Scouring the pages of a mouldering history, taking mental notes after scanning the archaic text and its ancient language, the mage decided it was time for Cait to be rescued by the castellan's most powerful household mage.

And, if that expedition proved successful, Nihal wondered if it might be time for the castellan's most powerful household mage to pledge a troth to Caitrin of Blackheath.

CHAPTER SEVEN

Inghean the Seasick

Inghean could have believed she had been transported atop the mountain of the gods. If she had subscribed to the myths that her sister, Caitrin the dark, found so compelling, Inghean could have thought she was residing on the peak of Mount Olympus. Her body was ensconced in a cocoon of sensuous milky warmth. The silken sound of a lyre-harp played from somewhere behind her. The tune was a sweet and heartbreaking melody that she had never heard but had always known.

But Inghean was not a believer in the myths her sister revered.

She opened her eyes to see she was surrounded by angels: three blonde young maids wearing thin togas of near-transparent gauze. The women were all comely, full in the hip and round on the bosom. Each fixed Inghean with a smile that was unquestionably sincere. Behind each smile, she could detect the promise of the most fulfilling lust and delectable debauchery. Even though it wasn't her habit to share physical intimacies with other women, Inghean found herself yearning to discover what pleasures these blonde maids could bestow.

Two of the three maids were in the sunken goat's milk bath with Inghean. The third prepared more liquids, oils and balms at the foot of the bath. The two with Inghean were rubbing her limbs and kneading heady-scented chrisms into her shoulders, arms and breasts. When their hands slipped further down her bare body, and began to caress her thighs and loins, Inghean gave herself to the liquid urgency of the sensations. She shivered from the excitement of having deft fingers tease her most intimate regions. And she wondered if the bath maidens knew how much pleasure they were provoking.

The air was a warm balm, fragranced by the honeyed goat's milk in which she lay. The columns and pillars above her stretched toward the faraway painted ceilings. With mild surprise she noted that everything around her appeared to be decorated with the colourful images of dragons.

Carved and sculpted dragon heads festooned the columns and pillars.

Pictures of swooping and diving dragons decorated the skyscape painting of the ceiling's mural. The pictures showed wingless lindworm, nesting wyvern, brooding basilisks and endless varieties of other less familiar dragon species. There were dark-green Smok and Ljubljana, night-black Coca and garishly coloured Orientals.

Heavy hanging tapestries covered the walls. Each tapestry was identical and emblazoned with arms Inghean recognised: a front-facing dragon, silver on a gold background, with its claws and teeth coloured red.

'I'm on Gatekeeper Island,' she thought.

A moment's panic touched her breast. Despite the weary ache in her muscles, she tried pushing the bath maids away so she could climb out of the bath.

'Relax,' a gruff voice commanded. 'You're on land now.'

Inghean glanced toward the speaker and gasped. The woman was pale with a shock of short, spiky hair as dark as winter coals. She was, Inghean thought, incredibly beautiful. Beneath the smears of sooted grime on her brow and forearms, her complexion looked to be as pale as the goat's milk in which Inghean lay.

A wyvern sat on her shoulder. The size of a parrot, it was a two-legged dragon, vibrant green in colour with scales of dark red on its breast, belly and beneath its wings. Its eyes were huge and as dark as onyx. A wicked barbed tongue danced over its lips.

'Sexy,' muttered the wyvern.

'Greetings, Inghean of Blackheath,' said the woman. She extended a hand and said, 'Welcome to Gatekeeper Island.'

'Welcome,' echoed the wyvern. 'Welcome.'

Inghean sighed. 'I can't believe we made it here. I had the most horrendous trip. How long ago did we land?'

'Your birlinn arrived in our harbour an hour ago.'

The beautiful woman smiled. She was dressed in a sleeveless yellow tunic, belted at the waist and accessorised with matching sandals. The arms of Gatekeeper Island were embroidered over her left breast. Being sleeveless the tunic was, Inghean thought, a manly form of garb. But she also thought it was somewhat manly for the woman to have a talking wyvern sat on her shoulder.

The two-legged dragon had its barbed tail curled behind the beautiful woman's back. Occasionally it turned and sniffed at the dark-haired woman's head before turning to regard anything and everything with its huge, dark eyes.

It was, Inghean thought, a truly enchanting wyvern.

The creature studied Inghean as its mistress knelt down beside the bath. The barbed tongue slithered across its reptilian lips. Inghean could have sworn the creature was smiling as it studied her.

'Inghean,' the wyvern sighed. 'Inghean.'

Overwhelmed by a thousand different questions, Inghean took the woman's offered hand. She tried to sit up. The bath maids held her firmly, but not unkindly, in the warm balm of the goat's milk.

'I am Meghan, daughter of Georgiana.' The woman

spoke the words with lofty importance. Even though she was kneeling Inghean could see her chest swelling out as she made the bold assertion. 'I'm dragonmeister of Gatekeeper Island.'

Surprisingly, the woman's fingers were calloused and dirt-stained, as though she usually worked in some form of physical labour, rather than whiling away hours in the company of scantily-clad maidens beside a goat's milk bath. Inghean did not know what she'd expected from a dragonmeister but she hadn't thought the woman would be wearing a tunic that looked like men's work clothes. Nor had she expected the dragonmeister to be presenting herself with scuffed sandals, scraped knees and a soot-smudged brow.

'Your grace,' Inghean began.

The protocols of courtesy and etiquette commanded that she should kneel or bow or curtsey to a dragonmeister. But she was laid in a goat's milk bath and her muscles felt too weak to drag her from the velvet embrace of the liquid so she could demonstrate her fealty. It didn't help that the bath maids were still caressing her bare flesh and seeming to hold her in place with the promise of greater pleasures to come. Inghean made another half-hearted attempted to pull herself from the milk and then gave up when the dragonmeister placed a steadying hand on her shoulder.

The touch was a caress that left her weak with desire.

Her pulse quickened as the woman's strong and roughly calloused hands scratched against Inghean's bare flesh.

'Call me Meghan,' the dragonmeister said easily. 'Meg if you prefer. And save your energies rather than trying to sit up.' She gestured toward the three bath maids and said, 'Let Minerva, Melinda and Miranda soothe you and help you recover from your ordeal. It strikes me that you had a trying journey. You're clearly not a seafarer.'

That was an understatement, thought Inghean.

She thanked the dragonmeister for her consideration and tried not to let her thoughts dwell on the two days she had spent leaning over the side of the birlinn, heaving and retching and making herself ill with seasickness. She didn't want to brood on such details because it seemed suddenly important to make a positive and desirable impression on the woman.

Meghan remained knelt by Inghean's side.

Absently she reached out and stroked Inghean's hair. Her fingers combed through the russet-red curls with a tenderness that was heart-warming. Inghean could almost feel the echoes of affection and bright blessings pouring from the dragonmeister's fingertips.

'Relax and let these bath maids help you recover from the ordeal of your journey,' Meghan whispered. 'They're experts in the art of sensuous massage. They will help your body repair and they will help your spirit find its correct alignment.'

Inghean had no idea whether her body needed to repair, or whether her spirit needed to find its correct alignment. But she did know that the bath maids were gifted in the art of touching and caressing and that felt like the sort of attention she currently needed.

Silky smooth fingers slipped against her body.

As Meghan spoke of her spirit finding its correct alignment, Inghean became aware that those caressing fingers were growing more intimate. She gasped softly as one maid's hand slid up her inner thigh. The breath caught in her throat as she felt knuckles brushing against the lips of her sex.

The touch was a light and intoxicating balm.

It was almost as gentle as the slippery caress of fingertips that teased at her areola. Her nipple responded to that touch. The bud of flesh grew swollen and hard. Inghean felt ill with the sudden rush of arousal that needed to explode from her body. She whimpered in response – not sure whether she was strong enough yet to cope with such stimulation.

The maid to her right beamed with innocent lechery.

The maid to her left pressed closer. Inghean could feel the woman's flesh urging against hers, with only the thin layer of milk-soaked cotton separating their bodies. The music of the lyre-harp seemed to grow in intensity. Then those sounds began to fade as though they had erupted.

When the maid to her left eased her body away,

Inghean realised a pair of fingers had slipped into the forbidden confines of her sex. She felt freshly weakened with a rush of raw lust. Her heartbeat tripped languidly as eddies of excitement stole through her body.

Both of the bath maids were smiling encouragement as Inghean ascended another crest of satisfaction. The third maid poured another balm of warm milk into the sunken bath and then stirred it with one slender hand.

Inghean sighed.

Because Meghan was squatting, the sunken bath meant Inghean's head was at the same height as the dragon-meister's crotch. If she had turned her gaze slightly, Inghean knew she would have been staring beneath the hem of the woman's short tunic. Even though that idea held an appeal of daring and excitement, Inghean used every ounce of willpower to resist the impulse.

Meghan stroked her fingers through Inghean's hair. 'Do you feel sufficiently recovered, Inghean of Blackheath?'

'Sexy,' croaked the wyvern agreeably.

Inghean nodded.

'Do you feel sufficiently recovered to help me with a small dilemma that's been brought to our shores with your birlinn?'

Inghean shrugged. She wasn't sure what sort of dilemma could have arrived on the shores of Gatekeeper Island with the birlinn, but she was willing to help the dragonmeister in any way possible.

From the corner of her eye she could see the milky invitation of the dragonmeister's upper thighs. At the top of those thighs there was a scrub of dark, inviting curls.

Inghean drew a deep breath.

'Pussy,' chirruped the wyvern.

Inghean blushed. 'I'll help in any way your grace commands.'

The dragonmeister shook her head. 'Just call me Meg.' She leant close and placed her lips close to Inghean's ear. 'And,' she murmured softly, 'if you help me resolve this dilemma, I'll make sure that you and I get a chance to become better acquainted whilst you're gracing our land with your presence.'

Inghean's nipples stiffened.

She was thankful for the milky white bath water which managed to conceal the more obvious symptoms of her arousal. It was momentarily embarrassing when one of the maids in the bath noticed the stiffness, but Inghean saw the woman's sly smile and she realised that the maid was discreet enough to not mention what was happening.

And, as this was likely the maid that had been slipping fingers into the welcoming tightness of her sex, Inghean figured she should be beyond any embarrassment about something as unremarkable as stiff nipples.

She wanted to turn and ask Meg questions, confirm that she understood what was being intimated. But the dragonmeister was standing up and the soft and seductive figure she had presented was lost beneath a façade of shouting and gruff-voiced bravado.

'Bring in the prisoners,' Meg bellowed.

'Prisoners,' the wyvern agreed.

'Let's find out what the hell has been going on here.'

A clatter of boots and metal rang from far away. As the noise began, Inghean realised the melody of the lyre-harp had faded to silence. She looked around and decided the harpist had left the building.

For the first time, Inghean saw she was in a temple.

Given the décor she supposed it was a temple raised to pray to the dragon gods. She supposed it was the temple at the southernmost tip of Gatekeeper Island: the temple she had often seen through a spyglass from the high towers of Blackheath. She was surprised to find it was even more imposing and elegant than she had ever imagined.

She was even more surprised to realise that the bath maids were still teasing her naked body. Oil-slippery fingers had returned to her breasts. The stiff nipples were teased with velvet caresses that made her ill with vicious lust. Her stomach muscles clenched with a cramp of raw desire. Inghean turned to glare at the bath maid touching her and was met by a challenging smile of cool indifference.

More fingers had moved to the tops of her thighs.

Inghean wanted to pull away, or push the hands

from her body, but she still felt weak. Also, because the sensations being administered were so exhilarating, she couldn't bring herself to drag her body from the inquisitive touches that caressed her breasts and loins.

Fingers smoothed through the curls that covered her sex.

They touched lightly against the sensitive lips. She could feel them hovering on the brink of penetrating her centre once again.

She held her breath, not sure whether she wanted the hands to move away, or if she yearned for them slip inside again. It was only when a lazy thumb rubbed over the thrust of her clitoris that she realised that she favoured the idea of having the bath maid's fingers enter her wetness.

'Bring the prisoners before Inghean the red,' the dragonmeister called.

'Inghean,' the wyvern on her shoulder chirruped enthusiastically, as though supporting her cries. Its wings fluttered in excited little flaps. 'Inghean,' it called again cheerfully. 'Inghean the sexy.'

Meg placed a finger on the wyvern's snout, silencing the creature abruptly.

Inghean tried to distance herself from the sensations exciting her body. She glared at the two bath maids teasing her intimate parts and sat more stiffly in the bath. But, no matter how ferociously she glared, the two women continued to touch and tease as though they knew she secretly desired their caresses.

With a metallic clatter of boots and armour, three men were paraded before her. The trio were forced to their knees in front of her sunken bath.

It was, she thought, like the start of some bizarre erotic fantasy.

She recognised two of the men.

Even though Gethin had a cut cheek and a broken nose it would have been difficult to forget him. He stared at her with an expression that was somewhere between contempt and lust. She might have been unsettled by the obvious animosity in his glower if one of the bath maids had not chosen that moment to slide a finger against the puckered ring of her anus.

A spasm of pernicious excitement rippled through her body.

Inghean was left quivering with the knowledge that she needed to experience more of that sensation. She trembled from the thrill and allowed her body to sink further beneath the balm of the goat's milk.

When she glanced up she recognised Owain amongst the three prisoners and wondered why he was naked. She wasn't complaining about his nudity. He presented a pleasing spectacle with his imposing presence. Considering the way the bath maids were exciting her, Inghean thought all three men should have been standing naked before her so she could further indulge the erotic aspects of the fantasies tumbling through her thoughts.

But it was still something of a puzzle as to why he wore no clothes. She opened her mouth to ask the question and then decided the answer would probably not be as interesting as the one being presented by her imagination.

The third man, a dark and swarthy figure with a bruised eye and a menacing scowl, was a complete stranger to Inghean. She didn't recall seeing him aboard the birlinn, although she felt sure she had seen him somewhere in Blackheath. However, no matter how hard she studied him, she couldn't recall where she knew him from.

Despite the three men having their wrists bound with hemp, they were each accompanied by two burly hostlers. The hostlers were dressed in a uniform of leather breeches and hauberks. The surcoat of each man bore the arms of a white dragon, red in tooth and claw, sitting on a gold background. Inghean noted that each hostler carried a ceremonial bullock dagger on their left hip.

'Who the hell are these men?' the dragonmeister demanded. 'Do you know them?'

Inghean realised the question was being thrown at her. She started and tried to brush away the hands of the bath maids but the girls merely giggled at her efforts. As soon as they were able they returned their fingers to the lips of Inghean's sex. Warm and eager hands touched her nipples and then rubbed the thrust of her clitoris. The sensations were too pleasurable for Inghean to continue fighting against them. She decided she would simply have to endure the sexual caresses whilst she answered the dragonmeister's questions.

'When your boat landed these three were involved in a vicious melee,' the dragonmeister explained. 'If my hostlers hadn't intervened I don't doubt one or more of them would be dead by now.'

She paused and considered Inghean with an earnest frown. 'There's one rule here on Gatekeeper Island. One law that is obeyed at all costs: no one ever hurts a dragon. If anyone ever breaks that law, the best they can expect is life imprisonment. More likely, I'd insist on the death penalty.'

Inghean swallowed, shocked by the solemnity of the woman's words. This statement had not been made by sexy, spiky-haired Meg. This was the word of the dragonmeister.

'This obviously wasn't as important as injuring dragons,' Meg conceded. 'But it still looked like a serious situation and, as dragonmeister, it's my job to punish the guilty and protect the innocent.' She turned to Inghean and said, 'Who are these men? Which of them should I punish? Which of them should I protect? Or do you think I should just throw all of them into the catacombs and let the ghosts and dragons settle their issues beneath the surface of the island?'

Inghean raised herself slightly out of the milk bath. It was a struggle to pull away from the bath maids and she felt a pang of genuine upset when the two fingers tickling inside her sex lips were tugged from her body. She was aware that she was exposing her breasts to the three prisoners and the six hostlers but that consideration seemed immaterial. All the Blackheath notions of propriety she had brought with her did not seem to apply on Gatekeeper Island.

'I don't know that one.' She gestured toward the dark-bearded stranger. Rivulets of goat's milk trailed from her pointing finger. 'I didn't even know he was onboard the birlinn.'

'I'm Alvar, son of Erland,' the stranger declared.

He looked set to say more but Meghan had nodded to the hostlers escorting him and he was brusquely dragged from his knees and led away.

'Take him to the westernmost dungeons,' the dragon-meister called after them. 'I'll meet with him later and get his side of the story.'

The stranger protested noisily. He tried to slam his feet against the marble floor of the temple in an attempt to stop himself from being transported from the room. He hurled insults and threats and promises of dire consequences for all.

And no one heeded a word of his warnings.

Inghean was annoyed to note that the stranger's

departure forced a smile across the face of Gethin ap Cadwallon. She identified him next. She wasn't sure if Gethin was still pretending to be someone else but she didn't see any need to lie to the dragonmeister. If he was still trying to travel in secret she was happy to expose him as visiting nobility.

'That's Gethin ap Cadwallon, High Laird of the West Ridings.'

'That's what he's been claiming too,' Meghan sounded disappointed. She glanced at the pair of hostlers holding Gethin and said, 'I've heard of this one. He's highborn. Free his hands.'

'About time,' grumbled Gethin.

Once the ropes were cut from his hands he began to rub his wrists as though encouraging circulation to return there. He remained kneeling although he shrugged his shoulders from the reach of the hostlers that had guarded him. His brow was furrowed into a frown of sour disapproval. His features were set in an expression that looked like he was awaiting an apology.

The dragonmeister walked past him and stood before a naked Owain.

She took a moment to examine him.

'Cock,' chuckled the wyvern.

Inghean got the impression that the woman was sizing him up in every possible way. Knowing Owain's prowess as a lover, Inghean could have confided that he was unlikely to disappoint if the woman was thinking of taking him into her bed. She could even have suggested that Owain might make for an intriguing plaything if the dragonmeister wanted to share him in the bath with her and the bath maids. The thought of making such a bold suggestion made Inghean squirm with a rush of wet and wanton arousal.

And when the bath maids returned to caressing her body, she made no attempt to stop them. Slender, slippery fingers teased her inner thighs. The lips of her sex were touched, tickled and teased. A sheen of perspiration erupted on Inghean's brow as the fresh tremors of an impending climax began to build inside her loins. And, when the two maids began to slip fingers into the tight confines of her sex, Inghean had to bite her lower lip to suppress a roar of approval.

'Who's this one?' Meghan called.

It took her a moment to find the words for a response. The teasing of the bath maids was so intense she had to focus and will the memories to come to the forefront of her thoughts.

'That's Owain,' Inghean said. 'Owain the fuh–' She stopped herself abruptly. That was not how she intended introducing him to the dragonmeister. 'Owain is the dragon handler.'

'Fucker,' agreed the wyvern.

For the first time, Meghan seemed to be impressed. She

raised an eyebrow and considered Owain with obvious interest. Hunkering down before him she said, 'You're the one who brought *Y Ddraig Goch* to the island?'

Owain nodded.

Inghean fought against a pang of jealousy. Meghan was squatting in front of Owain the same way the dragonmeister had hunkered before her. She wondered if Owain would be enjoying the promise of the same surreptitious view she had stolen. She felt ill with the idea that Owain would be excited by the sight of the dragonmeister's sex.

'We have one *Y Ddraig Goch* here already,' the dragonmeister explained. 'He's a male. A big, beautiful bull of a beast. He was brought to the care of my mother, Georgiana, when she was dragonmeister.' Meghan spoke with a rush of enthusiasm. The forced formality of her previous tone was forgotten. 'We call him Billy, although his full pedigree name is William Crimson Wings of Powys. He's nested in a former stables beside the monastery on the island's northernmost peninsula. I think he's been waiting for the day when someone would bring –'

She stopped, as though she had suddenly remembered herself.

She turned and studied Gethin. His hands had been cut free but he was still kneeling. Meghan glanced at Inghean and asked, 'Am I supposed to be nice to the highborn one?'

'Dirt and dragon dung!' Gethin grumbled. 'Who the fuck put a woman in charge of this island?'

Meghan acted with surprising speed. She slapped him across the face. The blow sounded so hard it rang from the stone pillars. She looked as though she had deliberately aimed her blow so that she caught his broken nose and scarred cheek.

Inghean felt a moment's pang of sympathy for Gethin. That emotion quickly evaporated when she saw that Gethin was smiling through his pain. His expression was made menacing with bitter anger.

'Isn't that just marvellous?' he muttered darkly. His tone was flat. He stood up and shrugged his shoulders back. His posture was so stiff with the unspoken threat of malevolence that neither of the hostlers tried to restrain him. 'I can see you don't want me here,' Gethin snarled. 'I can take a hint, dragonmeister. I'll just take my boat and my bright-red dragon and I'll leave you alone on your precious island.'

Meghan stared at him with wide-eyed fury.

He acted as though he hadn't even noticed her displeasure.

'It seems such a shame to part the last remaining pair of red dragons in the world,' he sighed. 'But I suppose rare and exotic breeds of dragon are common enough. It's not like they'll ever die out and become extinct, is it?'

Inghean could see Meghan was stung by the words. Her spine stiffened. Her fingers tightened into a fist.

'I thought *Y Ddraig Goch* was a gift,' Meghan growled.

'Gift,' her wyvern repeated. 'Fucker.' The creature's eyes sparkled with glossy excitement.

Gethin ignored the wyvern. 'And I thought I'd be treated with some of the courtesy that is due to a high laird bearing gifts of diplomacy,' he told Meghan. 'But, instead of receiving courtesy, I've been slapped about the face and tied up and treated like a peasant bed-swiver.'

His cheeks were flustered with barely concealed outrage.

'Trust me, dragonmeister, I know better than to throw unwanted gifts on ingrates who treat me like that. I'll return to my homeland and see if I can find some other way to show the North Ridings, Blackheath and Gatekeeper Island how the House of Cadwallon responds to such hospitality. I'll leave now.'

He turned and marched toward the grand entrance way for the temple.

A range of conflicting emotions flashed across Meghan's face.

Inghean could see the woman wanted to let him go. But it was also obvious that she wanted to keep hold of *Y Ddraig Goch*. Studying the woman's face, Inghean thought it was almost possible to see the moment when Meghan made the decision to call after him.

A frown of self-contempt knitted her brow. Her upper lip wrinkled into a sneer of disgust. She slammed a curled fist against the broad muscle of her upper thigh.

'Fucker,' croaked the wyvern.

'You must forgive me, Laird Gethin ap Cadwallon.' Meghan spoke with a forced light heartedness. She stepped quickly to grab his bicep. With a subtle nod of her head she was gesturing for the bath maids to leave Inghean and join her by Gethin's side.

Obediently, and hurriedly, they slipped from the milky waters.

Gethin continued to scowl.

'The arrival of your birlinn was somewhat unexpected,' Meghan went on. 'And the conflict between yourself and the others put me in something of a predicament. I had to act in a judicial capacity. And I'm sure you would want to know my justice here on the island is honest and unbiased.'

Inghean and Owain exchanged a glance. They both knew that Gethin would not care whether Meghan imparted biased or unbiased judgement as long as it fell in his favour. From the way he scowled at her, Inghean guessed that Owain was not going to say those words aloud.

'I still have no –' Gethin began.

Meghan didn't let him finish his words. 'Allow my three most senior temple maids to bathe you and help you recover from the trials of your journey.' She brushed a finger against his cut cheek and feigned a wince of sympathy.

Gethin did his best to flinch away from the contact.

'You must be tired and distressed after such a long journey with so much unwanted adventure,' Meghan went on.

Again, he opened his mouth to reply.

And, again, Meghan didn't let him finish what he was saying.

'We'll gather together for a feast this evening in the dragon hall,' she exclaimed brightly, 'and I can give you a more heartfelt apology for the absence of courtesy you've experienced since landing here.'

He hesitated and Inghean knew that Meghan had clearly started to sway him.

Her hand pressed lightly against his chest. She leant close and pressed a light peck of a kiss against his cheek. The three bath maids, two of them still perspiring goat's milk onto the marble floor, leant close against him. Each woman touched and caressed and stroked him with a reverence that was almost obscene to watch.

'I'm still very distressed from the way I've been treated,' Gethin told Meghan.

'You have every right to be,' she agreed. 'I hope the temple maids will help to soothe your temper, and show our heartfelt apologies for the ill-treatment you've received at our hands.'

'Blow job,' agreed the wyvern.

Meghan placed a warning finger on its snout.

One of the bath maids stroked the front of Gethin's hosen.

Inghean saw that was the moment when he turned his head from challenging Meghan. He seemed to have been won over as he was led away from the temple with a promise to discuss the situation further at the banquet in the dragon hall.

Meghan followed the quartet as far as the temple doorway and then left the maids to take Gethin away. She walked slowly back from the temple doorway, her forehead wrinkled by a brooding frown. Her sandals slapped loudly against the temple's marble floor. She marched over to where Owain remained kneeling on the floor.

'You work for that prick?' she asked incredulously.

Owain sighed, as though he was tired of addressing this particular question. 'I don't work for Gethin.' He spoke with thinly concealed exasperation. 'I'm a dragon handler. I was employed to ensure the safe delivery of *Y Ddraig Goch* to Gatekeeper Island.'

Meghan was nodding. 'You don't work for him? You're just employed by him? I'm glad we got that cleared up. It could have become confusing. What the hell was happening onboard the birlinn when you pulled into the harbour? Am I going to get the same riddle from you about that? You weren't trying to kill someone: you were just trying to end their life.'

'I wasn't trying to kill anyone,' Owain said firmly. 'I was trying to stop Gethin ap Cadwallon from slaying Alvar of Erland whilst he was unconscious. I don't know what bad blood sits between those two but I didn't want any of it on my hands.' He glared at Inghean and said, 'They say that the dragonmeister invariably becomes crazy before she ends her tenure. This bitch is proof of that.'

Meghan recoiled as though she had been slapped.

Owain pulled himself up from the floor. The hostlers that had been holding his shoulders looked as though they were going to try and detain him. A glance at his menacing scowl was enough to make them think better of such folly. With anger obvious in each stride, Owain started towards the temple entrance way.

'I haven't given you permission to leave,' Meghan called after him.

'Then give me permission now,' he hissed. 'I've got to make sure *Y Ddraig Goch* is still safe and well.'

'You really care about your dragon, don't you?' She sounded surprised.

'I'm a dragon handler,' he called over his shoulder. 'It's my duty to care. So, with your permission, I'd like to go and tend to my charge.'

She nodded primly.

And then he was gone.

Inghean thought it a shame that Owain had left them because she had hoped Meghan and her could have shared him and played with him. Then maybe she would find a way of satisfying some of the urges that still nestled in her loins after all the teasing that had been administered by the bath maids.

Meghan pointed a finger toward an ornate and decorative stand. Obediently, the wyvern that had been on her shoulder flapped its wings and flew to the stand. Casually it began to preen itself, rubbing its snout against the polished red scales of its breast.

Absently, the dragonmeister climbed into the goat's milk bath with Inghean.

She didn't bother to remove her tunic or sandals. She seemed suddenly weary and less imposing than the formidable woman who had dominated the temple a moment earlier.

'I hope you're capable of giving me the same rejuvenating massage that my bath maids just gave to you,' Meghan sighed. She whispered the words against Inghean's ear, her lips kissing gently against the lower lobe.

Unable to resist the invitation, Inghean placed her arms around the woman and drew her into a welcoming embrace. She had not expected the journey to Gatekeeper Island to be fun. Knowing her body's dislike for travelling on water, she had thought the whole experience would be a chore of nausea, compounded by civic duties and weighty responsibilities.

For the first time since her consciousness had returned, Inghean was stung by the realisation that she hadn't thought about Caitrin and Tavia since she had awoken on the island. She hadn't been acting as a proper chaperone aboard the birlinn and she hadn't been looking out for them on the island.

The oversight struck her as being almost unforgiveable.

She was supposed to be acting as the chaperone to her younger sisters and she had no idea what had become of them. She sat up in the bath, removing her embrace from Meghan, allowing goat's milk to cascade over her bare breasts and pour down her skin.

'Where are my sisters?' she asked. 'Caitrin the dark and Tavia the fair. Where are they?'

The dragonmeister laughed. She placed a hand around Inghean's wrist, urging her to return to the bath. 'Don't worry about your sisters. They're safe at the northern end of the island. They're in the charge of the monastery's senior abbot, Robert of Moon Valley.'

CHAPTER EIGHT

Robert of Moon Valley

'This way to the dragon horn,' whispered Robert of Moon Valley. 'Stay close.'

He led them briskly through the cellars beneath the monastery. The air was cold and dusty. The lingering scent of fading memories and maturing wines filled each and every corner. The passageways were long and narrow and made deeper by inescapable shadows. Oft-trodden black soil coated the floors. Those walls that were not hidden behind the wine racks, all laden with dusty bottles, looked as though they had been hewn from solid stone by the hands of giant, skilled craftsmen.

Robert of Moon Valley was able to taste the sexual anticipation with every step they took toward his private cell. He led the way with an ease and familiarity that came from knowing every inch of the subterranean passageways beneath this stretch of the island. He tried not to let his haste show and reminded himself there was no need to hurry. The passageways beneath the monastery were his territory and there were few on Gatekeeper Island who knew their secrets better than him.

As he brooded on those secrets, he tried to think how best to deal with Caitrin and Tavia and the problem they presented. In their quest to obtain a perpetual source of dragon horn, it seemed the daughters of Blackheath's castellan had discovered where he resided.

That had been one of several secrets he had wanted to keep from them.

Damage control for this disaster, Robert conceded, would be costly, but he was adamant that the burden of cost would not fall on his shoulders. However, before he started to think about the personal repercussions and the financial implications, he was determined that he would reap whatever benefits came from having the two women finding him on this island.

His length stiffened inside the braies beneath his robes as he contemplated the main potential benefit. His sac drew tighter as he thought about the pleasures he and the twins would share together. They had proved an interesting distraction a month earlier. He was sure that there were other things the three of them could do together now that they were about to be properly reacquainted.

His hand gripped forcefully around the huge blazing torch he carried.

His knuckles whitened. It took an effort not to groan with anticipation.

When he did release a breath he could hear the sigh sounding from the walls with a hunger that was almost tangible. Even though the world beneath the monastery was composed of endless passageways of a darkness that clashed harshly against the light from the too-bright torches, his mind's eye was filled with the crystal-clear images of himself rutting naked with Tavia and Caitrin.

'You never said you were a monk,' Tavia told him. 'I might have treated you differently if I'd known you were a man of the cloth.' She giggled and added, 'I might have even said a prayer whilst we were doing it.'

Her words echoed hollowly from the stone walls. If he had been of a fanciful nature, Robert could have thought it was almost as though the pursuing shadows were calling to him. But he recognised the melodious lilt of Tavia's voice and knew he was being addressed by the blonde who had ridden him two dozen times or more during his week at Blackheath. He liked Tavia. There was something businesslike about the way she spoke, as though this was the polite interaction between equals before they got down to negotiating important terms for a deal.

Determined to have the upper hand in any negotiations he coughed to clear his throat. 'I'm not a monk.' He tossed the words coolly back over his shoulder. They bounced from the stone walls with a hollow chime of arrogance. 'I'm the abbot of this island. As a point of fact, I'm the senior abbot.'

They walked in silence for a few steps before Caitrin asked, 'Would you still be the senior abbot if it was found out you'd been trading in dragon horn?'

He stiffened at the question.

He stopped and turned to face her.

Because neither of the women was expecting him to stop they both came close to stumbling into him. Their faces were momentarily made orange in the blazing flare of the torchlight. They stared at him with eyes made dark and wide and etched with a smoky shadow of fear. It took an effort, but Robert forced a patient smile across his features before he spoke.

'Caitrin,' he began. 'Are you threatening me?'

Tavia punched her sister on the arm.

Caitrin gave Robert an indifferent glance. There was something in her hand that seemed to be dominating her interest but she had pushed her arms behind her back when he turned on them. He suspected it was the moonstone ring on the fourth finger of her left hand. It was an ugly and monstrous piece of jewellery that looked like a milky canker. It occurred to him that she had been absorbed with the thing, and paying undue attention to the ring, since the dragonmeister's hostlers had delivered the twins to the monastery. It was either a talisman or a gift from someone special, he reasoned. For some reason he thought it might be important to find out, but he didn't think this was the right moment to explore that line of thought.

'Caitrin,' he repeated. 'Are you threatening me?'

'Of course she wasn't threatening you,' Tavia said quickly. 'Caitrin was just –'

'Caitrin,' Robert repeated. He spoke over Tavia, silencing her as he glared at her sister. 'Are you threatening me, Caitrin?'

'I wasn't making a threat,' Caitrin assured him.

She kept her hands behind her back. He got the impression that she yearned to study the ring again. It always surprised him that jewellery could have such a hold over a woman.

'I wasn't making a threat,' Caitrin insisted. 'I was just curious to know if dealing in dragon horn meets with the approval of the dragonmeister. I wouldn't want myself or my sister to say the wrong thing to the wrong person whilst we're visiting Gatekeeper Island. That could prove embarrassing for all of us.'

He considered this for a moment, then nodded and resumed his brisk pace. Walking more swiftly through the narrow corridors he said, 'That's a sensible observation, Caitrin, and a wise precaution. And your curiosity deserves an honest response.'

He paused for a moment, trying to clear his thoughts

whilst composing the most politic way of responding to her question.

'There are powers on this island that would not be happy to learn that the senior abbot of Gatekeeper Island was dealing in dragon horn,' he admitted carefully. 'I do believe the dragonmeister is one of those powers and it would be wise not to mention our transactions to her.'

He sighed and his shoulders slumped.

'Not that the dragonmeister minds my pouring dragon horn down the necks of her temple prostitutes whenever we have visiting dignitaries pulling into Whitecap Harbour –'

He stopped himself from saying anything further, already worried that his tone might sound churlish or accusatory. There was no sense in his moaning about the petty side of the island's politics to a pair of vacuous mattress-warmers like Tavia the fair and Caitrin the dark. It was enough that the simple-minded bitches now knew when to keep their mouths shut.

The twins remained silent, with only their footfalls telling him that they were still following. Deciding the matter had been addressed, Robert led them around a corner and paused before the door that led to his private cellar. He motioned for the two women to stand silent behind him whilst he produced the large iron skeleton key from the thong around his neck. Hoping that neither of them noticed that his fingers were shaking, he slipped the key into the lock.

Tavia and Caitrin drew excited gasps.

'One word of warning,' he began solemnly.

Tavia studied him with a wide-eyed excitement that urged him to continue. Caitrin barely glanced up from her examination of the ugly moonstone on her finger.

He figured it would still be light above ground. It had been around midday when the women were first placed in his charge by the dragonmeister's hostlers and no more than an hour or two had passed since then. But in the cellars and corridors beneath the monastery, torches were needed to banish the pervasive and inescapable darkness.

'It's dark down here and these passageways and corridors are a warren of intersecting pathways that are only navigable by torchlight and experience. It's said that some of these tunnels connect with the island's easternmost catacombs, where the dragonmeister holds her most dangerous dragons. I don't know if I believe those catacombs are connected but I've heard the ghost of Vortigern, cursing the name of Georgiana of Roxburghshire, as his restless spirit lumbers through the shadows of these tunnels ...'

His voice trailed off and he glanced from Tavia to Caitrin hoping his message was being interpreted as a cautionary tale. To drive the point home he shook the torch he was holding and said, 'This light will show us the way back to safety when we've finished our business down here. But this is the only torch down here. That means the three of us will need to stay together.'

Tavia nodded eagerly.

Caitrin raised her hand. He thought she was going to ask a question. Instead she partially covered a yawn whilst glaring at him with truculent indolence.

Annoyed by her blatant rudeness, Robert pushed the door open and urged them to step inside. With his voice lowered he said, 'You'll want to come in here.'

With only the slightest suggestion of reluctance, the twin sisters did as he bade. Tavia went first. Caitrin followed in her wake.

Robert stepped into the room and closed the door.

He considered locking it and then decided that was one precaution that wasn't needed for his subterranean cell. He had just told both women that there was no escaping the tunnels beneath the monastery without the aid of a torch. If Caitrin or Tavia decided to try and make their own way back to the surface, he would be happy to let either of the Blackheath bitches roam through the darkness forever.

He lodged the torch into a sconce on the wall and then smiled with an expression that he hoped suggested reassurance.

The room was swathed in shadows.

The torch illuminated a cot in one corner. Its surface was covered with a tapestry throw. The tapestry was of an ancient design that showed gods and goddesses rutting freely whilst imbibing wine and playing panpipes. Robert noticed that some of the needlework on the tapestry had been darkened by the memory of damp stains. He wondered if there would be more stains on the throw before Tavia and Caitrin left the room.

His smile grew broader.

'I think we'd better get undressed.'

Tavia and Caitrin exchanged a sceptical glance.

Robert was shrugging off his robes, then stepping out of his braies and sandals. He placed the discarded clothes on the empty shelf of a wine rack beside the door and turned to face the two women. He removed everything except for the skull-headed iron key that hung from the leather thong around his neck.

Neither of the women had made any attempt to undress.

They stared at his nudity with expressions of prudish and pious distaste. They watched him without words as he stroked a fist up and down the length of his slowly thickening erection. Their obvious discomfort was almost amusing, he thought, especially when he felt confident that the three of them would be rutting before much longer.

'Are you not getting undressed?' he asked.

'Why on earth would we want to do that?' Caitrin asked. 'We came here in search of your dragon horn, not your cock.'

Tavia nodded agreement. She used a single lazy finger

to brush a fringe of flaxen curls from her brow. 'It's a bit forward of you to suggest that. I mean, I know the three of us rutted the last time we met ...'

Caitrin's cheeks flushed crimson at this reminder. She scowled at her sister.

Tavia blundered on. '... but even though we did that, it doesn't mean we're going to rut with you today.'

He stepped close to the women. Being naked between two fully dressed maids added to his excitement. His erection thickened and stood proud without him needing to massage fresh life into the length.

Caitrin seemed ready to flinch from his nudity.

Tavia, he noted, held her hands against her chest to stay herself from reaching down and caressing his shaft.

'I was thinking to protect your modesties,' he admitted. 'And I was thinking to protect your fine clothes.'

He stroked his knuckles against the scarlet silk chemise that covered Tavia's breast. She trembled beneath his caress. He could feel the nipple beneath the cloth stiffen with the touch of his fingers. Her eyes seemed to grow wider as though offering unconditional acceptance of whatever he proposed.

Turning away from her, Robert of Moon Valley reached out to caress the golden wool of Caitrin's kirtles. She fixed him with a single, solemn scowl. He couldn't bring himself to place his hand against her clothing. His erection throbbed with sudden need.

He coughed to clear his throat. 'The last time we three shared dragon horn, if you remember, we were all quite overtaken by its powers. Clothes were ripped and kirtles were torn, if you remember. I believe there was an occasional scratch against flesh as we each struggled to get close to one another.'

Tavia sighed. 'I remember.'

There was something in her tone that told Robert her memories of that day were fond ones and all connected to positive connotations. He watched as Tavia began to pluck at the laces fastenings on the breast of her kirtles. Her head was tilted coquettishly and she studied him from beneath lowered lashes. When she finally exposed her breasts his stiff erection ached with the need she inspired.

Caitrin gave her sister an exasperated glare, and then seemed to react as though she was being forced to undress against her will. Grudgingly she yanked open the laces that fastened her kirtles. She shrugged the garment from her body with an air of frustrated nuisance.

His hardness grew stiffer.

He barely noticed as Tavia seductively peeled away the layers of her clothing. The women were twins, both blessed with the same shapely breasts and equally welcoming curves. But his interest was ensnared by Caitrin's cool indifference and almost repelled by Tavia's eager enthusiasm.

He licked his lips as he admired the girl's rounded rear and the fleshy invitation of her dark-tipped breasts. Her flesh was milky pale and as smooth as a midwinter snowfall. The dark hairs that covered her sex were a secret forest of curls with the promise of infinite pleasures.

Caitrin took her sister's clothes, as well as her own, and placed them with Robert's robes on the shelf of the wine rack. She turned around to face Robert and he couldn't help but drink in the beauty of her nudity with frank and unashamed approval.

Tavia reached out, trying to take hold of his hand.

He brushed her fingers away.

'So where's this dragon horn you said was down here?' Caitrin asked. 'Please don't tell me you just lured us down here so we could look at your dick.'

He forced himself to smile for her and plucked the torch from the sconce. The fluttering flame illuminated the three of them. Their bare bodies seemed to undulate beneath the blaze. Shards of light danced from the pock-marked iron key around his neck.

He stepped between the two women.

Caitrin and Tavia each took a step back.

The orange glow of the flames made him think of the sun-kissed days and sultry nights he had spent sandwiched between the two sisters as the three of them explored and devastated a range of sexual boundaries. The memory of those hours, intense, sweltering and bold, made his hardness stand as rigid as though he had already downed a flagon of dragon horn. A huge grin split his face as he paused and asked, 'Did you miss me, girls?'

Cockily, he pointed toward the substantial length of his erection. Its aim wavered between the pair of them like a drunkard's crossbow.

'We missed your dragon horn,' Caitrin said flatly. 'Where the hell is it?'

He tried not to let the remark cause any irritation.

Prickles of gooseflesh covered Caitrin's bare skin, a legacy of the cellar's perpetual chill. She regarded him from beneath long raven lashes and there was a sneer of contempt drawn across her upper lip. Her attention seemed distracted, as though she was absorbed by something fascinating she found in the moonstone ring wrapped around the fourth finger of her left hand.

In that moment Robert knew he wanted Caitrin more than he wanted her twin sister. He wanted her because she clearly had so little interest in him. The prospect of giving her dragon horn, and then having her desire him and demand that they rut until her basest carnal appetites had been sated, struck Robert as being the thing he needed for absolute sexual satisfaction.

It didn't matter that Tavia was studying him with obvious sexual need. She had reclined on the cot he kept in one corner of his private cellar. She fixed him with a bold gaze as she kept one hand resting against her own breast whilst the fingers of her other hand teased idly between her legs. She was clearly toying with the thrust of her throbbing clitoris as her wide-eyed gaze sought his. She was so obviously and openly in need of him that it was almost off-putting.

'Where is the dragon horn?' Tavia asked. 'You did say we'd find it down here.' She gave him a sweet smile that was softened by her fair complexion and flaxen curls. Gesturing to her sister she said, 'We've done as you asked. We've undressed so that none of us get our clothes damaged when the drink takes effect.' She stroked her tongue across her lips and added, 'It would be wonderful to taste a sip of your dragon horn.'

He glanced expectantly at Caitrin and waited for her to nod.

She glanced up from the moonstone ring on her finger and flashed an insincere smile. 'Yes,' she agreed. 'What she said. That would be wonderful.'

He pushed his torch toward the rear wall of the cell. 'There!' he declared grandly. 'There's where I keep the dragon horn.'

Tavia shrieked with soft amazement.

Even Caitrin, he was pleased to hear, released a sigh of surprised approval.

'Fie!' Caitrin muttered. 'That's a lot of dragon horn.'

'So much,' Tavia murmured. 'God's truth!'

He could understand the wonder in their exclamations.

The torch had thrown light onto the cell's rear wall and the collection of wine racks that covered the rough-hewn stone. Each rack was laden with row upon row of earthenware casks. Each of the casks had a black scorched bottom with the initials DH scrawled into the ashes at the base.

'Is that all dragon horn?'

'Every last drop,' he nodded.

There were twenty-five earthenware casks in each row and the rows stretched from the floor up to the faraway ceiling. 'There's enough dragon horn on that wall to get the lairds of the East and the West Ridings rutting like newlyweds. There's enough there to have the sexless sisters of the Howling Forest bedding every Jack-o'-Lantern they can find in the Cursed Dells. There's enough dragon horn there to keep a senior abbot with simple tastes content if he lives to see the passing of two centuries.'

Studying the scorched base of one bottle, Tavia said, 'I want to try some.'

He stepped past her and plucked an earthenware cask from the nearest shelf. Pulling the cork from the neck he offered the cask to Caitrin. She shook her head and pointed to her sister.

Robert tried to accept this development with equanimity. He had wanted Caitrin. A part of him still throbbed with need for Caitrin. But the immediate desire to satisfy his basest urges held precedence. He pushed the cask toward Tavia and she took it with a trembling hand.

'Just take a small sip,' Robert warned. 'You know how powerful it can be.'

She nodded and raised the neck to her lips.

He saw her nipples harden as she inhaled the scent. As soon as Tavia had sighed with wet appreciation, Robert snatched the cask from her fingers and then took a swig himself.

'This smells almost as divine as your sandalwood cologne,' Tavia told him.

He could have told her that his cologne was sandalwood and ambergris, but he couldn't see the point in starting the argument. Instead he swallowed greedily from the bottle. The flavour burnt his throat and flowed through his veins with a searing heat. It tasted of the headiest pomegranate fire wine, but with a kick more powerful than the swipe of a dragon's wing. As the drink scorched its way through his body he was overtaken by the surge of arousal. His need to possess Caitrin was diminished to a forgotten memory. He was only interested in rutting with whichever woman wanted him.

One glance in Tavia's direction told him that she was certainly interested.

He thrust the cask into Caitrin's hands, unmindful of whether or not she intended to drink. Then he was diving onto the cot where Tavia lay and telling her that he wanted her.

The blonde welcomed him with open arms.

She had spread her legs and wrapped them around him as soon as their bodies touched. Her skin was soft and smooth against his bare flesh. The scratch of her neatly shorn pubic curls was a teasing abrasive against his hardness. The urge to hammer his pelvis back and forth repeatedly against her was almost irresistible.

But he forced himself to slow.

Familiar with the urges brought on by dragon horn, Robert often found himself fighting the desire to simply give in to the needs awoken by the drink.

He placed a hand between their bodies.

His fingers found the wet split of flesh where her sex sat broiling for him. The liquid heat tingled against his fingertips. She squirmed against him as he tried to wriggle one eager finger into her depths. His imagination was in overdrive because it felt as though the lips of her sex were suckling against his finger. As the tip disappeared into her moist confines, he heard Tavia sigh with heartfelt eagerness.

He moved his head forward so they could kiss.

Their mouths met in a wet exploration.

Her tongue slipped between his lips as he slid the finger deeper into her hole. She pushed against him with breathless urgency. One hand, blessed with silken fingers, encircled the engorged stiffness of his length. She guided him toward her wetness, seeming unmindful of the fact that he already had a finger pushed into her folds.

Spluttering the words between kisses she gasped, 'Please. Please do me.'

Robert was eager to oblige.

From the corner of his eye, he saw that Caitrin was getting dressed. His interest in her had previously been all-consuming. Now it teetered on being less than negligible. He realised his need for her had vanished with the first swig of dragon horn. And, with Tavia stroking her fingers against his shaft, he didn't think his desire for Caitrin was likely to return in the very near future. Nevertheless, he could see her glancing toward the doorway and he thought it would be prudent to remind her about the dangers of the corridors beneath the monastery.

They were in a room within an unlit labyrinth.

Anyone attempting to find their way through the corridors was risking a lonely and miserable death. The prospect of becoming lost was almost inevitable. The dangers that lurked within the darkness were not all imaginary. He knew it would be only right to remind her of those dangers.

And then he figured that he didn't care for Caitrin enough to tell her.

'Keep your fingers inside me,' Tavia breathed softly.

It was all the distraction he needed to forget about Caitrin the dark.

He frowned at Tavia, not sure she understood the practical implications of him keeping his fingers inside her. 'If I keep my fingers there ...' he began. His voice trailed off. He tried to think of a polite way to explain how the presence of his fingers would stop him from penetrating her. It was impossible to phrase the notion without explicitly naming body parts. He tried twice before realising he couldn't say the words.

Tavia kissed his cheek and whispered in his ear. 'Keep your fingers inside me,' she repeated.

She tugged his erection slightly downward.

Robert felt her place his length over the puckered ring of her anus. And then she was pushing herself against him. His eyes opened wide with surprise as the snug sleeve of her rectum stole over him.

He was being squeezed by the deliciously tight muscle of her backside.

He could feel himself sliding into her as his length swelled from the other side of her inner walls and pushed against his fingers.

Caitrin was dressed.

She placed the unstoppered cask of dragon horn on a cabinet beside the bed. Then she disappeared into the shadows. When she returned a moment later she held six casks of dragon horn she had taken from the shelves. She placed them carefully into a heavy linen bag that he kept in the room and then she hoisted it onto her shoulder.

Quietly, she stepped behind Robert and her sister as they rutted. She slipped silently through the cell door.

And, whilst he noticed that she was leaving, he was beyond caring.

His length was buried inside Tavia's backside. His fingers were deep into her sex. He was savouring the satisfaction his body craved and she was bucking against him and moaning encouragement.

Caitrin's act of theft was inconsequential and unimportant.

'I don't remember dragon horn being this good,' Tavia grunted.

Her nails were buried into his back. She was clutching him tight against her as she gripped his fingers with the muscles of her sex and clutched his cock with the muscles of her backside. 'I don't remember it being so ... so ...'

Her voice trailed off in a sigh of pleasure. A ripple of small convulsions crushed his erection and almost ripped the climax from his body. He staved off his own eruption with a huge effort of willpower.

And he continued to plough back and forth into the super-tight restrictions of her rear. Boldly, he slipped a second finger into her sex.

Tavia screamed and begged for a third.

It proved too much for him. His erection thickened and pulsed and spat hot jets of fluid deep into her rear. His balls were a momentary agony. A spasm clutched his groin as his ejaculate spat along the shaft of his cock.

Tavia's wail of gratitude echoed from the walls of the cell with a resonance that matched his own cry of pure pleasure. His sac clenched into a tight fist of release as the seed was ripped from his body. The pulse seemed to continue in ever-demanding waves of agonising delight.

Together the pair of them pulled apart and collapsed onto the cot with gasps of mirthless laughter. 'You two were playing me, weren't you?' he smiled. 'You and your sister had this set up from the beginning. One of you was going to rut with me. The other was going to steal casks of dragon horn. Am I right?'

Wordlessly, she reached for the dragon horn from the cabinet beside the bed. Taking a swift swig from the neck of the bottle she spat a mouthful of the drink into her palm and then massaged it against one breast and then the other.

His eyes opened wide.

'We were only playing you as much as you were playing us.'

'I knew you were playing me,' he grumbled.

He started to turn away but she reached for his head and then guided his face to her breast. The nipple was lacquered with a sheen of golden dragon horn. The liquid sat wetly on her skin.

'And you knew we were only playing, because we've both been having fun, haven't we?'

He nodded. Then his mouth was over her breast. And

he was lapping the heady flavour from her skin and discovering that his arousal was already returning with full and thrusting hardness.

She moaned beneath him, urging him to suck harder and faster and with more ferocity. Before he realised it had happened, Tavia had swabbed his shaft with a fresh fistful of dragon horn, and then she was guiding him into her sex.

The time he'd spent with the two sisters before had been exciting.

This moment was no less arousing.

Tavia took command of the situation and straddled him easily. She squatted on her haunches over him, whilst sliding up and down on the rigid length of his shaft.

The end of his erection trembled with an overflow of sensation.

She glided up and then down, groaning as though the pleasure of each movement was nothing short of climactic. He supposed, given the way dragon horn could intensify pleasures, it was likely that she was suffering such a heady rush of perpetual satisfaction.

Listening to her beg for more, hearing the way her cries became fuelled by demands for him to fill her and take her and ensure her satisfaction, Robert figured her pleasure might be more intense than he could imagine.

'Ride me,' she insisted. 'Ride me hard. Come inside me.'

He groaned and prepared to give in to the need for a swift release.

He knew that the second climax she squeezed from him would be painful. But he couldn't stop himself from submitting to the desire she raised in him. Perspiring heavily from the exertion, he thrust himself into her with increasing fury as he prepared to release his eruption inside her wetness.

Tavia sighed.

He lay breathless and wordless for a moment.

His heartbeat raced as though he had just cheated death. He clutched her like a drowning man clutching a lifeline. As the intensity of his passion subsided he realised she was returning his embrace carefully – almost as though she was battling contempt or distaste. But he reasoned it was not the first time he had rutted with a woman who despised him. One of the pleasures of dragon horn came from knowing that it could make a maid act against the dictates of her own common sense.

Tavia traced her fingertips against his chest. 'What are you thinking?'

'I'm thinking your sister is an idiot,' he said softly. 'Did she think I wouldn't notice her stealing out of here and taking six bottles of my dragon horn?'

Tavia said nothing. Her fingers stopped teasing through the hairs on his chest. She grazed her knuckles against the iron skeleton key and then withdrew her hand. The façade of pretending to be interested in him was dropped. She had worn the smile of a coquettish and sultry seductress. Now she fixed him with a frown of undisguised irritation.

'There's a real danger she could get lost in the passageways down here,' Robert said honestly. 'I suppose I can get a party of monks to patrol the catacombs with torches but there's no guarantee that we'll find her.'

'Caitrin will find her way out of these passageways,' Tavia assured him. 'She has a natural sense of direction.' The blonde paused and fixed him with a curious stare. 'May I ask a personal question?'

He shrugged. 'You can ask.'

'How's dragon horn made?'

He frowned. It wasn't something he wanted to share. The process behind dragon horn was a closely guarded secret known to only a handful of mystics and no one else on Gatekeeper Island.

He shook his head.

'I couldn't possibly tell you. Ask me another question.'

She smiled and placed a finger against the end of his thickening length.

Glancing at the sly smile in her eyes he could tell that she was about to make a suggestive remark or a provocative proposal. He didn't know if she would suggest having him explore her anus again, or if she had something more depraved in mind. But he could tell, even by Tavia's broad-minded standards, it would be something unusual and depraved.

Even though his length ached from the exertion of two climaxes in such quick succession, he knew he would happily acquiesce to whatever she proposed.

'Well ...' Tavia began.

She got no further.

CHAPTER NINE

The Mage's Eye

Nihal had been trudging through the tunnel for hours. It was long and dark and stank of mouldering fish. It led from the dungeons of Blackheath and headed beneath the depths of the Last Sea. Supposedly the tunnel extended to the bowels of Gatekeeper Island with its subterranean corridors and dragon-filled catacombs, but Nihal had only the word of a ledger written in the language of the ancients to prove that much. With no sign of the tunnel's end in sight, and knowing that a break was needed, the mage drew a deep breath and summoned the necessary magicks for resuscitation and nourishment.

'Gods of the Great Ones,' Nihal grumbled, 'give me light.'

The cavernous pathway was immediately lit. The walls, embedded with seashells, looked as though they had been carved from the bottom of an ocean. Stalactites dripped from the rough ceiling above. A sheen of briny wetness coated every surface. The remnants of a flailing fish splashed in a large puddle away from the centre of the tunnel. A fat grey crab scuttled from one seawater puddle to another.

'Gods of the Great Ones,' Nihal intoned in the language of the darkest mages. 'Give me food. Give me drink. Give me a crystal ball through which I can claim the vision of the mage's eye.'

The summoned items appeared with remarkably little ceremony.

A small wooden table and a stool materialised in the middle of the dimly lit tunnel. On the table there was a plain plate of beggar bread, a round of cheese and a selection of summer fruits. Beside the fare there was a pewter jug filled with mead and an empty flagon. The front of the flagon was inscribed with the words: *NIHAL – most powerful wizard in the whole of Blackheath*. The rear of the flagon bore the inscription: *WITH LOVE FROM CAIT*.

Nihal drummed impatient fingers against the solid surface of the table awaiting the arrival of the crystal ball. When it slowly winked into existence the mage scowled.

'About fucking time.'

Sitting at the table, poring over the crystal ball whilst tearing a chunk of beggar bread from the loaf, Nihal murmured incantations, insisting that the mists should disclose their secrets. When the secrets were finally disclosed, the mage released a groan of agonised disappointment.

'Not again, you fucking slut.'

Nihal's wail of despair echoed from the cavernous roof of the tunnel.

'You couldn't keep your legs together if I transformed you into a mermaid, could you? Your snatch has taken more cock than the eunuch-maker's blade.'

The mists within the crystal ball showed Robert of Moon Valley pounding into her. The senior abbot of Gatekeeper Island was riding up and down with a hypnotic and mechanical rhythm. The woman beneath him groaned with an enthusiasm that was either heart-felt or fuelled by dragon horn, or made louder by both those stimulants.

Nihal's shoulders slumped.

'Say a prayer for me, abbot,' the woman giggled.

Nihal frowned.

The woman had not spoken with Cait's voice. Understanding came with a surge of relief. The woman beneath Robert of Moon Valley was not Cait: it was her slutty sister, Tavia. Cait was clearly in the room – or at least, the mage's eye she wore on her ring was in the room – but Nihal knew Cait would not be a part of something so lewd or tawdry. Cait was pure and chaste and, Nihal knew, Cait had standards.

Through the crystal ball, Nihal watched as Cait stole earthenware casks from a shadowed wall and secreted them into a heavy bag she carried. Each of the casks had the initials DH scratched into the bottom of its scorched base.

Nihal's shoulders slumped again.

Cait wasn't rutting with perverted abbots in the bowels of Gatekeeper Island. Instead, Cait was stealing contraband whilst her sister acted as a diversion by rutting with the person who owned that contraband.

'You really are a classy maid,' the mage muttered before taking another mouthful of untasted beggar bread. The bread was made softer with a sip of honey-sweetened mead. Unable to stop studying the scene, Nihal caressed the smooth surface of the crystal ball.

'You're a classy maid who shall be mine.'

Caitrin slipped out of the abbot's cell after giving Tavia a conspirator's wink. The bag containing the earthenware was surprisingly heavy. Its cumbersome weight threatened to spoil her covert exit. She held the bag with her left hand to keep the casks from rattling together. Outside the cell, in the darkness of the underground corridor, she kept her left hand clamped over the bag and used her right hand to find the thread she had left to retrace her route out from the underground warren of passageways and tunnels.

After being escorted from the birlinn, Tavia had handed her a ball of thread. She told Caitrin to remember the story of Ariadne, Theseus and the Minotaur and it was not a difficult story to recall. In truth it was one of Caitrin's favourite myths because it had always struck her as a triumph of female strength over masculine domination. She had always loved the idea of wily Ariadne masterminding a scheme to defeat something as complex as a masculine man-made maze and the menacing Minotaur. It was especially pleasing that she used something as simple and innocuous as the traditionally female tools of sewing thread.

Later, when Robert of Moon Valley had mentioned that his stash of dragon horn was stored in the centre of an underground maze he had used the word 'labyrinth' and Caitrin had again been reminded of the story of Ariadne, Theseus and the Minotaur. She had retrieved the thread and discreetly tied one end to a door in the monastery before allowing the senior abbot to escort her and her sister into the underground tunnels and corridors. As they walked to the cell she had allowed the thread to spill behind her as a perpetual reminder of the safe route to the surface.

Now she tied the other end to a cask of dragon horn and dropped it beside the doorway in case Tavia needed the lifeline to return to the surface. The trail of thread would also serve, she thought, as a convenient way of finding her way back to the cell should she decide to liberate any more casks of dragon horn before leaving Gatekeeper Island.

Not that she thought they had needed the thread.

Robert of Moon Valley seemed to leave a stink of sandalwood and ambergris in his wake that was almost as tangible as the weight of the thread that Caitrin had left to mark their route.

From the shadows she heard the murmur of faraway footfalls.

She ignored the noise.

She was sure it had nothing to do with the ghosts that Robert had mentioned, nor did she think there was any likelihood of errant dragons lumbering through the connecting corridors within the catacombs. Even when the sound came again, she told herself it was nothing to cause concern. She even refused to acknowledge the prickle of gooseflesh that tickled the nape of her neck because she knew tunnels and caves were renowned for making unusual noises.

A part of her wanted to know how Tavia had possessed the foresight to make such a convenient suggestion. She had mentioned the myth of the Minotaur and supplied an appropriately large ball of thread – details which Caitrin was happy to acknowledge were now proving to be her lifeline. She suspected her sister's insight involved Tavia's relationship with a seer. And, whilst she supposed she had no right to complain about the arrangement, Caitrin didn't advocate or approve of the dark arts. Admittedly, Nihal had restored her virginity too many times for Caitrin to claim piety about the use of magicks. And whoever had been responsible for putting the thread in her hands was also responsible for her now possessing six casks of dragon horn – and that was an acquisition that deserved gratitude. But it was still disquieting to think she was walking at the behest of powerful forces and driven by the agenda of someone she barely knew.

She missed her footing in the darkness.

The earthenware casks clunked noisily together.

She held her breath, squeezed the sack tighter against her side, and continued holding the thread as she tried to find her way upward.

'Caitrin?'

She almost dropped her bag when she heard someone hissing her name. A glimmer of light from behind made her turn. She was momentarily panicked into thinking it might be ghosts or dragons or Jack-o'-Lanterns. Then she saw a burly figure holding a modest torch and stooping for fear of bashing his head against the broad wooden beams that supported the ceiling.

There was something comforting and familiar about his shape.

'Caitrin of Blackheath?' he called. 'What the hell are you doing down here, woman?'

'*Owain*,' she reminded herself. '*His name is Owain. He's not Muscles. And he's not High Laird Gethin ap Cadwallon. He's Owain the dragon handler*.'

'Owain?'

She wanted to ask him how he had escaped from the dragonmeister and the hostlers. He had still been brawling with Gethin and Alvar when the birlinn landed in Whitecap Harbour. He had been dragged brusquely from the vessel and she had feared for his safety at the hands of the guards of Gatekeeper Island. But she and Tavia had also been taken from the boat and sent to the monastery. There had been no opportunity for her to intervene and insist, in the name of her father the castellan of Blackheath, that no harm should befall him. And yet, although she wanted to be sure he had been unharmed at the hand of the dragonmeister and her staff, the first question that came to Caitrin's mind was to ask why he was naked.

'You've got no clothes on.'

He walked lazily toward her, seeming untroubled by his nudity. The long length of his exposed penis shone dully in the fluttering flame of the torch. The dark thatch of his pubic curls was made denser by the shadows.

'I didn't get the chance to dress after you and I were together on the birlinn.'

His discreet choice of words made her warm for him. They hadn't been rutting: they had been *together*.

They hadn't been banging like farmyard swine: they had been *together*. Acting without thinking she stepped into his embrace. His exposed length pressed lazily through her kirtles against her thigh. She wanted to shiver but she resisted the urge. She didn't want to make it too obvious that she found him attractive.

'I was concerned for you,' she said carefully.

His arms encircled her waist. She allowed them to stay there.

'What are you doing down here?' he asked.

'One of the monks brought us down here to show us his cell.'

'Us?'

'My sister. She's still with the monk now.'

'And you?'

'I've never liked being underground. I was making my way back to the surface.' She shook her head to stop further questions. She wasn't sure she could bring herself to explain that she was stealing casks of an illicit and forbidden potion from the senior abbot of the island's monastery. There didn't seem to be a way of explaining her situation without sounding like some sort of monster.

'Why are you here?' she asked quickly. 'I thought you'd been taken to see the dragonmeister.'

'I've seen the dragonmeister.' Owain started to step away from her, as though the subject was not one he wanted to discuss. 'And now I've got some business to address before I get on with my duties for the care and resettlement of Drusilla.'

She grabbed for him and pulled him back into her embrace. 'Address me first, dragon handler,' Caitrin insisted.

She reached between their bodies and found the substantial length of his shaft. He was long and thickening to her touch. When she pressed closer, pushing her lips up to meet his, the shaft began to grow hard. Whatever bad mood had soured his disposition when she mentioned the dragonmeister it seemed to be banished by the suggestion of what they could do together.

'Didn't I satisfy you enough aboard the birlinn?' he asked.

'That was an age ago,' she complained. 'And, are you seriously telling me you're refusing a direct command from Caitrin of Blackheath?'

'I'm a dragon handler from the West Ridings.' The arm around her waist drew her closer to him. The thickness of his erection pressed at her with an urgency that stole the breath from her lungs. 'I don't take instruction from Caitrin of Blackheath.'

She placed her lips close to his ear and asked, 'Don't you take *any* instructions, dragon handler? Not even when Caitrin of Blackheath gives you the instruction to pleasure her as long and as hard as you're able?'

He chuckled and dumped the end of his torch into the soft-soil carpet of the corridor. The end penetrated the soil and stood impressively erect. Caitrin wondered if that was a good portent for what she could expect from him now.

The sound of his mirth was a soft reminder of the pleasures they had previously shared. Her nipples hardened for him as the inner muscles of her thighs grew moist with fevered desire. Her stomach was tightened with the delicious thrill of heightened anticipation.

'Caitrin of Blackheath?' He murmured her name as though it was unfamiliar. 'Caitrin of Blackheath? I'm sure I've heard about her. Was she one of the shipboard wenches that was there to service the sailors? There were so many onboard concubines I'm surprised that birlinn stayed afloat. There were so many onboard concubines it was hard to differentiate one from another. Was Caitrin the one with the nickname? Didn't they call her Horny-Caitrin? Or was it Forny-Caitrin?'

Caitrin raised a hand to slap at him.

Owain grabbed her wrist and pressed himself against her. Their lips met in a delicious union of exploration and greedy tasting. She realised he was pushing her against the wall as his body pressed over hers. His physical presence was so large and broad it was wonderfully daunting. The wrist he held was pinned against her side.

Her bag fell to the floor.

The earthenware casks clunked loudly together but the sound was lost beneath her cry of easy acquiescence for him. She struggled to catch her breath. His tongue slipped between her lips. The weight of his massive erection pressed forcefully against her thigh.

Her need for him grew stronger.

'Did you really have difficulty recalling me?' she teased. 'I thought you would have remembered.' She held his erection in one hand. Her fingers tightened their hold around his shaft. With her free hand she clutched at the linen of her travelling kirtles, raising the fabric to expose herself to him.

'I remember how hard you rutted,' he said. It sounded as though he was spitting the words from between clenched teeth. 'But I also got the impression you'd rut harder if you were angry.'

She laughed and placed the end of his shaft over the gaping mouth of her sex.

The subterranean corridor was not particularly chilled but she could feel a shiver teasing the surface of her flesh. The warm light from Owain's torch bronzed their bodies and darkened the shadows. Caitrin braced herself for the pleasure of having him slide deep into her sex.

She could see he was half-kneeling before her. She pressed her back against the wall of the tunnel. And then she reached around him to clutch at his buttocks. He was so close that, when she inhaled, she could drink in the scent of his nearness. The manly taste of his perspiration was an incendiary spark to the fuse of her arousal. She could taste the flavour of pomegranate fire wine that sweetened his breath. She trembled in his arms.

'Up against the wall, Caitrin?' he murmured. 'You're taking me like a low maid or a tavern slut.'

'I'm taking you,' she warned him. 'But not if you continue to insult me.'

He chuckled and brushed a tender caress against her cheek. 'One of these days you and I shall find ourselves together in a sumptuous feather-filled bed and it will be an unusual experience.'

'You make it sound as though we'll be doing this repeatedly,' she scoffed. 'I'm only rutting with you again because I didn't get a chance to find out if you were any good the last time.'

He pushed his mouth over her ear. 'You'd rut with me every hour if you had the chance,' he muttered. 'You know how well we rut together. You're addicted to my cock.'

The words filled her with a thrill of raw need for him. It took every effort not to lower herself onto his erection and accept the rush of pleasure that she knew would come. 'Just rut with me,' she hissed. 'Stop trying to engage me with clever wordplay. You don't have the skills for that. You're just an empty-headed dragon handler.'

'Tell me I'm wrong,' he breathed. 'Tell me you're not addicted to my cock.'

She groaned.

The end of his length nestled against the lips of her sex. Its weight was a maddening temptation urging her to do more. She wanted to slide down, onto him and around him, so that he filled her hole with his thickness. But the idea of doing such a thing would have been tantamount to admitting that she was addicted to his cock. And it seemed important to Caitrin that Owain should not know she harboured such a craving for the pleasures he could provide.

Also, and this was the reason why she told herself she wasn't doing as he bade, Caitrin believed that idea of taking such a commanding position would have been unladylike. It would have shown her to be dominant and she didn't want Owain to see her as being commanding or dominant or bossy.

'Rut with me, dragon handler,' she grunted. She buried her nails into his bare buttocks and tried to pull him toward herself. 'Do me now and do me hard. Don't make me demand this from you.'

Laughing softly, he pushed forward. His length slowly separated the lips of her sex. Then he slid into her velvet depths.

Caitrin groaned.

She had remembered that he was large. But she had

forgotten he was so large. Her inner muscles felt as though they were being stretched to the point of tearing. She stifled a scream of absolute pleasure and struggled to remain standing whilst Owain continued to push his formidable length into her most intimate depths.

Her fingernails buried deeper into his buttocks. The muscles beneath her palms tensed and stiffened whilst his length seemed to thicken in her confines. The waves of pleasure began to ripple through her body.

Still he continued to plough slowly into her sex.

She briefly wondered if it would ever end. She fancied that his length would continue sliding deeper and deeper until the echoes of delight had snatched the consciousness from her dizzied thoughts and left her in a quivering heap of satisfaction. It did not sound like the most unpleasant fate a person could suffer. The idea held a nihilistic appeal that she would be happily rutted to death – skewered on the impossible length of Owain's huge shaft.

As that delicious idea passed through her thoughts, he began to pull himself from her. This time the ripples of satisfaction were just as devastating. The rush of blissfully liquid sensations was almost more than she could bear.

Caitrin bit back a sob of pure gratitude.

'You were desperate for me, Caitrin of Blackheath,' he observed.

She swallowed twice before responding. 'I was no more desperate for you than you were for me.' The words were torn from her throat on ragged breaths. 'You were the one parading yourself around Gatekeeper Island in a state of nakedness, flaunting yourself for me.' She tried not to make her tone argumentative but it was impossible not to challenge him. 'And I'd thank you to remember –'

He pushed back into her.

Whatever she had been about to say was forgotten as an exquisite explosion of sensations flushed through her sex. She tilted her head back and stifled the desire to scream for fear that her cries would be heard by Tavia or Robert of Moon Valley.

When Owain pulled back she felt the joy increase.

When he pushed back into her she had to quash the urge to cry out by jamming a hand against her mouth.

'Too much,' she gasped. It pained her to make the admission. 'This is far too much. It's more than I can take, Owain.'

'Do you want me to stop?' he asked.

She glared at him. 'Of course not. Finish me, dragon handler. Rut me hard and finish me well, if you can.'

She suspected it was the sneering challenge in her voice that made him push into her with more force. He raised his pelvis upward with such ferocity she could feel the floor being taken from beneath her feet. Her back rubbed against the hewn stone wall and the thrill of cataclysmic pleasure convulsed through her bones.

That he was pushing into her again and again was

enough to make her weary from the climaxes bursting through her sex. Her inner muscles clenched and convulsed with so much force it was almost painful. Tears of sated wetness wept down her thighs. A sheen of perspiration suddenly soaked her entire body. She gritted her teeth as the echoes of torrential satisfaction burst from her loins. Unable to stop herself, she screamed.

He continued to ride harder between her thighs.

She stopped clutching at his thighs. Instead, she pressed her hands against his shoulders and tried to push him away.

'Too much,' she told him. 'Please. No. I've come. I can't come again. Not yet. Not soon. Please stop.'

She saw he had heard her words. But he pushed into her with one final apocalyptic thrust. His length stiffened and then grew thicker. He groaned and placed a kiss against her lips.

Caitrin held her breath knowing what was about to come.

His shaft spurted a rush of white-hot seed into her depths.

The liquid seared into her most private parts and she almost fainted as the thrust of his climax threatened to be too satisfying. His fat length continued to thicken and pulse, filling her with his seed and pushing her repeatedly past the threshold of the climaxes her body was able to endure.

In a daze, she felt him slide his dwindling length from her sex.

Droplets of his seed and her wetness trickled down her thighs and fell to the soil beneath their feet. She allowed him to lay her down on the floor, sure that she wouldn't be able to remain standing after having enjoyed such extremes of satisfaction.

Her knees had buckled and she doubted they would ever again be able to support her. Her heart raced like a fevered illness. Her body was suddenly drained of all energies. She languished in a state between the need to fall into a satisfied sleep and the desire to repeat the experience immediately.

She stretched in the darkness. Her knuckles brushed against the bag containing the earthenware casks. It occurred to her that there was a way she could immediately enjoy a repeat performance of the divine experience he had just bestowed upon her.

She sat up excitedly and fumbled for the bag.

'Here,' Caitrin said eagerly. 'We must try this. We must try this now.' She grabbed at the discarded bag and fumbled to retrieve one of the earthenware casks from inside. Pushing it toward him she said, 'Have a drink.'

He pulled the stopper from the neck and sniffed warily. 'Fire wine? You think I'll get hard again from drinking fire wine? You really were a virgin if that's how you think men –'

'It's not fire wine, you half-witted dragon handler,' she snapped. 'It's dragon horn.'

She had meant the words to come out as a joke. She had thought he would be amused by her harsh tone of voice and impressed by the fact that she had access to something as forbidden and mysterious as dragon horn.

Instead, the words sat between them like a challenge.

The flames from his torch seemed to recede until she could no longer read his face from the shadows. He had been animated before, but now he sat as stiff and unmoving as a carved gargoyle. The air, which had previously been rich with the promise of fresh pleasures and burgeoning intimacy, was now stale and cold and hostile.

'Dragon horn?' he grumbled ominously.

She swallowed, aware that the mood between them had changed faster than a slap. A moment earlier she had thought they would be playfully teasing each other about the prospect of another bout of passion. Now it was as though she was trapped in the underground labyrinth with a genuine Minotaur.

'Dragon horn!' he repeated.

He snatched the earthenware cask from her fingers and hurled it toward the darkest shadows. Caitrin heard it shatter before she had a chance to cry out and tell him not to do something so wasteful.

'What did you do that for?' she demanded. 'Do you know what I had to do to –'

'Carys forgive me,' he spat. 'What have I done?'

'You've just broken one of my casks of dragon horn,' Caitrin told him. 'Don't you know how valuable –'

'Do you know how harmful dragon horn can be?' he growled. His face was wrinkled into a mask of disgust. 'Do you know how many unsuspecting maids have had their innocence taken from them by charlatans pedalling that filth?'

'I had no –'

'Do you know how many innocent dragons have suffered through fools believing that stuff comes from the horns of dragons?'

Caitrin's mouth worked silently for a moment as she tried to formulate a response to his question. She had no idea how dragon horn was manufactured. She had never given the process any thought. She knew few names related to the things they described. There was no real fire present in a mouthful of fire wine. Beggar bread did not contain traces of beggar. There was no trace of summer in the finest summer fruits. But, if she was being honest with herself, she supposed she had been one of the fools who had thought the manufacture of dragon horn had something to do with the horns of dragons. It had never occurred to her that there was no horn from a dragon in a cask of dragon horn. And she wouldn't have suspected that harvesting those horns might be detrimental to the health of the dragon involved.

Seeing the concern on Owain's handsome features she realised she had upset him. Her heart beat faster with self-recrimination and renewed passion. His compassion for the creatures he was charged with handling made her realise he was more than just an attractive man and a competent lover. He was a decent person.

'I had no idea dragons were being harmed,' she told him. 'If I'd thought –'

'If you'd thought, we wouldn't be in this situation.'

He snatched another earthenware cask from the bag and hurled that into the shadows. The sound of the pottery shattering echoed hollowly from the depths of the darkness.

Caitrin flinched from the noise.

She wanted to stop him. She wanted to tell him that some of those casks belonged to Tavia. But she didn't have the heart to say the words.

'Is this from *his* private supply?'

He sneered the word 'his' with such contempt Caitrin felt ill. 'From whose private supply?'

'Robert. Robert the bastard of Moon Valley.'

It was sickening to hear him speak with such obvious loathing. She nodded and said, 'He's the monk that Tavia's with. He's senior abbot here at Gatekeeper Island.'

A flare of bright fury flashed in Owain's eyes. 'He's the abbot? Didn't you say he's down here now?'

'I can take you to see him. He's this way.' Blindly, she clutched for the thread from the wall. She didn't mind that her clothes were dishevelled, and bearing the obvious signs that she had been rutting whilst she wore them. She was so eager to bridge the gulf that had grown between them she was desperate to do whatever was needed, regardless of the personal cost. She clutched at the thread and followed it back into the shadows from where she had originally come.

Owain walked behind her. The fluttering of his torch-light lengthened and shortened their shadows on the walls. Aside from the crackle of flames he was silent as he walked beside her.

'Here,' she told him, when they reached the door. 'He's in here.'

Owain pushed past her without thanks. He raised one bare foot and kicked. His heel landed squarely in the centre and the door burst open. The thunder of splintering oak resonated from the stone wall. It resounded hollowly down the passageway and rang loudly in the cramped confines of the private cell.

Tavia gasped. She snatched a length of sheeting to cover her modesty.

Robert of Moon Valley, the bastard of Moon Valley as Owain had called him, had been laid with his head between her spread thighs. He pulled his face away, momentarily revealing the juicy pink split of Tavia's sex.

He turned to glare at the interruption, his jaw dripping with remnants of Tavia's excess wetness.

His eyes grew wide when he saw Owain.

Whatever words he had been about to exclaim in protest died on his lips.

'Robert of Moon Valley,' Owain marvelled softly. 'It's been a long time since we last had a chance to converse, hasn't it?' He glanced sourly at the split of Tavia's labia and said, 'I do hope you enjoyed your last meal.'

Robert scrambled away from Tavia.

He scoured the immediate area of the cell.

Caitrin thought it was obvious he was looking around for something he could use to defend himself against the surprise visitor, but there was nothing close to hand. She could see the partially drained cask of dragon horn but it struck her that his attempts to retrieve a cask of dragon horn would not pacify Owain. More likely it would exacerbate the dragon handler's obvious anger.

'Owain,' Robert began. He was backing into shadows, his gaze still flitting to the corners of the room. 'I know you and I have unresolved issues, but surely we can settle our differences in a civilised way, can't we?'

'Of course we can,' Owain agreed solemnly. He stepped into the room. 'We can easily settle our differences in a civilised way. I can kill you. And you can die.'

Robert glared in dismay as Owain approached. Drawing a shuddering breath the abbot wailed, 'No!'

'No!'

Momentarily disoriented, Nihal glanced up at the cry. Watching Owain rutting with Cait had been painful. Admittedly, she might have been closing her eyes and pretending she had the mage of Blackheath between her legs. But even if she had been thinking as much, Nihal still thought the sight of her infidelity was unbearable. Seeing the pair creep closer to the abbot's cell had been unsettling. But Robert's cry had not seemed to come from the crystal ball. Nihal thought the cry had come from somewhere ahead in the cavern.

'I was almost there,' Nihal whispered bitterly.

Clutching a tight hold on the crystal ball Nihal growled '*Atra*.'

The world within the crystal ball was plunged into darkness. A shriek from somewhere ahead in the cavern, somewhere surprisingly close, told the mage that all the torches and lights surrounding Cait had been extinguished.

A flash of Nihal's bitternut wand was all it took to make the crystal ball vanish from existence. A second flash of the wand and the table and chair and the remnants of the fare had disappeared. As the light in the corridor began to fade, Nihal started running toward the end of the tunnel.

'I'm almost there, Cait. I'm almost with you.'

CHAPTER TEN

Inghean the Voyeur

Gethin ap Cadwallon was being pleasured by the three women.

Inghean tried to watch with a disinterested eye but it was difficult not to be drawn into the scene and aroused by the spectacle. Melinda, Minerva and Miranda were all naked and doing their best to coax the climax from his fat, stubby length. The quartet had become a sea of writhing pink flesh, muttering the soft sounds of sex and the indulgent groans of encouragement. Whilst Inghean had first mistaken the three women for mere bath maids, it was clear that they were highly trained temple prostitutes. She realised they were disciplined in the celebrated arts of pleasure. They were each able to excite men and women to the point of climax. And they made no attempt to disguise their vocation as they shamelessly indulged every whim of the High Laird of the West Ridings. Judging from the demonstrative sighs each one released, it was clear that they took a great deal of personal satisfaction from their work.

Inghean found herself envying their vocation. She told herself, if she had not been the highborn daughter of the castellan of Blackheath, she would have wanted to be a temple maid.

Melinda oiled Gethin's bare flesh with balms and chrisms. Minerva worked her mouth around the thick shaft of his erection. Miranda whispered intimate suggestions into his ear. They teased him with touches and caresses that made Inghean jealous of the high laird's good fortune.

Although the pleasure he was receiving looked enviably humbling, Gethin basked in the midst of the three women like a man who believed such attentions were his divine right. His grin was broad and self-satisfied. His stubby erection remained fat and swollen. Inghean could see it was tipped by a bulbous purple end that throbbed contentedly. The flesh glistened with the glossy wet lubricant of Minerva's saliva. Gethin constantly encouraged the three women to get closer and add to his pleasure. Between kisses, whispers and shared intimacies, he quaffed lustily from a flagon of fire wine.

He looked like a man who belonged in the dragon hall.

The walls were adorned with carved statues of legendary dragons. The statues were life-size and colourful. Red and green wyvern perched on the tops of pillars and columns. Serpentine Orientals, rich in deep azures and fiery oranges, climbed the walls. Statues of Smok, Ljubljana and Coca stood by the door, each holding ceremonial swords.

Because the statues were so large and so lifelike, Inghean thought the effect was equally mesmerising and disconcerting. If she hadn't thought Meg was busy trying to maintain a façade of diplomatic conviviality for Gethin, she would have mentioned her unease.

Meghan released a soft sigh of disapproval. In a whisper meant only for Inghean she said, 'If that swarthy little wretch hadn't brought us *Y Ddraig Goch,* I would have covered him in goat's blood and tossed him into the easternmost catacombs.'

'Catacombs,' the wyvern on her shoulder chuckled. 'Catacombs.'

Inghean shivered.

The brutality of the suggestion was almost enough to sour her smouldering excitement at the sight of Gethin and the maids. During the short time she had been on Gatekeeper Island, she had already learnt a lot about Meghan's dragons. The mention of goat's blood didn't bode well.

The dragons nested in two separate sets of catacombs beneath the surface of the island. In the easternmost catacombs the dragonmeister kept a Bedgerid of Orientals.

The Orientals included three-toed Japanese dragons and five-clawed Chinese dragons. These were known as the most dangerous beasts on the whole island.

In the western catacombs, Meghan kept European dragons. These included a dozen varieties with breeds ranging through Portuguese Coca, Polish Smok, Catalonian Víbria and a flock of chattering Wessex wyvern.

But, of all the dragons on Gatekeeper Island, only the Orientals were considered dangerous. And it was well-known the Orientals had an avaricious taste for goat's blood. If Gethin had been daubed with goat's blood and tossed into their Bedgerid, Inghean knew the carnage in those catacombs would have been brutal and final. The thought sent a chilly shiver rippling down her backbone.

'Catacombs,' the wyvern on Meghan's shoulder croaked again.

The creature had a habit of latching onto some spoken words, as though it enjoyed the flavour of them. At other times it would say words that struck Inghean as totally random, or as though they had been plucked from the forefront of its mistress's mind.

'Catacombs.'

Meghan stroked its snout and the beast fell silent. 'Shush,' she whispered. 'He's not really going to the catacombs.' She scowled with obvious disgust at Gethin and murmured, 'I doubt even my Orientals could digest that.'

Inghean regarded the woman warily. She still thought

Meghan was irresistible but there was now a snake of doubt crawling through her bowel. It was like discovering a dangerous side effect to a favourite wine, or a potentially lethal spice that was the key ingredient for a particularly delicious feast. Maddeningly, the suggestion of danger did not make Meghan less attractive. If anything, Inghean thought the woman seemed even more appealing than she had before.

Inghean pressed her thighs tight together and tried not to think about the unbidden desires the woman spurred in her loins.

The dragonmeister of Gatekeeper Island lounged in a gold throne at the head of the dragon hall. She wore a short-sleeved yellow smock belted at the waist to show off her desirable curves. The breast of the smock bore the arms of Gatekeeper Island: a front-facing dragon, silver on a gold background, with its claws and teeth coloured red. The hem of the smock barely covered the tops of her thighs and, having already shared a moment in one of the temple baths with the woman, Inghean had the sneaking impression that Meghan was naked beneath the smock.

The idea inspired a thrill of raw desire. The inner muscles of Inghean's sex began to clench in ripples of swelling need.

The wyvern, a comical splendour of dark green and bright red, remained on Meghan's shoulder with its barbed tail curled around her neck. Its huge onyx eyes followed every movement in the hall. Occasionally a dark, barbed tongue slipped across its lips and the creature repeatedly chattered words as though it was a part of a larger conversation.

'Fucker,' the creature cooed agreeably. 'Goat's blood. Catacomb fodder. Steal *Y Ddraig Goch*.'

Inghean shivered.

Meghan had instructed Inghean to sit at her right hand. Together they watched the temple maids pleasuring Gethin ap Cadwallon. They watched the spectacle as though it was a demonstration of celebrated actors performing scenes from the sacred tableaux or working their way through the pageant plays.

Even Meghan's pet wyvern seemed intrigued by the performance. Its large, dark eyes shone excitedly as it watched the four in the centre of the banquet hall. Occasionally the creature crowed, 'Fucker,' to demonstrate its enthusiasm. Each time the wyvern said that word Meghan hid her smile behind a politic hand.

'You don't trust him?' Inghean asked quietly.

'Of course not,' Meghan sneered. 'It's Gethin ap Cadwallon. He has a kingdom-wide reputation for dishonesty. He's patently untrustworthy. There's even talk that he might be a dark mage.'

Inghean considered this reply. 'He's not a dark mage,' she announced confidently. 'The castellan has his mage test all visitors so there's no danger of an expedition to Gatekeeper Island being led by a dark mage.'

Meghan did not look like she was convinced.

Inghean was going to say something further but her attention was drawn to the temple maids. Melinda, Minerva and Miranda were blonde and buxom and their unclothed bodies looked lithe and inviting and exciting. As the three cajoled and caressed the High Laird of the West Ridings they giggled indulgently whenever he confided a thought to them.

Miranda repeatedly replenished his flagon.

Minerva, lowering her mouth over Gethin's erection, constantly turned to smile at the dragonmeister as though she was trying to solicit the woman's approval.

Occasionally Inghean met the challenge in Minerva's gaze and she was left trembling from the intensity of that expression. It was, she thought, as though she had been touched by a suggestion of the eroticism that was supposed to be shared between Minerva and Gethin or Minerva and Meghan. It was a darkly exciting expression that she did not think should have been shared by herself and the woman.

Inghean cleared her throat. 'You're bestowing a lot of pleasures on a man you neither like nor trust,' she observed. 'Is there a reason you're doing that?'

'It's a longstanding tradition for Gatekeeper Island,' Meghan explained. She said the words in a tone that was weary and matter-of-fact. 'It's lore for the dragon-meister to show such hospitality to all guests regardless of whether I consider the visitor to be worthy or worthless; deserving or dragon dung; despicable or desirable.'

As she said the final word, she treated Inghean to a glance of brooding intensity.

Inghean wanted to say something in response but she couldn't find the words.

This was nothing like the celebrated banquets her father had hosted at Blackheath. In the feast hall at Blackheath the emphasis was always placed on the honour of rank and the rules of courtly privilege. Visiting dignitaries were esteemed by the legend of their personal acts of valour or the honour of their family entitlement. Those perceived to be lacking in merit were seldom offered the hospitality of the banquet and the welcome of the feast hall. Only visiting dignitaries and trusted allies were invited to share repast at the banquet table. And, she remembered, at her father's table it was customary for guests to remain dressed and not start rutting with such salacious abandon.

But, as she studied the dragon statues guarding the walls, and savoured the silken sounds of a lyre-harp being lazily caressed, she realised she was no longer at her father's banquet hall in Blackheath. She was far away from those familiar surroundings and the conventions she had always known. On Gatekeeper Island, sitting at the right hand of the dragonmeister in the fabled dragon hall, Inghean realised a whole world of new possibilities was now open to her.

It was a revelation that stirred excitement in her loins.

'Does this ceremony trouble you?' the dragonmeister asked quietly.

Inghean glanced up to see Meghan's hand was on her thigh.

The dragonmeister studied her with an expression of knowing concern. The weight of her fingers scratched tiny sparks of excitement that lit the kindle of her arousal. Her sex began to broil with lewd excitement. She tried to quell the insistent internal need she harboured for the woman, but it was a fight she knew she could never win.

'Trouble me?' Inghean repeated. She shook her head. 'No. This is just different to the banquets we have at Blackheath.' She longed to stare into Meghan's eyes but she couldn't wrench her gaze from the scene of Gethin and the temple prostitutes. She felt as though she had been hypnotised by the spectacle. The rhythmic thrust of the laird's hips was a metronomic match for the way Minerva's head bobbed up and down over his lap. 'It's *very* different to the banquets that we see at Blackheath,' she repeated.

Meghan laughed. She clutched Inghean's thigh more firmly.

The snakepit of uncurling excitement within Inghean's

stomach writhed with fresh eagerness. She savoured the sensation and finally wrenched her gaze from the sight of the three temple prostitutes teasing Gethin.

Meghan was smiling for her. Her lips were kissably close.

'I find the sight incredibly arousing,' Meghan confided. 'Even though I think Gethin is one of the most loathsome spectacles of masculinity I've ever encountered, I do enjoy watching my temple maids pleasuring him. It sparks a need within me.' She met Inghean's gaze and asked, 'Is it affecting you in the same way?'

Inghean's mouth worked soundlessly for a moment. Knowing an answer was needed, and deciding she had to answer honestly, Inghean nodded.

Meghan took the movement as an invitation to kiss. She leant close. Her breath was a whisper of honey-fragranced anticipation. Her silky lips brushed against Inghean's mouth.

Meghan's fingers brushed at Inghean's chest. She was treated to the sensuous caress of the dragonmeister's fingers teasing at her stiffening nipples. With the spike of desire that came from that contact, Inghean knew she would happily obey any command that the dragonmeister dared to issue. She held her breath, expectantly savouring the tingle of arousal that came from having enjoyed the woman's caress.

'Pleasure me,' Meghan whispered.

Inghean started in surprise. The words sounded so much like what she had been hoping to hear she wasn't convinced Meghan had really given the instruction.

'Pleasure you? Do you really want me to?' She realised what she had said and then added quickly, 'Do you really want me *to do that*?'

'Could you? Would you?'

The dragonmeister sounded as though she was begging. Her eyes flashed a heartfelt plea before she glanced briefly back toward the banquet table. Inghean followed Meghan's gaze and saw that Minerva was still trying to lick and suck at Gethin's erection even though he was busy trying to guide his length into the welcoming haven between Miranda's thighs.

'Gethin keeps glancing in this direction,' the dragonmeister explained. Her voice was a low and intimate whisper. 'If he sees that we're both unoccupied he'll want at least one of us to help indulge his voracious appetites and I'm damned if I'm going to service that worthless cousin-knocker.' She laughed bitterly and said, 'The hospitality of the dragonmeister can only stretch so far. If he thinks that we're involved with one another he'll be far less likely to try and interrupt. If he thinks we're pleasuring each other he'll keep his distance.'

Inghean's stomach churned at the idea of pleasuring Meghan.

'Fucker,' the wyvern crowed. The creature stamped impatiently on Meghan's shoulder. 'Fuck the redhead.'

Inghean would have been happier if the dragonmeister had wanted to be intimate because of genuine desire, rather than to act as an excuse for avoiding Gethin. But she supposed, if it gave her a chance to be with Meghan, she was willing to take whatever opportunity was available.

Taking the initiative, she moved closer to Meghan. She eased herself from her seat and slipped between the woman's spread legs.

Meghan remained seated, spine pressed against the back of the throne and her legs parted wide to allow Inghean to kneel on the floor before her. She combed her work-dirtied fingers through Inghean's fiery red hair, gently guiding her head lower. Inghean allowed her face to be moved from the woman's kisses, between her breasts, and then pushed over the dragonmeister's lap.

The short hem of the dragonmeister's smock had folded back.

Inghean was treated to the alluring sight of the dragonmeister's sex.

A scrub of short, dark curls shadowed her cleft. The lips, dark pink, wet and inviting, pouted from the thatch of dark hairs. Inghean hesitated. She glanced up at the dragonmeister and was warmed by her encouraging smile.

'You wouldn't really have Gethin ap Cadwallon harmed, would you?' Inghean asked.

Meghan reached down and caressed her cheek.

The touch was tender and warm. The hairs on the nape of her neck bristled with the caress. She basked in the gesture of affection and braced herself to accept whatever Meghan said.

'I'm the dragonmeister of Gatekeeper Island,' Meghan explained. 'I spend a lot of time trying to be strong and independent and, occasionally, I might say something that could be construed as off-colour.'

She had the good grace to blush. Inghean felt momentarily shamed for doubting the woman's integrity.

'*Scītan*,' muttered the wyvern.

The dragonmeister ignored the creature. 'But I would never hurt a visitor to this island,' she told Inghean. 'All I ever offer is pleasure, hospitality and satisfaction.'

With one hand she reached down to caress Inghean's cheek again and then guide her face lower. Her other hand rose into the air so she could rest a warning finger on the wyvern's snout.

Inghean allowed herself to be guided.

She supposed she wasn't wholly comfortable with the answer that the dragonmeister had given. It was likely Meghan was telling the truth, but the wyvern's exclamation had cast a shadow of doubt over the statement's veracity.

However, whilst it was important to have raised the question, Inghean thought it was more essential to get her face closer to the centre of the woman's sex.

Meghan was an exciting and alluring woman. The promise of pleasure lingered perpetually around her, like remnants from the heady perfumes that her temple maids wore. The chance to give Meghan a taste of the satisfaction she deserved, and possibly enjoy the reward of receiving reciprocal pleasure, thrilled Inghean with a dagger of exciting arousal. Extending her tongue, lowering her face to the woman's sex, Inghean tasted her.

Meghan gasped.

If her mouth had not been otherwise occupied, Inghean would have echoed the woman's moan of approval. The sensation of sliding her tongue against the silky nether lips, tasting the salted wetness of Meghan's sex and feeling the tremble of her excitement, proved to be a debilitating combination.

She pushed her face closer, lapping greedily at the glossy wet split of Meghan's hole. The woman's dark curls tickled at her nostrils. They were rich with the subtle musk of the woman's perpetual excitement.

The dragonmeister urged her pelvis upwards, spreading her thighs a little more so that Inghean could get closer. 'That's it,' she sighed. 'That's just what I need.'

'That's it,' agreed the wyvern. 'Tongue my hole.'

Inghean placed a hand on each of the dragonmeister's

milk-smooth thighs as she pushed her face closer to the woman's centre. When she inhaled she could only drink the heady scent of the woman's musk. There were no other tastes or flavours in the world. There were certainly no other tastes or flavours that she wished to experience in this moment. When she traced her tongue against the glossy split of the dragonmeister's wetness, Inghean empathised with the woman's tremor of mounting excitement.

Behind her she could hear Gethin's cries of nearing satisfaction.

It was clear that the High Laird of the West Ridings was being taken to an extreme of pleasure he hadn't previously experienced. With his roar of approval, Inghean sensed that she was also hearing the surging cry of the man's climax.

He roared and groaned. He cursed his gratitude in the name of the Great Gods of the West Ridings. The temple maids groaned with him. They sighed and screamed with theatrical jubilation. But all of those noises were happening behind her.

More important were the noises being made by the woman above her.

Meghan was trembling as though she urgently needed the release that was building inside her body. The wetness at her sex became more copious and Inghean realised she was swallowing the rich juice of the woman's excitement.

'Go on,' Meghan urged. 'Get me there, and then I'll do you.'

The idea left Inghean quivering. She could imagine the dragonmeister's masculine fingers and feminine tongue working together on her sex to produce a rush of powerful satisfaction. It was an exciting prospect that made her catch her breath before returning her mouth to the woman's hole and devouring her.

She lapped against the wet flesh.

She drank the juices that perspired from the dragonmeister's sex.

She felt the first tremulous quivers as the woman basked in the thrill of a climax. Fingers clutched tight against her head. There was a moment when the pain of being clutched in the woman's talons was sharp and almost too much to tolerate. And then, with the douse of musky spray that spattered over Inghean's face, Meghan was loosening her hold and relaxing in her seat.

'My turn to do you,' Meghan muttered cheerfully. She tore the delicacy of her sopping sex away from Inghean's mouth. 'It's my turn to do you and I'm determined that you're really going to enjoy –'

'If I may interrupt, ladies.'

Inghean turned around to see that Gethin ap Cadwallon stood over her.

The High Laird of the West Ridings was still naked. His stubby penis looked small and inauspicious now that his arousal had been spent. He glanced first at the dragonmeister, then at Inghean, then back to Meghan.

'I appreciate you're otherwise preoccupied,' he told Meghan. 'But there is something I'd like to discuss with you as a matter of urgency.'

'Of course,' Meghan agreed.

She pulled herself from the throne.

Inghean was appalled to be separated from the succulent temptation of the woman's sex. As Meghan walked away, Inghean realised she was also losing the prospect of being pleasured by the woman.

Her dislike for Gethin ap Cadwallon briefly intensified.

'I'd been hoping you and I would have a chance to become better acquainted,' Meghan said, intertwining her arm with that of the High Laird. 'I was worried that we might have got off to a poor start.'

'Swarthy fucker,' the wyvern croaked.

Meghan took Gethin's hand and pressed it warmly between her breasts. Her gaze was locked on his. Her eyes were large and gave no indication she had heard or understood what the wyvern's cry suggested.

'I don't know if you're aware,' he began carefully, 'but it's my intention to rule the Ridings.'

Inghean placed a hand over her mouth to disguise her shock. Gethin ap Cadwallon was talking about war. He was talking about destroying a truce that had been in place for centuries. He was talking about an end to the way of life she had always known.

Meghan nodded diplomatically for the High Laird of

the West Ridings. 'It's only to be expected that a man with your ambition would want to stretch his command to cover the broadest area possible. You clearly have the acumen to control more than a single Riding.'

He preened beneath her praise. His chest puffed out and his jaw tilted upwards. He looked like a man posing so that his profile could be minted on coins. 'I could exercise my deserved rule over the Ridings far more easily if you pledge allegiance to me.'

'Go on,' the dragonmeister insisted. 'I'd be interested to hear more.'

'Witless fucker,' the wyvern croaked.

Meghan placed a firm finger on the creature's snout. It immediately fell silent.

'Look at this map,' Gethin said, pointing to one tapestry.

Inghean was surprised to note that he was gesturing toward a tapestry that showed a map of the fiefdom. It was guarded by a pair of crimson *Y Ddraig Goch*. On the tapestry, the vaguely triangular arrangement of the mainland was divided into thirds to show the Ridings. The mainland was topped with the diamond shape of Gatekeeper Island sitting on the other side of the Last Sea.

Unable to resist, Inghean stepped closer to see the detail that had been placed to show Blackheath, the Howling Forest and the River of Merr. Toward the bottom of the map she could see the edges of the Silver Sands.

Suddenly angry, she tore her gaze away from the map.

'I already control the West Ridings,' Gethin said, pointing to the area. 'But I want the whole kingdom.' His finger went to the diamond of Gatekeeper Island. He studied Meghan with a broad and encouraging smile. 'An army of your dragons could take the North Ridings with a single attack. The Blackheath Cavalry is stationed overseas at the moment. There's only the Order of the Dark Knights at Blackheath and, although they're a skilled unit, they're no match for your dragons.'

'My dragons are powerful creatures,' Meghan agreed. She looked set to say more.

Gethin ap Cadwallon didn't allow her to continue.

'Once the north has fallen, the combined strength of a twin-pronged attack – your dragons from the north and my battalions from the West Ridings – could help us take the east and –'

'You've clearly given this a lot of thought,' Meghan broke in.

Gethin's frown was severe. He was a man who seemed not to appreciate interruptions. It looked like it took an extreme effort for him to remain civil and respond in a courteous tone of voice. 'This is our destiny,' he agreed stiffly. 'Together, I believe we can –'

'You need to give me some time to think about it,' she told him.

'Witless fucker,' agreed the wyvern.

'What is there to think about? You'd be the queen of my army of dragons. You'd be the head of my most ferocious military arsenal. Who wouldn't want the prestige of such an enormous hon–'

'You need to give me some time to think about it,' Meghan repeated firmly.

A flash of disappointment wrinkled Gethin's brow. Inghean could sense the confrontation that was about to erupt when she watched Melinda step between the pair.

'Perhaps you should give the dragonmeister time to consider your offer?' Melinda suggested. She took a cask from the tray being held by Miranda and offered it to the High Laird of the West Ridings. With a smile of coquettish playfulness she said, 'This is from the abbot. He has it blessed beneath his monastery and it works as well as the reputed effects of dragon horn.'

It took a moment before Gethin's frown softened.

He snatched his ferocious glare from Meghan and studied Melinda.

Inghean wanted to swoon with relief as she realised the moment of confrontation had momentarily passed.

'Dragon horn?' Gethin said the words as though he had never encountered them before. Inghean supposed it was possible he had never heard of the drink previously, although she thought it unlikely. She was convinced that everyone in all three Ridings knew about dragon horn.

'What effects does dragon horn supposedly have?' Gethin demanded.

Melinda didn't get the chance to respond.

Minerva had taken the initiative and stepped in to help banish the growing danger of a confrontation. 'This is from the abbot?' she purred the excited question to Melinda. She glanced at Inghean and Meghan as she took the cask, sniffed the open neck, and shivered theatrically.

Inghean noticed that the woman's nipples flushed a dark shade of magenta as her nostrils flared to inhale the drink's fragrance. The buttons of flesh grew fat and stiff. A sheen of perspiration made her body glisten in the fluttering candlelight of the dragon hall. It occurred to Inghean that if this was dragon horn it was a powerful blend of the aphrodisiac.

Turning to smile at Gethin, Minerva nodded eagerly and offered him the cask.

'You should try this, High Laird Gethin ap Cadwallon,' she urged.

Melinda pulled the cask from her fingers and sniffed. Her eyelids lowered in an expression of sleepy ecstasy. She clutched Gethin's arm and nodded with an enthusiasm that matched Minerva's. She pressed her naked body close to his. 'We have to try this, high laird,' she pleaded. 'Please don't make us beg.'

'Very well,' Gethin grumbled.

He snatched the cask and doubtfully lifted the neck

to his nostrils. His erection immediately returned to its former length and hardness. Inghean even thought it likely that the flesh was a little longer than it had been before. It was possible it was even a little thicker.

'I suppose I can enjoy another taste of your hospitality,' Gethin allowed grudgingly. His steely gaze met Meghan's. He raised his finger and scowled at her. 'But I warn you now, dragonmeister, I shall discuss this matter with you further before I leave Gatekeeper Island. If you do not consent to being my willing ally I shall have to make plans to force you into being my unwilling ally.'

Meghan's smile was fixed as she nodded courteous agreement and said, 'Of course, High Laird Gethin ap Cadwallon. That will be your privilege.'

The wyvern on her shoulder bristled and said, 'Goat's blood.'

CHAPTER ELEVEN

Caitrin the Captive

Caitrin felt a chill of unease tickle down her spine as the cuff was wrapped around her wrist. By the time she realised what was happening, and had tried to pull away, the second cuff was being snapped into place. She tried to wrench her hands free but the cuffs appeared to be attached to chains set firmly into the stone wall.

Without the key, escape would be impossible.

Not knowing where the insight came from, she suspected the key that would get her released would be the same key that Robert wore around his neck. It seemed to be the key that unlocked everything. It was the key he had used to unlock the hidden doorway in the abbey. It was the key he had used to unlock the door to his underground cell. It would be the key he used to unlock any manacles or handcuffs he placed on a kidnap victim.

She vividly remembered the length of pitted iron with the black age spots pock-marking the dull metal. It had a head fashioned to look like a demonic skull. The memory made her shiver as though the cell they now shared was icy cold.

'Don't struggle,' Robert soothed. 'And don't panic. Here. Take a drink of this to soothe your nerves.'

She grudgingly accepted the cask, placed it to her lips, and swallowed. It felt like the first opportunity she'd had to enjoy a drink in ages. After the rush of darkness had overtaken them in Robert of Moon Valley's private cell, things had happened with surprising speed.

Owain had gasped a surprised, 'What the –?'

He got no further before there was the sound of a cask smashing heavily against something hard.

Owain groaned with fury. The sound of his anger echoed groggily from the unseen walls. Because the noise was followed by the pungent stink of fire wine filling the room, Caitrin guessed that Robert of Moon Valley had smashed a cask of dragon horn over Owain's head.

She felt sick with worry that he had been injured by the cowardly attack.

Tavia had shrieked.

It was a long and terrifying squeal of dismay – a sound that Caitrin had never thought she would ever hear from her sister's lips. Tavia was invariably the more level-headed of the sisters. Tavia was usually the one with a practical solution to a problem and a pragmatic approach. Tavia was not the sort to shriek with such an ear-splitting cry of horror.

The sound echoed from the walls of the abbot's cell. It rang shrilly in Caitrin's ears.

Robert had started to rush past Caitrin. She knew it was him because she could smell the sandalwood balsam he used as a cologne. Before she had always thought the smell was masculine and alluring. Now it was a smell she associated with easy and regrettable sexual interludes and the prospect of deception. It was a smell that she thought defined Robert of Moon Valley.

Robert snatched Caitrin's wrist, his grip surprisingly firm, his strength was unexpected and uncompromising. Without a word of warning he yanked her into the depths of the darkness.

'No!' Caitrin called. 'Let go of me!'

'Stop it,' Tavia called. 'Let me go. Stop pulling me. Stop it, I say.'

Caitrin guessed Robert was also dragging her sister along in the darkness. She was shocked to think that there was so much physical strength and capability contained within the fragrant abbot. He had struck her as being a man more suited to displaying prowess in the bedroom rather than having any other physical abilities of note. Yet here he was effortlessly dragging her and her sister into the shadows of the subterranean corridors.

'Let go of me, you lackwit,' Tavia insisted. 'I swear

you'll suffer for this if you don't let me go. Unhand me now. Let me go.'

He continued dragging her into the darkness as her cries echoed from the invisible walls. Caitrin was reluctantly impressed by his ability to blindly navigate the unseen territory, but she was loath to make that admission even inside the privacy of her thoughts.

'Let go of me or I swear I'll bite your hand off.'

Robert of Moon Valley grunted with discomfort. He paused long enough to push Tavia into the deepest shadows of the darkness.

She shrieked angrily in protest, cursing him and calling him a string of names that were offensive and insulting and probably quite true.

Then her cries seemed to diminish as she was engulfed by the blackness and Robert began to drag Caitrin in an opposite direction. His fingers squeezed tight around her wrist as he propelled her through the inky unlit gloom of the subterranean corridors.

'Don't you think of biting me,' he warned, 'or I swear I'll leave you to make your way in this darkness all alone with the ghosts and the dragons.'

Caitrin did not need to hear a threat like that twice.

It was only a few minutes later, after lurching blindly through dense-darkened corridors, when she realised she and her sister had been used as distractions to help Robert of Moon Valley escape from Owain.

Clearly Robert wasn't convinced that he had put Owain out of commission when he struck him with the cask of dragon horn. And Caitrin thought his plan showed a mentality that was unnervingly cunning.

Even in the darkness, an experienced animal-handler like Owain would have been able to follow the sounds of Robert's footsteps as he tried to find sanctuary in the catacombs. But with his egress confused by the shrieks of Tavia's screams in one direction, and the bellows of Caitrin's cries and protests from another, there was a good chance that Robert could escape from Owain's clutches as he navigated the familiar terrain of the underground tunnels. Besides, there were so many cells and rooms leading off the corridors that it was unlikely the dragon handler would have been able to find his way to very one in which Caitrin now found herself confined.

Tavia was wrong to dismiss Robert of Moon Valley as a lackwit, Caitrin thought. The man had many faults and failings but being a lackwit was not one of them. Even though Gatekeeper Island was home to vicious Oriental dragons, Caitrin suspected that Robert of Moon Valley was one of the most dangerous creatures she could expect to encounter on this side of the Last Sea.

The cask was snatched away from her lips.

'Don't go drinking too much of that,' Robert grumbled. 'No one should be quaffing a full cask of dragon horn just to slake their thirst.'

She coughed with surprise. He'd given her dragon horn? Her mouth worked soundlessly as she realised the effects of the drink were already beginning to make themselves felt on her body.

Her nipples stiffened. Heat surged in her loins. The inner muscles of her sex clenched and rippled with greedy need. What sort of sick trick was he playing to chain her to a wall and then give her dragon horn?

'You bastard,' she hissed.

He pressed a finger over her lips.

Whatever other protest she had been about to make was silenced. The pressure of the finger on her lips filled her with an unbidden desire for him. She longed to encircle his finger with her lips and suckle against him in the greedy and licentious fashion of the low maids from the Blackheath taverns. She could smell the richly scented remnants of arousal on his fingers. She suspected the scent was either the musk from her sister or the flavour of Robert's excitement. The acknowledgement of those thoughts only made her need for him more furious.

But it was a need she didn't want to suffer.

'You absolute, despicable bastard,' she sighed.

He chuckled. 'Keep your noise down.' His voice was a whisper. 'I'm fairly sure we're out of earshot from Owain but I'll gag you if I have to. Don't think I won't do that.'

She glowered at him, dimly aware that her silent venom was making no impression in the darkness.

And, to her shame, she realised she wanted to rut with him.

Of course she knew that the arousal had come from drinking the dragon horn. She had quaffed dragon horn and it had made her want someone – anyone – who was able to satisfy her body's carnal demands. As much as she found Robert of Moon Valley to be spiritually and morally repellent she couldn't argue that her body wanted him to satisfy the urges he had awoken in her loins.

Robert pushed his mouth close to her ear.

She could smell the ascetic tang of his perspiration. The memory of sandalwood and ambergris lurked beneath the surface scent of his sweat. When he spoke she was touched by the weight of every word as it brushed against her skin.

'If you try to give away where we're hiding, I'll leave you here frustrated and chained in the dark,' he whispered. 'Those manacles are strong. Those chains are unrelenting. And these corridors are a labyrinth of inescapable darkness. Don't try to think that there's a way for you to get out of this situation without me being a part of it. You're here until I say otherwise.'

She trembled at the thought. She would have gasped if she hadn't feared that the sound would make him think she was defying his instructions.

'Kiss me if you agree to my terms,' Robert insisted. 'Kiss me if you agree to stay silent and do everything I demand of you.'

Her lips found his face.

She tried willing him closer, desperate to devour him and show that she was ready to sate her need for him. His kisses tasted of dragon horn and she guessed he had been sipping the elixir with a view to recharging his arousal. She supposed, as she savoured the bitter remnants of the second-hand flavour, it was easy to guess his plans.

He was going to use her.

The thought made her squirm.

Robert of Moon Valley clearly needed to lie low in the subterranean cellars. He needed to wait for a while as Owain either searched fruitlessly for him or decided he had gone into hiding and couldn't be found.

Rather than cowering alone in the shadows, he had obviously decided it would be more comfortable to spend his time in the cellar in the company of a willing sex partner. Caitrin would have thought it was a perfect plan if she hadn't been forced into the role of being Robert's reluctant sex partner

His fingers found her breasts.

She realised he was teasing her – heightening her excitement to a point where it was beyond unbearable – but it didn't occur to her to complain about the temptation. She strained against the chained manacles, desperate to get closer to him and frustrated by the metal bindings that stopped her from being able to embrace him and urge him to use her the way she craved.

'We may as well play down here for a while,' Robert murmured. 'I'd grown weary of your sister's insatiable demands. But you seemed to be playing hard to get in my cell.'

She blushed at the memory and was thankful that the darkness was so impenetrable because it concealed her embarrassment. She hadn't wanted to give herself to Robert. She wasn't sure if she had been saving herself for Nihal, tempted by the prospect of learning more about Owain, or simply repulsed by the arrogance of the abbot.

Caitrin supposed, if she had been saving herself for Nihal, she had almost spent herself wholly on Owain when she met him in the tunnels. The memory of those few tender moments she had enjoyed with the dragon handler filled her with a surge of fond recollections. The emotions were so strong it almost made her want to decline the offer of pleasure that Robert's teasing suggested.

But she knew she was under the thrall of the dragon horn.

She could more easily have refused the sun its rightful passageway across the sky than she could have resisted her body's rising needs under the influence of dragon horn. She could have more easily found her way blindfolded from the subterranean cell where she was currently imprisoned.

All she wanted was to have her rising desires satisfied.

And, although she despised Robert of Moon Valley, she knew he was the perfect man to help sate each and every one of those carnal needs.

She pulled toward him and was stopped by the chains. Even though the restraints forced her hands behind her back she still strained to get closer to him, desperate to let him know that she was his for the taking. Eventually, when she realised that neither the chain nor the stone were going to relent, she collapsed back against the wall with a sob of despair.

'What's the matter?'

From the shadows it sounded as though he was taunting her. His voice was a haughty challenge. He resided just beyond her reach.

She sobbed with frustration and said nothing.

'Caitrin? Tell me what's troubling you. Perhaps I can help.'

She scowled and bit her lip. He was taunting her. She could hear it now and she knew he was taunting her in the cruellest way imaginable. He had conspired to make her drink the dragon horn and now he was waiting for her to beg for him to satisfy her needs. If she hadn't been chained to the wall of the cell Caitrin would have slapped him senseless and pummelled him with her fists.

Determined to keep hold of her dignity, she said nothing.

A finger teased the shape of her nipple.

The touch came through her kirtles. It was a light caress that would have barely been felt under other circumstances. Because she was so acutely attuned to every sensation, Caitrin felt the brief contact as though a greedy lover was sucking hungrily against her breast. The pleasure was magnified to a hateful intensity that had her moaning with raw need.

'Tell me what's troubling you, Caitrin,' he insisted. 'I'm sure I can help if you just let me know what I can do to best satisfy you.'

Another hand reached out for her.

The neckline of her kirtles was pulled down. The cover of her chemise was tugged aside. Both nipples were exposed and tormented by unseen hands. The prickle of divine sensations was exquisite and inescapable. Her senses had been sharpened by the drink and every movement against her body was intensified into a rush of sublime ecstasy.

A thrill of delightful pleasures sparkled from the tips of her breasts. The shards of joy seemed to erupt in an explosion of greedy sensations based in the centre of her belly.

Miserably – a mood that contrasted harshly with the splendour of sensations her body was enjoying – Caitrin knew she was going to submit to Robert of Moon Valley. She knew she was going to submit to him because her body was being more insistent than her mind.

She sniffed back a tear of self-recrimination.

She didn't want to beg him to take her. But she felt sure that act of submission would inevitably come if he continued to tease her so mercilessly.

'Tell me what's troubling you, Caitrin,' he sighed. 'Pretend I'm the mage from Blackheath. Everyone knows that you always confide in that crimson-cowled spook.'

Caitrin was about to respond angrily, disliking the way Robert of Moon Valley insulted Nihal. She remembered something she had said to the mage the last time Nihal restored her virginity. '*I can always close my eyes and pretend that it's you and not him between my legs.*' The words struck her now as being the most useful tool she could use in defence against Robert of Moon Valley.

But she wasn't sure who she should be imagining between her legs.

Robert's fingers tore at her kirtles.

The sound of the fabric ripping was as shocking as a slap in the darkness. She clenched her teeth, not sure if she wanted him to stop or continue. Inquisitive fingers slipped between her thighs and stole against the sultry heat of her sex.

It was dark enough in the cell that she didn't have to close her eyes to pretend Robert was someone else. There was so little light in the subterranean cells that she couldn't even make out shapes or silhouettes.

But Caitrin didn't know whether to pretend Robert of Moon Valley was Nihal the mage or Owain the dragon handler. Maddeningly, she felt torn by a greedy need to have both suitors.

'I want you to take me,' she told Robert. 'I want you to take me. And I want you to make it good.'

He needed no further prompting.

She heard him slurp at the cask of dragon horn and he pushed her to her knees, the manacle chain proving long enough for such an act. A thick penis pushed against her face. Caitrin had no way of using her hands but she worked her mouth against the thick length. She stroked her tongue up and down, savouring the taste of him and enjoying the heightened sense of pleasure that came from listening to the man above her sigh with approval.

Nihal or Owain? she wondered.

Both suitors had advantages and disadvantages compared with the other. Caitrin didn't know whether she should be considering these traits whilst she pleasured a third person or if that was a sign that she had now sunk to new depths of depravity.

The briny flavour of Robert's pre-seed filled her mouth. The wetness made her swallow more quickly. She found the taste was simultaneously noisome and exciting – not unlike Robert. She wanted to ask him if she could have a mouthful of dragon horn to take the taste of him away from her lips. But she resisted making that request, not sure how insatiable her appetites were likely to become if she swallowed any more of the outlawed drink.

Caitrin knew Owain the dragon handler would be appalled if he had thought she was drinking dragon horn. She also knew that Nihal would be livid at the idea of her casually quaffing dragon horn and then rutting with whoever happened to be nearby. Even though it hadn't been deliberate she figured both of her current suitors would be furious with her for ending up in this situation. Since she had only ended in this situation because she and her sister were trying to steal a forbidden aphrodisiac, Caitrin supposed it was fair to call it a predicament of her own devising.

Two fat fingers pushed against her sex.

She gasped and parted her thighs.

Robert was a demanding lover and surprisingly dexterous. She didn't know how he was able to have his shaft in her mouth and two fingers pushing between her labia. She wasn't sure she wanted to build the mental picture in her mind's eye.

For Caitrin it was more satisfying to pretend that she was being pleasured by Owain and Nihal at the same time. In her imagination her two suitors had combined forces and were working together to please her.

She told herself she was sucking eagerly on Owain's length.

She touched the thrust of his exposed glans with her tongue. Her lips moved over the hard pulsing veins that sculpted his length's shape. Robert must have swigged some more dragon horn from the cask because his shaft felt sufficiently large so it could almost have been mistaken for Owain's.

Almost.

Between her spread thighs she pretended that Nihal was fingering her to a climax. The mage's fingertips were long, slim, slender and inquisitive. The mage's fingertips would have been far more skilful in the way they slipped softly against the silken inner muscles of her sex. But Caitrin was prepared to imagine that Nihal was having a bad day as the mage struggled to finger her to a climax.

The idea of being taken by both suitors at the same time was compelling and thrilling. As soon as it filled her thoughts Caitrin gave herself over to the idea. The pleasures she was enjoying were immediately intensified.

She took as much of Robert's length into her mouth as she could accommodate. It was a fat cock with a large swollen end.

She relaxed the muscles of her throat and let him push to the back. It was a technique she remembered learning at the hands of Robert when he had first introduced her and her sister to dragon horn.

But, even though she was only doing what he had taught her a month earlier, Caitrin now felt as though she was performing this same divine service for a far more worthy recipient.

The fingers between her legs pushed insistently against her wetness. The intimate caress was joined by the pressure of a warm tongue sliding against her flesh.

Caitrin groaned.

If it had been Nihal pleasuring her, she knew the rhythm of the fingers would have been almost melodic as they slid in and out. There would have been an enchanting music to the caress against her inner muscles, as though the mage was playing an instrument and the pleasures taking over her body were the resultant plainchant or clausula.

But it was dark and it wasn't really Nihal and Caitrin knew she was having to pretend that Robert's inferior prowess was really the mage's superlative touch. And all those considerations were pushed aside as the first orgasmic rush of pleasure flooded through her system.

It came on strong and with unexpected force.

It came with such ferocity that, for an instant, she felt as though the room was illuminated. Surprisingly, as she imagined the room to be lit, she could see that she was being pleasured by Nihal and Owain.

The pair were both naked and both working to please her.

The sight of them both made the intensity of her climax all the sweeter.

Owain, she thought. She focused on the name as though making a silent prayer. *Owain or Nihal*, she thought. *If either of you can save me, please hurry up and come to my rescue.* She arched her back, sucking more greedily on Robert for a moment, and then she spat his shaft from her mouth.

The memory came back to her like a blinding revelation. She wondered how she could have forgotten something so important until this moment.

'*If you ever need me,*' Nihal had said, '*all you have to do is call my name. Simply take yourself to the peak of a climax, close your eyes and then whisper my name. If you do that, I'll be with you.*'

Caitrin couldn't decide if the words had been some coded expression of the mage's love, or if they were the requirements for a true spell. As the second climax pushed through her body, she knew there was only way to find out: she clenched her teeth and closed her eyes.

'Nihal,' she prayed softly. 'Nihal.'

The room was briefly lit. Caitrin caught a glimpse of a crimson-cowled robe with a dark hood covering the face.

'What the fu–?' Robert began. He didn't get to finish his sentence.

'Gods of the Great Ones,' roared the mage. '*Transportum!*'

The final word was bellowed with a roar of disapproval. A flash of lightning-bright whiteness flooded the dungeon. Caitrin had time to see the scowl of surprise flash across Robert's face. And then he had disappeared.

The mage stood where Robert of Moon Valley had been.

'Nihal,' she whispered. 'The spell worked.'

Nihal shrugged and knelt on the floor beside her. 'I wasn't that far away, Cait. I've been following you since you left.' The mage's fingers touched her hand. Caressing her mage's eye ring, Nihal said, 'I've been watching over you through this.'

Soft lights filled the room.

She lowered her gaze, suddenly embarrassed to be seen in such a state of used vulnerability before the mage. Her kirtles were torn. Her breasts were exposed. Her sex was open and engorged and desperate for penetration.

'You've been watching me?' she muttered. 'You must despise me.'

Nihal placed elegant fingers beneath her jaw and tilted her head upwards. 'I could never despise you, Cait. I love you.' After placing a kiss on her brow the mage said, 'I take it you were doing as we'd once agreed: closing your eyes and pretending you were with me.'

'I was pretending I was with you,' Caitrin admitted. Blushes darkened her cheeks. She couldn't bring herself to explain that she'd also been pretending there was someone else in the room. 'I was pretending,' she agreed carefully. Realising that something important had been overlooked, and uncomfortable that she would have to apologise to the mage if she didn't quickly change the subject, Caitrin asked, 'What's happened to Robert?'

'Do you care?'

'No. I'm just curious.'

'He's been sent to the dragon hall. That's the dragon-meister's banquet hall,' Nihal explained. 'I transported him there.' There was a chuckle of malign glee in the mage's voice.

'You've transported him to a banquet hall,' Caitrin repeated. 'What's so amusing about that?'

'I also sent his nemesis to that hall, that puffed-up lackwit Owain the dragon handler.'

Caitrin blanched. She pulled against the chains that still held her to the cell wall. 'You've transported Owain to the banquet hall? But he was unconscious. Robert will kill him whilst he's laid out and vulnerable.'

Nihal looked momentarily perplexed. 'You care for this Owain?'

'I don't want to see him murdered whilst he's unconscious.' She set her jaw determinedly and clutched at Nihal's hand. 'You have to transport us to this dragon hall. I'm not going to stay here whilst Owain is murdered for sport.'

With a sigh of resigned frustration the mage pulled away from Caitrin's grasp and muttered a handful of words in a foreign language.

The manacles at Caitrin's wrists fell away as though they had never been there. They clattered heavily to the floor and she immediately began to rub life back into her aching wrists.

'I'm not transporting us anywhere,' the mage grumbled. 'I despise transportation spells.' Seeing the scowl of disapproval in Caitrin's glare the mage said quickly, 'But it will only take us a few short moments to find our way up to the banquet hall from here.'

Caitrin was not so easily appeased. 'I don't like the idea of Owain being in danger from Robert. We have to hurry.'

Nihal sighed. 'Yes. It would be terrible if any harm befell that muscled wanh l.'

CHAPTER TWELVE

Commander Owain of the Royal Guard

When Robert struck him with the cask of dragon horn, Owain did not lapse into blank unconsciousness. It was far worse than that.

He remembered everything.

Breaking through the darkness and the pain was a rush of pale-blue light. The brightness became a spring sky flecked with faraway clouds and falling fistfuls of rice. He was laughing and the echo of his mirth was shared by Carys, the beautiful bride on his arm.

'No,' Owain murmured. 'Not this. Please, not this.'

The memory was too vivid. The colours were so strong they stained his retina. The deafening peal of golden, church bells clanged monstrously in his skull. The floral fragrance of her bridal bouquet was a heady perfume of richly scented roses and cloyingly sweet lilies. The weight of her hand on his arm was as cold as the caress of a predatory serpent.

'I love you, Commander Owain of the Royal Guard,' she murmured.

He heard himself say, 'I love you too.'

The words tasted like the blackest treachery.

Not that it would have been difficult for anyone to love someone as beautiful as Carys. On an ordinary day, with her dark hair and olive complexion, she was stunning to behold. Her eyes were large and inviting. Her lips were ripe and warm. Her breasts were full and round. Her legs were long and coltish.

But this was no ordinary day.

This was her wedding day and she had spent six hours painting her fingernails, preparing her hair, having her body washed, scrubbed and oiled, and all so that she could look at her most radiant for him, her bridegroom. Dressed in virginal whites, festooned with garlands and boughs of pale, white roses, her smile sparkled in the spring sunlight.

It was a smile that was destined to dazzle him.

He supposed he looked equally impressive. He was dressed in the full military regalia of a commander of the Royal Guard. His powder-blue surcoat and navy hosen were accessorised by black leather boots and enough silver trappings so that each step jangled musically. His ceremonial longsword shone like a barb of captured sunlight. The breast of his surcoat was adorned with the symbol of the kingdom's royal household, a single red crown on a shield divided into thirds by a Y-shaped split. The sign-makers and arms-painters described the background as *tierced in pairle field*and Owain knew the badge represented the king's rule over the three Ridings.

It was an honour to be part of such a prestigious regiment.

But it was a greater honour to have just been wed to the beautiful Carys.

The cheering guests outside the church were singing the praises of the happy couple and pouring blessings onto them. The promise of a bright future had never been more brilliant. The laughter and gaiety of the moment could have stretched on forever.

On the horizon he could see a storm cloud building.

Equally dark, supposedly a lucky omen to see at any wedding ceremony, was the dark-robed apothecary he could see lurking in amongst the crowd. Commander Owain of the Royal Guard had no idea where the tradition was born but he was not one to fight against the beliefs of such rites and rituals. He had heard that some couples invited stable hands, to represent a marriage blessed with industry, and others were given a marriage bed strewn with flower petals to encourage fertility and fecundity. If Carys, or her family, believed that a dark-robed apothecary was meant to bring luck he was happy to accept the gift.

Owain wanted to break through the crowd and hail the apothecary and shake the man's hand and give him the golden pfennig that properly betokened good fortune. But the day was his wedding day and Carys was holding his arm too tight and he didn't want to be separated from her.

Fellow officers from the Royal Guard were amongst the wedding party. Their blue and silver uniforms looked resplendent in the sunlit haven of the church's garden. Sunlight danced in painful shards from their polished buckles and the glistening pommels of their ceremonial longswords. Their grins were easy and genuine as though they were wholeheartedly happy for the wedding of their unit's leader. Their banter was hearty but softened by dutiful respect.

Carys pulled him close to her lips and whispered, 'Take me to our bridal bed.'

He started in mock surprise. 'Now? Are you serious?'

'Of course,' she laughed. 'We're married now. Finally we can be together with the blessing of the gods.'

His mouth was still close to her ear. 'What would we do in our bridal bed?'

She kissed his cheek. 'It's our wedding day,' she whispered softly. 'Find us a wedding bed in the next half hour and you may honestly slide your cock into any hole you find hidden beneath my braies.'

He had been embarrassed to find himself hard within his breeches. He stumbled awkwardly through the throng of guests that led from the church doorway, all the time trying to cover himself with the hem of his military surcoat.

Carys laughed at his embarrassment and he loved her for the tinkling sound of her merriment and the way she regarded him with a combination of hungry innocence and untarnished lechery.

Unconditionally, and without reservation, he loved her.

'If the guests can gather in the wedding hall,' he called loudly, 'Carys and I will join you shortly.'

There was a bellow of rowdy approval, as though the guests knew his intentions and all thought it was hilarious that he and his bride should want to rut before attending the commemorative feast. Then the best man was pushing an earthenware cask into Carys's hand and urging the guests to head toward the church's banquet hall which had been booked for their celebrations and Carys was leading Owain, and he was being pulled back to the church where they had both declared their vows.

The chime of the bells had subsided.

The shadow of the church was ominously dark.

For the first time Owain had a chance to properly study the building and its architecture but his interest lay in matters other than the wattle and daub walls beneath the whitewash paint. The interior featured an aisle-less nave and an apsidal chancel. The light inside the church was made colourful by the stained-glass windows. The air still smelled of wedding flowers and celebratory perfumes.

And all he really noticed was his beautiful new bride.

Carys led him to one of the chambers on the north wall. She held his hand and moved with the familiarity of a regular church attendee. Carefully she pushed open an oak door set in one of the whitewashed wattle and daub walls.

'Our wedding gifts are stored in here,' she explained. 'I think you should take me in here.'

'In the church?' he asked doubtfully. 'Isn't this sacrilegious or something?'

Carys had laughed and snuggled against him as soon as they were inside the small room. She smelled of blossom spring flowers. She pressed kisses against his throat and rubbed a hand against the swelling lump at the front of his breeches.

'What could possibly be sacrilegious about a couple in love showing their affection?' Her question would have sounded reasonable and innocent if she hadn't decided to lick her lips afterwards. The knowing sparkle in her eye contrasted with the innocent white of her bridal gown. The animal lechery in her gaze – meant for him and him alone – made the swelling in his loins ache with renewed force.

A grunt from the corner of the room startled him.

Y Ddraig Goch sat there watching them. The bright-red dragon allowed a barbed tongue to slip over its dark reptilian lips. It was almost as though the creature was parodying Carys's sultry intimation.

'A dragon?' he marvelled. He rushed to the creature's side and began to pet it. His fingers naturally fell to the creatures pointed ears. Atop its head they looked like small, miniature horns. The dragon purred excitedly as he caressed its head. 'Someone gifted us with a red dragon? Who do we have to thank for this?'

Carys was by his side, patting the dragon with him.

'This was a gift from the people of the West Ridings,' she explained. 'It's one of the last female dragons in the West Ridings. It's been named Drusilla by the princess and she's ours now.'

'Drusilla the dragon,' Owain murmured.

The dragon chased its barbed tongue against his wrist. The caress was soft and warm. For some reason the touch thrilled him with a spike of further desire for Carys. He turned to face his bride, knowing he could think about the wonderful gift of the dragon later.

'I want you,' he told her.

'I want you too,' she insisted. She took a sip from the cask she had been holding and blinked with startled wonder as the drink took its effect. He watched intently as her wine-wet lips again shaped the words, 'I love you, Owain.'

Without hesitating he went to kiss her.

She allowed the contact for a moment.

Then she was pushing his face away and lowering her mouth over his groin.

'Carys?' he asked doubtfully.

She shook her head and gave him a look of roguish devilment. 'Let me do this for you,' she whispered. Her tone was made breathless with hungry urgency. 'This is my wedding gift to you.'

He wanted to tell her that he didn't need such a gift, but there was no way he would be able to say those words. He wanted to tell her that he didn't feel right having his member exposed in front of *Y Ddraig Goch* but that would have just sounded ridiculous.

Instead it was easier to simply let his new bride devour his length, sucking and slurping greedily as she produced the most divine sensations from the head of his shaft through to the swelling fatness of satisfaction that grew in his balls.

Up to this point theirs had been a chaste relationship.

He had courted her with her parents' permission and made sure they did nothing together that could be deemed to contravene the strict regulations of her chosen religion. They had kissed. They had held hands. They had even talked of the joyous day of their marriage when they would be able to share a bed together.

But they had done nothing more.

Carys slurped and sucked and swallowed with greedy abandon. She had him excited to the point of near-climax when she first mentioned allowing him to slide into any hole he discovered hidden inside her braies. When he felt the silken sensation of her lips working around his hardness, Owain had to curl his hands into fists to fight back the encroaching orgasm that threatened to shudder from his shaft.

But his resistance was no match for her determination. Carys stroked him with her hands. She bobbed her head up and down, taking as much of him between her lips as her mouth could accommodate. She made the encouraging sounds of a woman who has found her vocation. When she eventually sucked the orgasm from him, Owain almost sobbed with relief.

His shaft pulsed and throbbed and sang as the climax was torn from his body.

'How was that?' she asked.

He shook his head. There weren't words.

'I want to pleasure you,' he told her. He was leaning close to thank her and show his appreciation. 'I want to pleasure my new bride.'

She pushed him away. 'Go and find your best man,' Carys hissed. 'He gave me this dragon horn. He can get us some more. Find your best man and get some more dragon horn. That will pleasure me.'

'Dragon horn?'

He'd heard of dragon horn. He was a commander of the Royal Guard so he was used to hearing subordinate soldiers discuss all manner of contraband items. But he hadn't expected his blushing young bride to know about the nefarious elixir.

'It was a gift from your best man,' Carys explained. She showed him the empty earthenware cask. The initials DH had been scratched into the sooty black residue on the bottom of the cask.

'I didn't know you were aware of such things,' he muttered.

She kissed him.

Her mouth tasted of his cock. Owain wasn't sure if that was a good thing or not. It was a rich and exciting flavour to find on her lips. But it was such a contrast from the chaste and innocent Carys he had fallen in love with, he didn't know how to reconcile the old versions of Carys with this new version within his thoughts. He wanted to ask more questions, curious to know how much she knew about dragon horn and what she knew of its purported effects. But he could sense that more questions would spoil the mood of the moment and, with this being their wedding day, he didn't want to give them cause to despair about a single second of the day.

'Will you be alright here on your own?' he asked uncertainly.

She laughed and snatched a pack of candles from a

cabinet beside the other wedding presents. 'I should be fine here for a short while,' she admitted. 'Now hurry up and find some more dragon horn. I've heard that dragon horn can spark a fire within a woman's nether regions that is so strong it makes her thighs sweat rivers.' She glanced toward his spent length which still protruded from his hosen. 'I've heard that a taste of dragon horn can harden a healthy man's hardness and lengthen his longing.'

Hearing the words tumble from her lips, and anxious to please his new bride the way she had pleased him, Owain rushed from the chamber.

'Go and find another cask of dragon horn,' she called after him. 'I'll wait for you here until you return.'

He rushed out of the church, heading toward the banquet hall where he had last seen his best man ushering the guests. In the church yard, from the corner of his eye, he saw the dark-robed apothecary. It occurred to him that this would be the ideal time to thank the mysterious figure for giving the day his blessing. But, because he was desperate to find his best man, Owain ran to the banquet hall.

The soldiers from the Royal Guard greeted him with a hearty welcome.

He diplomatically thanked them for their good wishes, quietly scouring the room for his best man. He got waylaid by the minister who had performed the blessing.

And then he was cornered by the bride's parents, all of whom wanted to talk with him and wish him and his new wife every happiness for the future.

As he quickly went from one group to another, conscious of the way the time was dragging on, he realised there was no sign of his best man.

He did think of asking the soldiers from his regiment if any of them kept a cache of dragon horn. But to make such a request would be tantamount to admitting that he needed potions and elixirs to maintain a healthy presence in the marital bedroom and there was no way he would ever say something that could be interpreted in such a way to his subordinates in the Royal Guard.

Defeated, and annoyed that his best man seemed to have disappeared, Owain hurried back to his new bride to share the disappointing news that he hadn't been able to locate any dragon horn.

He heard her cries of mounting pleasure as he entered the nave and he figured she was enjoying the pleasures of the candles she had discovered. A tight smile of approval spread across his face as he realised he had fallen fortunate in marrying a woman who enjoyed her sexual pleasures and would be happy to content herself with something as innocuous as votive candles whilst he was absent.

The smile remained fixed like a rictus on his face as he pushed open the chamber door and surveyed what was happening.

It was, he thought bitterly, the most distressing tableau a groom could ever be cursed to see.

Carys was naked and arranged on all fours. He wedding dress had been discarded and lay in a crumpled heap besides the gifts.

There was a cracked flask of dragon horn on the floor beside her and he immediately knew that the drink had been at the root of this development.

A man whose face he couldn't make out knelt between his wife's parted thighs, sliding his length easily in and out of her, while the hooded figure wearing the cowled black robes of an apothecary stood before her. His robes were open at the loins. The sprout of his manhood protruded from the sandy scrub of his pubic hairs. Carys held the base of his stubby erection between her finger and thumb as she licked and sucked and swallowed him with unseemly haste.

Owain remembered hearing that it was supposed to be lucky to have a dark-robed apothecary at a wedding. He supposed, on this occasion, it had certainly been lucky for Carys and it had not been unfortunate for the apothecary. The thought threatened to make him shriek a babble of hysterical laughter into the room.

Owain realised the lips Carys used on the apothecary's length were the same lips she had used to tell him she loved him. They were the same lips she had used to tenderly kiss his cheek, as though she harboured genuine affection for him.

'No,' he muttered.

Carys turned around to glare at him. Surprise registered in her eyes but because she still held the apothecary's erection in her mouth there looked to be little contrition in the expression.

The apothecary pulled himself away. He secured the robe around his waist and shrugged a vague apology. 'I can see I'm intruding here,' he told Owain. He glanced at Carys and said, 'Since you've got your dragon horn, I'll just take *Y Ddraig Goch* like we agreed on and remove its horns.' He reached for Drusilla and then glanced toward Owain. 'I guess you and your new wife have some private talking to do.'

Owain slammed a fist into the man's face.

The apothecary went down hard.

'No,' Owain said. 'You're not taking my dragon. And no one is removing her horns.' He frowned, realising the dragon didn't have horns. It was only the way her ears were shaped that made them look like horns. And then he realised such considerations were immaterial compared to the treachery he had just suffered.

It took an effort of willpower to resist the urge to wail at the unfairness of this development.

'Owain,' Carys sobbed. 'This isn't what you think.'

As she spoke she continued to slide back and forth against the man with his length buried into her rear.

Owain glanced at the man's face and was not surprised by what he saw there.

For the first time since entering the room he saw it was Robert of Moon Valley. Robert of Moon Valley had been his best friend. Robert of Moon Valley had been the best man at the wedding celebration. Wryly, Owain supposed that Carys would now be in a position to judge if Robert really was the best man.

He drew back his fist, ready to punch his former best friend.

Robert held up a steadying hand. 'Just let her finish me,' he insisted. He was chuckling good-naturedly. 'She is so tight I can't believe you'll have this for the rest of your life. You really are a lucky bastard.'

Owain took a deep breath and prepared to launch the most formidable blow his strength could deliver.

'No,' Carys moaned. 'You weren't supposed to see this.'

He wasn't listening. He was readying himself to hit Robert of Moon Valley and he didn't think anything could stop him.

Movement from where the felled apothecary lay caught his attention.

There was a flash of crimson light and he was immediately held immobile.

It had not been an apothecary, he realised. Instead, Owain saw that he had punched a dark mage. The dark mage was retaliating by hitting him with some sort of paralysing spell. From the little he knew of the powers of dark mages such spells could affect the body and they could scrub memories from the mind.

'No!' Owain roared.

With a valiant struggle Owain managed to spit out some final words before unconsciousness stole over him. He levelled a warning finger at Carys and said, 'Our marriage is annulled.'

She sobbed a protest but he wasn't listening. He had turned to face the best man.

'As for you,' he told Robert of Moon Valley.

For a moment he couldn't find the words. Robert of Moon Valley continued to ride in and out of Cary's perfect pink backside. His thick length plundered the dark haven of her sex. The sight of that treachery filled Owain's throat with the taste of heartbreak.

'One day, I shall have my revenge,' Owain declared.

And that was where the memory usually ended.

It was only on this occasion that Owain recognised the face of the dark mage pretending to be an apothecary. He was staring at the man he now knew as Gethin ap Cadwallon.

Consciousness returned and with it came a rush of light.

Owain had expected to find himself where he had been knocked out – on the soil floor of a subterranean cell beneath Gatekeeper Island. Instead he found himself in the arena of a banquet hall. Tall sconces on the walls and ornate chandeliers overhead lit the room with a sickening brightness. The walls were decorated with magnificent sculptures of dragons, gazing imperiously down upon him. The statues included Smok, Ljubljana, wyverns and Orientals. Some of them held ceremonial swords. Others snarled with vicious menace etched perpetually into their still features.

It was not, he realised, just any banquet hall.

This was the dragonmeister's dragon hall.

He tightened his stomach against the thrill of nausea that came with returning consciousness. The colours of the tapestries on the walls were a vibrant dizzying blend. Around him, sitting on distant and faraway seats, he saw the concerned features of the dragonmeister, Inghean of Blackheath and the temple maids of Gatekeeper Island.

But more importantly he could see Robert of Moon Valley.

Dressed as an abbot, his former best man was now bearing down on Owain and wielding a mace.

CHAPTER THIRTEEN

The Dark Mage

The abbot and the dragon handler winked into existence in the centre of the dragon hall. There was a moment's confusion as the pair assessed their circumstances. It seemed, to the eye of a keen observer, that the abbot was the first to understand the enormity of the situation. It seemed, to the eye of a keen observer, that the abbot was also the first to understand that there was a potential opportunity in being wholly alert.

The dragon handler simply lay slumped across a banquet hall bench. His nude frame looked like a contemptible example of manly perfection. His pectorals were too broad. His legs looked too muscular. His manhood was an obscene size and girth.

Gethin shivered in revulsion.

The abbot, loosely draped in the monastic robes of the island's holy order, charged at the unmoving Owain.

Clearly an opportunist, the abbot snatched a convenient mace from the claws of one of the dragon statues that adorned the walls. He raised the weapon above his head and released the bellow of an outraged berserker.

The roar was enough to make the dragon handler stir.

'Interesting,' mused Gethin ap Cadwallon. 'Very interesting.'

The dragonmeister sat up in her throne. It was difficult to tell whether she was startled by this development, unsettled by the violent confrontation that was about to ensue, or if her disquiet came from a combination of both those factors. She shook her head, attempted to close her legs and tried to push away the horny redhead that had been lapping greedily between her thighs. This latter movement was obviously something of a chore because Inghean of Blackheath seemed anxious to remain locked against the dragonmeister's sex.

One of the temple maids shrieked in protest. She dropped a cask of their precious dragon horn to the floor where it shattered into a thousand separate pieces. The pungent scent of fire wine tainted the air.

Gethin caught the scent and wrinkled his nostrils with disapproval. He had no need or use for dragon horn. He was more than capable of exercising his arousal without drinking potions or elixirs.

The redhead, Inghean of Blackheath, glared at the fight. At first she looked surprised to have been pushed away from where she had been suckling at the dragonmeister's sex. Now she held a horrified hand over her mouth, as though trying to contain a scream of protest.

Robert of Moon Valley slammed the mace down at Owain's face.

By some unprecedented stroke of good fortune the dragon handler managed to roll away from the blow. The mace – a mean-looking spiked ball on a short length of chain – shattered its way through a wooden seat.

Splinters exploded from beneath the impact.

As the abbot tried to wrench the mace free from the bench, Owain scoured the hall for a convenient weapon. His gaze fell on a ceremonial longsword held in the claws of one of the stone dragons that decorated the walls.

Gethin ap Cadwallon, High Laird of the West Ridings, snapped his fingers. He mumbled the sacred words that turned the flow of time to the crawl of treacle.

The world inside the banquet hall slowed to a near-standstill.

'Dark magicks,' crowed the dragonmeister's wyvern. 'Dark magicks. Dark mage.'

Gethin scowled at the beast. If it hadn't been a dragon he might have been able to silence its irritating voice. Annoyed that he had to tolerate the creature he turned his attention to Owain and the abbot.

The two men in the arena of the dragon hall continued to fight, but it was a battle where every movement was exaggerated and dragged out to an interminable age. Every action took an aeon from inception through to execution.

Owain hauled the longsword out from the clutches of the statue on the wall.

The abbot lazily pulled his mace from the splintered bench where it had been embedded.

The slow motions of each man were mimicked by everyone else within the banquet hall. The temple maids clutched at each other as though fighting to make their movements through a thick syrup. The dragonmeister waved a lethargic hand in the air as she began to call for Owain and Robert to cease their hostilities and put down their weapons. The redhead watched the scene with an expression of unmoving bewilderment which made her features momentarily gormless and stupid.

In short, Gethin thought, they all acted as though they were properly held in the thrall of a dark mage's control of time.

His smile broadened.

Of all the spells he knew, the control of time was one of his favourites. It allowed him such a great opportunity to use and usurp those who stood between him and his goals. Standing in the dragonmeister's banquet hall, he figured he could enjoy exploiting the one person who currently stood between him and his most heartily desired goal.

But first, he thought, there was a puzzle that needed resolving.

Owain was going in to strike the abbot.

The abbot had wrenched his mace free from the bench. By happenstance more than planning the spiked ball of the mace struck Owain in the chest. The dragon handler staggered backward from the force of the blow. A rose of blood blossomed on his sternum.

'They apparated in here,' mused Gethin. 'And neither of them are magi. They could only have apparated in here if there was a mage close by. That means there's a mage on Gatekeeper Island.'

It was a disconcerting development. A mage on Gatekeeper Island could challenge him and potentially thwart his plans to force the dragonmeister to help him rule the Ridings.

He stepped toward Meghan and the redhead with whom she was currently so enamoured. Clutching a fistful of Inghean's long red curls he pulled her face close to his and stole a kiss from her lips. Her mouth tasted of the rich musky honey of the dragonmeister's sex. He savoured the taste before pulling her into his embrace.

'Did you bring a mage with you, my lovely?' he demanded. He spoke slowly so that she could understand him in the time-slowed world where she resided. 'Other than me, I mean. Did you smuggle a mage aboard that bloody birlinn that brought us here?'

She studied him with lackwitted disbelief and a blatant dearth of comprehension. Her willowy figure swayed in his arms. Her firm, well-rounded breasts pressed against his chest. The nearness of her stirred a pleasant desire in his loins that he knew she could easily satisfy.

'A mage?' she repeated.

He nodded. He was prepared to accept that some of her slowness came from the fact that he had adjusted the speed of time's progression in the banquet hall. But he figured part of it was also down to the fact that Inghean of Blackheath was never likely to be renowned for her thinking skills.

The woman shook her head.

Speaking with a dream-like lethargy she said, 'There was only myself, my sisters, you, Owain and that stowaway.'

He scowled at her mention of the stowaway. Discovering Alvar of Erland aboard the birlinn had been an unpleasant surprise. If not for Owain's intervention, Gethin conceded, it could have proved fatal. However, Alvar was merely a seer. He wasn't a mage. His abilities were impressive to some mortals, Gethin allowed. But Alvar was a long way from having the skills of a mage.

'The only other people aboard were crew from the ranks of Blackheath's merchant navy,' Inghean continued. 'There was no mage.'

She regarded him uncertainly, her brows knitting with

a frown of obvious puzzlement. It was clear that she was no longer seeing him as Gethin ap Cadwallon, High Laird of the West Ridings. She now saw him as Gethin the dark mage. As understanding slowly flooded her features she said, 'No mage, that is, other than you.'

He brought her closer and stole another kiss from her lips.

The second-hand taste of the dragonmeister's sex excited him. Savouring that forbidden flavour reminded Gethin that he could exploit this situation as fully as possible now he had shaken off his guise of being a high laird and had returned to his true form. If there was another mage on Gatekeeper Island he would deal with the problem when it became necessary. But, for now, there were more important needs that had to be addressed.

His erection sprouted to full hardness.

He considered Inghean for a moment, trying to decide whether the pleasure she had given him at Blackheath was worth revisiting. Admittedly, she had been passionate and accommodating. Her slender frame and full breasts made her physical form desirable. The tight wetness of her sex was a delight he could happily endure again. From previous experience he knew that there was a delicious satisfaction to rutting with someone who was experiencing the passage of time at a different pace. The sensations defied description.

However, when he licked his lips and tasted the

remnants of the dragonmeister's flavour that lingered there, he cast Inghean aside and grabbed Meghan by the arm. If he was going to have any woman in the dragon hall, she was the one he wanted.

'High Laird Gethin ap Cadwallon,' the dragonmeister blurted.

He could see the confusion flutter across her expression. As she shook her head to clear her thoughts he could see her acknowledge the necessary levels of understanding to grasp the situation.

She could clearly see that a spell was slowing time within the dragon hall. It was also obvious that she could see a change in him and knew the man she was now addressing was no longer High Laird Gethin ap Cadwallon: he was Gethin the dark mage.

'What's going on?' she demanded. 'What do you want from me?'

'Fucker,' spluttered the wyvern. 'Oily little fucker.'

If there had been a blade close to hand, Gethin might have decapitated the bloody thing. Instead, because he knew that such an action would only set the dragonmeister's resolve against him, he said, 'I only want one thing from you, my lovely. I want the dragonmeister's fealty.'

Hearing the dull, metallic clang of metal on metal they both glanced toward the battle between Owain and the abbot.

Lines of dark crimson trailed down Owain's chest from where the mace had struck. The injury, although ugly, did not seem to be greatly troubling him. It certainly wasn't slowing his mastery with the longsword as he deftly separated the abbot from the mace he had been wielding.

The abbot snatched a shield from the wall. It showed the silver-on-black arms of the Order of Dark Knights. Silver swords were crossed over a stone tower. The abbot cowered behind the shield's protection as Owain assailed him with an onslaught of hard and heavy blows.

The dragon handler grinned with manic glee as he delivered each downward swipe. His deliberate intention to kill seemed etched into his tight, menacing smile.

'You have to stop this,' Meghan insisted. 'I won't permit unnecessary bloodshed on Gatekeeper Island. It's forbidden by the dragon gods.'

He shrugged. 'That's not my battle going on down there, my lovely. I don't know what bug scurried up Owain's backside. And I agree that magicks have brought them both here. But those two are there and fighting because of some other mage on this island.'

'The abbot is Robert of Moon Valley,' the dragon-meister supplied in the drawn-out drawl of a woman still locked in a world of slowed time. 'He's not a mage.'

Gethin nodded when recognition came to him. He knew Robert of Moon Valley. He was Owain's former best friend and the best man from that doomed wedding.

Robert of Moon Valley was a dragon horn dealer, a man of low reputation and now he was pretending to be an abbot so he could command the monasteries of Gatekeeper Island. Robert of Moon Valley was clearly many things but the man was not a mage, which suggested there was still someone on the island that could thwart Gethin's plans.

'Why are they fighting?' Meghan asked.

He shrugged. 'I reckon Owain is fighting because he likes holding a sword in his hand. I'd always thought he was trying to compensate for something, although I can't see what.' As he said the words he cast a knowing glance at the considerable length that swayed between Owain's legs.

'You're a mage,' Meghan blurted. 'You could stop this.'

'I'm a mage but I can't interfere with the magicks of another mage,' he reminded her. 'Surely you know how magicks work?'

'You could do something.'

'I've slowed time.'

'That won't stop them killing each other. That just means it will take longer before they die.'

To Gethin's mind there was no difference between living longer and not dying immediately, but he was in no mood for arguing semantics. It was easier to address the first comment she had made. 'You're right to acknowledge that I'm a mage,' he said agreeably. 'But I'd rather hear you tell me that I'm a mage who you're going to obey.'

She bristled at the suggestion.

'I'm dragonmeister of Gatekeeper Island,' Meghan declared. 'I obey no man.'

Gethin's smile tightened.

'I could make you do my bidding like a puppet,' he explained. He examined his fingernails with a distracted air. 'You can see the way I'm controlling time in this banquet hall, can't you? Surely, if I can control time so easily, you can see how easy it would be for me to control you?'

She said nothing.

Her lips were pursed in a scowl of automatic refusal.

'But I don't need to use my magicks to make you do my bidding.'

'Really?' Her voice was a haughty challenge of defiance.

'I've brought *Y Ddraig Goch* to this island,' he began.

He could see she was about to interrupt. A part of him knew that she was about to tell him that a man who had embraced the power of the dark mage was a man who could never control dragons. The laws of the known universe forbade any single person being able to command dragons and being able to simultaneously work with magicks. The two abilities were as unable to coexist as night and day, sunshine and moonlight, or good and evil. But Gethin didn't need to hear the dragonmeister make those observations. He already knew about the immutable laws of their universe. That was why he was controlling the dragon handler and not the dragon.

'She's the last female *Y Ddraig Goch* in existence,' he said quickly. 'If you make me take her from this island, you've consigned that species to extinction.' He raised an eyebrow before asking, 'Do you want that on your conscience, dragonmeister? How does that sit with the island's rule that no one is permitted to harm a dragon? Do you want to be remembered as the dragonmeister that allowed the last of the red dragons to die without issue?'

It didn't look as though Meghan gave her response any consideration. Her acquiescence was so sudden it was almost comical. 'How do you want me to obey you?' she asked.

'Turn around and bend over,' Gethin demanded. 'I want to take you from behind whilst I watch this fight.'

She did not obey immediately. Instead, she curled one hand behind his neck and kissed him. After whispering the words, 'I'd hoped you would suggest something like this,' she turned and presented her backside to him as she bent at the waist.

The sight of her, exposed to him and ready to do whatever he wanted, was invigorating. The short length of the dragonmeister's tunic rose to reveal the inviting curves of her buttocks and the gaping split of her sex.

It was an intoxicating sight.

The dark curls that covered her sex were slick with

saliva from the redhead's constant kisses. The lips had curled back to reveal the dark pink flesh of her arousal. Gethin could smell the musky scent of her excitement as soon as she bent over. He considered the puckered ring of her rectum and then tensed the muscles of his groin to stop himself from being overcome by a rush of need for that particular deviance.

He placed himself behind her, resting one hand on her hip and gently coaxed her to glide back toward him.

Over the top of her bowed head he could watch the ongoing battle between Owain and Robert of Moon Valley. The fight continued to progress in a lethargy of slow motion that was amusing and also allowed him to savour every nuance of the confrontation.

Owain continued to slash blows downwards.

Robert continued to cower behind a raised shield.

A blonde rushed into the arena as fast as the slowed time would allow. Gethin assumed she was one of the temple maids and he figured she was calling for the pair to stop. She wore the red and gold kirtles that he had thought were the colours of the Blackheath women – although he conceded that he had never been particularly interested in female fashions. It annoyed him that he didn't immediately recognise her.

But, in truth, his attention was focused on sliding the head of his length back and forth over the gaping hole of the dragonmeister's sex. Whilst it was an intriguing development to watch the blonde try to intervene in the fight below, he was more concerned with the idea of enjoying the pleasures the dragonmeister could bestow on him.

From the corner of his eye Gethin watched Owain stay his sword arm.

Gethin didn't know if this was because the man feared accidentally injuring the blonde, or because he was trying to obey her request. Either way, Gethin could see it was an error of judgement on the part of the dragon handler.

Robert of Moon Valley took advantage of Owain's hesitation. He pushed the blonde aside with a brutal and uncaring thrust. She looked like she was trying to hold on to the abbot. Her grip snagged at something around his throat.

Robert of Moon Valley acted without consideration for such minor discomforts. With a surprising demonstration of skill, Robert slammed the shield into Owain's face. Then he disarmed his opponent by smashing the shield against Owain's sword arm.

Gethin was surprised.

He had expected Owain's victory to be almost certain. The man was a former commander of the Royal Guard. But now it looked as though the abbot might snatch a surprise triumph from the battle.

'You know how to entertain visitors,' Gethin told the dragonmeister.

He wrapped a fist around the thickness of his shaft and pressed the end over the centre of her sex. She was warm and slippery. He knew, when his length did slide into her, the pleasure would be enormous.

A part of him hoped that Owain and Robert could continue fighting with weapons. The idea of rutting with the dragonmeister whilst the two near-naked men wrestled together made him fear that his sexuality might be called into question. But, he reasoned, so long as he was enjoying himself, he didn't suppose it mattered how that pleasure looked to outsiders.

The dragonmeister pushed herself back against him.

As Gethin slid into the velvet warmth of her sex, he acknowledged that pleasures seldom came to be more satisfying. Her sex was tight and oily. The heat of her muscles radiated through him in a divine and delicious rush.

She moaned appreciatively as he filled her.

Gethin didn't know if the sound was borne from her genuine appreciation or if the sighs of approval were affectations the dragonmeister had picked up from associating with temple maids. It excited him to think that she was enjoying the sensation of having his shaft fill her hole. But he supposed he could enjoy himself with her whether she was having pleasure or not.

Determined to savour the experience, he pulled himself back and then pushed into her. Every movement caressed his length with a rush of delicious sensations. She was gripping him with a tightness that bordered on being uncomfortable. Her inner muscles sparkled with a frisson that tickled into him.

It was almost enough to distract him from the excitement of the fight.

'Is this all that you want from me?' she asked. Her voice was a seductive purr. He could feel each syllable trembling through his stiffness.

'I told you before what I want.'

She said nothing.

He continued to glide in and out of her wetness. The slurping sound of their union reverberated through his length.

'I want you to lead your dragons in an assault on the North Ridings. I want you to command your dragons and help me to rule the Ridings.'

'You ask too much,' she told him. 'I'm dragonmeister. I'm supposed to protect the Ridings. I'm not supposed to provide support to those who would command every shire.'

'I ask a lot,' he agreed. He had fallen into the rhythm of speaking to her as his length slipped to and fro inside her. He measured every breath so that he didn't give away his excitement. 'But I don't think I ask too much. If you do as I ask, you'll be the dragonmeister that maintained the lineage of *Y Ddraig Goch*. If you do as I ask you'll be revered as the dragonmeister who helped unite all three Ridings beneath the lordly rule of Gethin ap Cadwallon. Considering those benefits, do you really think that I ask too much?'

She sighed. 'I'll do as you command, dark mage.'

Gethin had ridden in and out of her three times before he realised she had agreed. He hesitated, unsettled by what sounded like too easy a submission. She was the dragonmeister of Gatekeeper Island. Surely she should be resisting his demands.

He paused from sliding into her, aware that her oily tight warmth was on the verge of wrenching the climax from his length. His hands clutched tight against her hips as he struggled to stave the satisfied eruption that yearned to pulse through his length. Lowering his face to the side of her head, whispering in her ear, he asked, 'Did you just agree to my demands?'

'I said, I'll do as you command, dark mage,' she said flatly.

Had she acquiesced? Or was he hearing hollow platitudes that would be forgotten and dismissed as soon as she had an alternative plan? It wasn't in his power to read her innermost thoughts. He was a powerful mage but there were some things beyond his limits of understanding.

'Do I have your word that you'll do my bidding?' he insisted.

The dragonmeister said nothing. Instead it was her wyvern that responded.

'Obey Gethin,' muttered the wyvern truculently. 'Save *Y Ddraig Goch*. Help Gethin rule the Ridings.'

On hearing the creature growl those words, Gethin knew that the dragonmeister was going to do everything he commanded of her. He continued to ride her with a quickened pace and renewed enthusiasm. Grinning, he turned his attention back to the battle between Owain the dragon handler and Robert of Moon Valley.

The fight still looked like it could go either way now that Owain had recovered his senses, but Gethin wondered where the blonde had gone.

He remembered who she was now. With the dragonmeister's acquiescence, Gethin had finally been able to put a name to the woman's face. The blonde had been Tavia the fair.

CHAPTER FOURTEEN

Tavia the Lover

Tavia realised she was in love.

She rushed out of the banquet hall, disconcerted by the effects of the slowed time she had encountered there. It had been obvious that something was amiss within the building but she hadn't been able to decide exactly what had been troubling her. All the colourful stone dragons on the walls had been unsettling. She had still not yet had a chance to overcome her fear of the beasts and the ones she had seen in there were chilling.

Equally unnerving had been the sight of Gethin ap Cadwallon, rutting with the scruffy dragonmeister. She recognised him as the man who had been pretending to be a dragon handler back in Blackheath. He was the man whom Alvar had battled aboard the birlinn as they travelled across the Last Sea. And now he was revealed in his true form as a brooding and powerful dark mage.

His eyes shone with the giveaway crimson light of a dark magician.

Tavia had been aware that there was a very real danger of being harmed as she threw herself between Owain and Robert. The abbot was fighting for his life and Owain was clearly a proficient warrior.

But Alvar had assured her she was in no danger. Alvar had promised she would not suffer any harm or injury and, as always, he had been absolutely right. That was one of the many reasons why Tavia had decided she loved him.

'You damned genius,' Alvar muttered as she hurried toward him.

Tavia laughed as she rushed out of the dragon hall and into the day's fading sunset. The abbot's skeleton key trailed from her hand. She threw herself into Alvar's arms and they embraced. It was an embrace as powerful as the one they had shared in the northern catacombs beneath the monastery half an hour earlier.

Robert of Moon Valley had thrown her into the shadows, leaving Tavia to roam scared and frightened in the impenetrable darkness. She had been terrified that she would never again see daylight. But before the panic became insurmountable, Alvar of Erland had crept out of the shadows to save her. She had wondered at that moment if it might be love she felt for him.

As he clutched her in the darkness she said, 'I thought you were imprisoned in one of the dungeons.'

'I was meant to be imprisoned,' he admitted. In the dark shadows surrounding him she had heard the snap of a card being drawn from the deck he held. There was the soft lilt of his characteristic chuckle as he added, 'But I had a bet with the hostler guarding my gaol cell. He lost.'

'Did you cheat?' she asked.

'I won,' he replied. 'Isn't that what matters?'

She had wanted to argue that cheating was immoral and winning wasn't everything. But she knew that without his cheating he would not have been able to save her from a fate of scrabbling blindly through the darkness in the northern catacombs. Under those circumstances it would have sounded petty to prattle on about the morality of escaping from unjust imprisonment by cheating.

'Thank you for saving me,' she told him.

In the catacombs, he had kissed her. She could taste the fire wine on his breath. It was a rich and intoxicating flavour. Tavia supposed it should have been nauseating but, because it was so much a part of Alvar, she found it strangely warming. It was a part of the man she found more desirable than any other man she had ever known.

He gave her kirtles to wear, seeming to have known that she would be in need of clothes to protect her modesty. Tavia thought it was surprising that he had the garments but, whenever her thoughts dared to doubt Alvar's abilities, she heard the snap of a card being drawn from the top of the deck and realised she knew how his foresight had been built.

Hurriedly, she shrugged the kirtles over her bare body.

'Let's be heroes and save the day,' Alvar suggested.

He would elaborate no further except to say, when they had escaped the catacombs, Tavia was to hurry into the dragon hall and embrace Robert of Moon Valley.

She shrank from the suggestion.

'What's wrong?' he asked.

'Robert of Moon Valley is the man who tried to consign me to the darkness of the catacombs,' she reminded Alvar. 'I have no desire to embrace him.'

He shrugged. He snapped another card and then sighed. 'It needs to be done.' He snapped a further card and added, 'Do this small favour for me, and there will be time enough for us to thank each other after you've been heroic and embraced the damned bastard.'

Tavia couldn't understand how embracing Robert of Moon Valley could be construed as being an act of heroism. But there had been a lewd implication in Alvar's tone. She could see the same devilish glint shining in his eye when he eventually led her to the stairway that would take them upwards to the monastery above. And, although she didn't want to embrace Robert of Moon Valley, Tavia knew that her real reluctance to enter the dragon hall was because of the building's name. She still had a deep mistrust of dragons.

Alvar seemed oblivious to her unease.

His fingers, she noticed, were following the thread that Caitrin had laid in the catacombs. It occurred to her that he had known that she would leave this thread to guide their safe passage. It was amazing to think that his abilities as a seer had given him the foresight to know that this thread would be needed whilst they were still aboard the birlinn.

But Tavia was less concerned about how Alvar had helped them navigate the darkness and more eager to know how she could properly thank him for rescuing her from a fate of blundering through dark corridors for eternity.

She pressed herself against him and tried to steal another kiss.

'Later,' he promised. He clutched her in a tight embrace and squeezed one buttock with an urgency that threatened to contradict his words. 'Go to the dragon hall, embrace the abbot, and then meet me outside the building.'

'What will you be doing?'

He took her outside the monastery before responding and glanced toward the hulking ruins of the crumbling stables that stood beside the main building. Tavia noticed a dark-red dragon sat atop the stables glowering down at them. If not for the fact that it was bright red, and its barbed tongue occasionally slipped over its stern reptilian lips, it could have been a gargoyle or a piece of decorative stone.

She swallowed and stepped nervously backwards.

Alvar didn't seem to be looking at the creature. His attention was focused on the doorway that led into the ruined stables. Inside she could see the shape of a large cage covered with what looked like a green and white flag. She suspected it was the same green and white flag that had covered the cage containing *Y Ddraig Goch.*

'I'll follow you,' he said. 'And then you can thank me for saving your life.'

At the time, she had not believed she was acting with any heroism. At the time, Tavia had only done as Alvar asked because it meant she was escaping from the foreboding presence of the huge, red dragon that glowered down at them.

Now, Tavia could see, Alvar had stayed true to his word. He had followed her. He had also dragged the cage from the stables and was panting from the exertion.

Tavia tried to hand him the key she had taken from Robert of Moon Valley.

For some reason she had known exactly what she needed to do when she embraced the abbot. Her fingers had automatically encircled his neck. Her thumb had twined itself – almost accidentally – around the strip of leather he wore. When Robert of Moon Valley pushed her away, Tavia had found herself clutching the abbot's precious skeleton key.

It was, she remembered, a key that seemed to open everything.

Alvar shook his head. He pulled the green and white flag from the cage to reveal the red dragon caged within.

Tavia took a wary step back.

'This is *Y Ddraig Goch*,' Alvar explained. 'You're going to be the one who kindly releases the beast from this damned cruel captivity.'

She hesitated. 'Didn't I see this dragon sitting atop the stables?'

He shook his head. 'There's a male on the island. He's been hanging around her cage trying to rescue her since we landed, but apparently this cage is quite secure.' He frowned as he added, 'The likelihood is that it was sealed by the power of a dark mage.' Nodding at the dragon in the cage he said, 'This is the last surviving female and she'll be forever in your debt if you release her from her unjust imprisonment.'

As though agreeing with his words, the dragon cawed loudly.

Tavia swallowed down her nervousness. If Alvar said this was something she should do, then she knew it would be sensible to do as he asked. But fear of the dragon made her hesitate.

She offered Alvar the key and said, 'You should unlock the cage.'

He shook his head.

'The cage has been constructed by a dark mage. More specifically it's a dark mage who guards against me. The lock of this cage is charmed to resist my attempts to open it.'

Tavia considered this. For the first time, she realised Alvar was talking without needing to consult his tarot. She could sense that he urgently needed her to unlock the cage but still the idea of going so close to the dragon made her hesitate.

'Why does Gethin guard against you?'

'Because I'm the rightful heir to the West Ridings,' Alvar admitted. 'Gethin stole my title and my heritage. Gethin had me imprisoned under sentence of death. And Gethin believes, if I ever get a chance to get revenge, no powers of dark wizardry will be of use to him.'

'Are you still bent on revenge?' she asked.

Alvar considered this for a moment. 'All I want right now is to build a dragon horn empire with you. Even if the chance to rule the West Ridings was handed to me, I'd refuse the offer. You, Tavia the fair, are all I've ever wanted.'

It was as much as Tavia needed to hear. She put her fears of the dragon to one side and fumbled to slide the clumsy key into the lock of the cage. At first she didn't think it was going to fit. The key she had taken from Robert of Moon Valley seemed much too large for the small lock that secured the dragon's cage. But, after a moment's jamming the end against the hole, the magicks that controlled the key allowed it to slip inside and force the tumblers into acquiescence.

She pulled the door open.

The dragon stayed inside the cage, staring at her with large onyx eyes.

Tavia waited patiently for a moment. Nothing happened. She wondered if the creature was likely to charge at her, breathing flames and chomping at her with gnashing jaws. The idea was horrifying and she pushed it from her thoughts before it could make her tremble with unease.

Alvar took her hand. 'Thank you, Tavia the fair.'

'She's not coming out,' Tavia protested.

'She will,' he said softly. 'She'll come out in her own time.'

'What do we do until then?' she asked.

Alvar snapped a card from his deck. He grinned. 'The cards say you're going to thank me.'

She wanted to scowl at him. She wanted to tell him that the cards said no such thing. She wanted to remind him that there were dark magicks occurring within the walls of the dragon hall which needed addressing. But there was something about the shine in his eyes that made it impossible to dismiss his suggestion.

'Where am I going to thank you?' she asked.

'Here.'

'With the dragon watching?'

As though she had heard and understood Tavia's objection the dragon turned its head and waddled around inside the cage so it was no longer facing the couple. It flicked its barbed tail dismissively.

Alvar pulled Tavia close and kissed her.

She savoured the bristling caress of his beard against her face. It tickled and scratched, but that only served to remind her that she was being kissed by him.

'I do owe you my life,' she admitted between kisses.

He shrugged. 'You saved me from the gaol. I saved you from the catacombs. I think this means we're even.'

She shook her head. She was about to protest when he placed an arm around her waist and one behind her back and then lowered her to the floor.

Tavia made no attempt to refuse him. It was easier to simply melt in his arms and allow him to take the lead. Lying with her back on a carpet of well-trampled grass outside the entrance way to the dragon hall, Tavia was happy to let Alvar use her in any way that promised to give him satisfaction. Knowing he was a competent lover, she felt sure he would do all that was needed to make sure she enjoyed the experience.

His fingers had fallen to her crotch.

She had no idea that the kirtles he'd provided were split at the front but his hand found bare flesh. She parted her thighs to allow him easier access to her sex.

He chuckled softly.

The broad breadth of his fingertips smoothed against the silky folds of her sex. She raised her hips to meet him, expecting him to push his fingers between the sopping lips of her labia.

Instead of treating her to that pleasure, Alvar moved one finger over the rim of her anus.

Tavia held her breath.

He pushed one finger and then a second through the tight ring of muscle.

For an instant she was conflicted by the rush of pain and the spasm of pleasure. She stared at him, her eyes open as wide as the ring of muscle where his fingers now pressed, and she realised this was going to be enormously satisfying.

'Shouldn't we be saving those at risk inside the dragon hall?' she asked.

It was an insane question to ask at such a heightened moment of passion. But she didn't want him to think that she was selfish.

'We'll save them in good time,' he promised. 'Right now, we should be making time for this.'

The two fingers in her anus plunged deeper.

His thumb rubbed against the thrust of her clitoris then slipped inside the wanton split of her sex, it then came out lubricated, to smooth over the thrust of her clit again. The intensity of the pleasure was so sweet that, for an instant, Tavia could barely breathe.

She considered Alvar with unadorned adoration.

He kissed her again.

She fumbled to find his hardness. She had no doubt that he would be erect for her. His length pushed at the front of his hosen and weighed heavily against her palm when she found him.

Tavia squeezed her fist around the thick girth and was rewarded to feel him slide his fingers idly back and forth between the folds of her labia. She whimpered softly as she realised he was going to make this pleasure even more memorable than their previous encounters.

And then the thumb was back inside her.

'You're such a tease,' she complained. She could hear that the words were threaded with need. She bucked her pelvis up to meet his hand, allowing the lips of her sex to engulf him and swallow him.

Alvar shook his head.

'If I was a tease,' he countered, 'I'd do something cruel like this.'

His face lowered to her breast.

She hadn't even noticed that he'd unfastened the chest of her kirtles. His mouth circled the tip of one breast and he suckled against her nipple.

Tavia groaned.

His fingers were gliding back and forth with increased pace – filling her rear and then leaving her to feel empty. His thumb repeatedly pressed at the throbbing bulb of her clitoris, squashing it hard against the bone of her pelvis. When he released his punishing pressure on that greedy bead of flesh, he slid his fat thumb between the warm, wet and welcoming lips of her sex.

'Take me,' she pleaded. 'I want to feel you inside me when I come.'

'Come,' he countered. 'Now we're in a monogamous relationship I want to watch you come before I rut with you.'

She worked her mouth soundlessly.

For an instant she wasn't sure how to respond. She couldn't recall agreeing to enter a monogamous relationship with Alvar. She wasn't even sure when they had begun to have a relationship other than the occasional fumble as part of their mutual quest to liberate dragon horn from Gatekeeper Island. But Alvar clearly thought they were in some sort of exclusive relationship and she wondered how he was likely to react if he knew what she'd done with Robert of Moon Valley.

She had rutted with the abbot to ensure that he provided her and her sister with a supply of dragon horn. Even now, although she currently despised Robert of Moon Valley for trying to kill her, Tavia knew she would rut with him again if he offered her a taste of dragon horn in return. She would rut with the man repeatedly if it meant securing a constant supply of the aphrodisiac.

'Monogamous,' she repeated. 'Are we really monogamous?'

Alvar's chuckle should have been reassuring.

'I've seen the cards,' he explained. When he spoke the tremor of every syllable bristled through the tips of his fingers. She could feel the sensations vibrating against the inner muscles of her sex. 'Neither of us will ever have sex with anyone else. We'll always be exclusive.'

'Since when?' she asked carefully.

She strained to ignore the pleasurable responses he was igniting through her breasts and loins. It crossed her mind, if he said that this understanding had been in place since they first met, then such a declaration would cast serious doubts over her belief in his abilities as a seer.

'Since when?' she repeated.

'What does it matter since when?' he asked. 'Isn't it enough that I've seen the future and know that neither of us shall ever go with anyone else?'

She thought about this and opened her mouth to respond.

Alvar picked that moment to slip a third finger into her rectum.

The muscle, already overstretched, screamed from the sensation. When she climbed down from the rush of unexpected satisfaction she had almost forgotten what she was going to say.

'Are you sure the cards are telling you we'll be exclusive?' she insisted. 'If they say we're never going to go with anyone else, could that not mean one of us is going to die?'

He frowned. 'Quit with the sexy talk,' he said darkly. 'I don't think I can hold myself from orgasm if you keep putting forward such sexy ideas as my impending death.'

She scowled and caught the glimpse of his grin in response.

It was enough to tell her, whatever the future held for her and regardless of how long or short that future might be, she would be wise to spend as many moments as possible in the companionship of Alvar.

Tavia gripped his length tighter and guided it to her sex.

She nudged his thumb away from her hole as she placed the erection over her labia. And she gripped the muscles of her rectum tight around his fingers as he slid his shaft into the sopping centre of her sex.

It was the most satisfying sensation she had yet experienced.

Her rear was filled by the breadth of his three fingers. Her sex was spread by the thickness of his erection. The rush of satisfaction began as soon as he slipped into her. It culminated in a delicious wet explosion as soon as the scrub of his pubic curls scratched against the downy thatch of her own.

'When we're off this island,' he whispered, 'We're going to spend a year in bed drinking a cask of dragon horn each day.'

She whimpered.

It sounded like heaven. And, when he spoke, she could feel every word trembling through the sturdy length of his erection.

'When we're off this island, I'm going to satisfy you every morning, noon and evening from now until eternity.'

She nodded agreement. It was exactly what she wanted. And she didn't dare speak in response because she knew any sound she dared to make would force her to lose control and she would be screaming through another climax.

'When we're off this island,' he continued. 'We're going to take our relationship to new levels every day.'

The idea made her groan.

He was already rutting with her in the open air whilst he had three fingers buried into the tight muscle of her anus. How much further could they go to reach a new level? She wasn't sure what other boundaries they could stretch but she looked forward to smashing them all in Alvar's company.

That thought was enough to make her inner muscles clench and convulse with satisfaction.

And, as that pleasure rippled through her body, she felt her sex tear the climax from him. Alvar's hardness stiffened and then shivered. His shaft exploded with a wet and burning rush of ejaculate. The pleasure of her orgasm grew momentarily brighter. And then she was basking in the liquid rush of having his body pressed against hers.

She didn't feel him slide the fingers from her rear. She didn't even feel his spent erection slipping from the lips of her sex. She simply noticed that he was pressing a kiss against her throat and murmuring the words, 'Thank you,' with a surprising blend of tenderness and sincerity.

Her heart beat faster.

He pulled himself from her embrace and tucked his sticky, spent length back into his hosen. Climbing to his feet he grinned down at her and passed her a wink. 'The cards told me we'd just have time to do that before I performed the day's final act of heroism.'

She frowned, puzzled and unsure what he meant by the day's final act of heroism. Whatever it might be, she felt sure Alvar was the right person to perform an act of heroism because the man was an ideal hero. She felt sure of that fact because she now knew the emotion she felt for him had to be called love.

Alvar bent beside the unlocked cage.

The dragon still had its rear to them.

He reached inside and stroked the red flesh of the bristling beast within.

'*Cer i achub y triniwr dreigiau, Owain*,' he murmured.

The dragon lifted its head, as though understanding the words. It glanced briefly in Tavia's direction and then cawed before glancing back at Alvar.

Alvar nodded at the dragon as though showing agreement. '*Cer hedfana ac achub, Owain*,' he said gravely. The dragon crept warily out of the cage and then regarded its situation. '*Cer i achub y triniwr dreigiau, Owain*,' prompted Alvar.

With that final command, the red dragon took to the air.

Alvar extended a hand to Tavia to help her from the floor. 'Would you care to join me?'

'Where are we going?'

'Now that we've saved the day inside the dragon hall, I figured we'd take your skeleton key and go down to the catacombs to start liberating some casks of dragon horn.'

She hesitated.

'What are we going to do with the dragon horn once we've taken it out of Robert's cell?'

Alvar retrieved the tarot cards from his pocket. He snapped one to the top and studied it for a moment. Then he glanced up toward the dock on the horizon. A birlinn rested there, its black sails decorated with the silver arms of crossed swords over a castle tower. 'We'll put our first haul aboard that birlinn,' he explained. 'And then we'll go back for more.'

Tavia allowed him to help her from the floor. She had decided she would be happy to do whatever Alvar of Erland wanted. And if that meant they would spend their days dealing in dragon horn, it was a future that she could happily enjoy.

Alvar pushed Tavia to the wall just in time to stop her from being knocked over by the two figures that were hurrying into the dragon hall. She recognised them from behind as Nihal and her sister Caitrin the dark.

CHAPTER FIFTEEN

Inghean the Heartbroken

Inghean did not want the moment to end.

Gethin ap Cadwallon, his need for the dragonmeister sated, had gone off to pleasure himself with the temple maids. The three women now seemed oblivious to the torturous fight being acted out for their pleasure. They only seemed intent on servicing Gethin ap Cadwallon.

Owain and Robert of Moon Valley continued to fight. They exchanged lethargic blows and grunted with lazy industry. If Inghean had given the matter any thought she would have expected Owain to easily defeat Robert of Moon Valley.

But Inghean was lost in the arms of Meghan the dragonmeister. She was lost in the woman's arms and she wanted to remain there.

It helped that time had slowed to a crawl.

Inghean could kiss the dark curls from the brow of the

dragonmeister and savour the salty taste of the woman's perspiration. She had slipped two fingers into the wetness of the dragonmeister's sex and the woman responded with a similarly intimate embrace.

Their bare chests were pressed together, nipples sparking against one another like flints scratching stone. The frisson of skin touching skin kindled all manner of blazing needs in Inghean's loins. The sensations made the dragonmeister moan her name with obvious, blatant lust.

Inghean wanted to push the woman back into her golden throne and then devour the musky essence of her sex. She wanted to drink from the lips between the woman's thighs and bask in the heady honeyed perfume of her most intimate treasures.

But the dragonmeister clearly had other plans for this encounter.

Crawling onto the floor, she pushed Inghean back and then smothered her face with tiny kisses. She moved like a drunk, although Inghean did not think the woman's apparent stupor was caused by alcohol.

The fingers inside her sex squirmed against the overly sensitive inner muscles. Inghean basked in the sensation of thrill after thrill being fed into her hole. She sighed happily as the rush of pleasures became even more and more fulfilling.

Meghan's tongue was pressed against her sex.

Inghean could feel the warm, wet, slippery muscle

pressing against her flesh. The heated breath and eager movement of her tongue made for a debilitating combination.

Inghean bit her lower lip and suppressed a groan of absolute contentment.

The journey to Gatekeeper Island had not been an easy one. The travel across the Last Sea had left her drained to the point of exhaustion. The journey had meant leaving her home behind and putting her beloved husband out of her thoughts. But it had all been worth it for the chance to pleasure Meghan and for the benefits of being pleasured in return.

The dragonmeister's tongue lapped at her sex as the woman's stubby fingers slid in and out of Inghean's wetness.

In the background, Inghean could hear the sounds of Owain and Robert striking blows at each other as their never-ending battle continued. She cast a disinterested glance in their direction and watched as Robert unexpectedly pushed Owain backward.

He stumbled.

As he toppled to the floor he lost his hold on his sword. It clattered loudly and Robert pounced on the weapon.

Inghean blinked with surprise. She had not expected Robert of Moon Valley to gain the upper hand in the confrontation. If anything, she had thought Owain would run him through before the man had a chance to properly arm himself.

She considered shouting out, tempted to call encouragement to Owain.

But Meghan chose that moment to slip her fingers deeper, squeeze another rush of pleasure through Inghean's exhausted sex-muscles, and the idea of doing anything that didn't involve pleasure with the woman was driven from Inghean's mind.

'Stay with me,' Meghan whispered. 'Stay with me and we can do this every night for the rest of forever.'

'I want that,' Inghean agreed.

'And you want this,' Meghan told her.

The dragonmeister changed positions, pushing her crotch over Inghean's face and burying her head between Inghean's spread thighs. Her fingers remained deep inside Inghean's hole. She rubbed them slowly back and forth whilst her tongue danced a lazy tune against the raging pulse of Inghean's clitoris.

But it wasn't just the pleasure of having the dragonmeister devour her sex.

Inghean was amazed by the pleasure she got from nuzzling at the woman. The short dark scrub of Meghan's sex was a divine fragrance that she found delicious and enriching.

Placing her hands on the well-muscled thighs of the woman's legs, holding her open as she pushed her nose against the centre of her sex and drank, Inghean did not think she could be in a more beautiful place.

'I want to stay here forever,' Inghean sighed.

'And I want you to be my – Nihal?'

Inghean frowned, wondering why the dragonmeister hadn't finished her sentence and why she was calling her by someone else's name. She glanced up and saw Meghan staring toward the entrance way of the dragon hall.

As Inghean watched, her sister and Nihal rushed through the doorway.

'You have to save him,' Caitrin told the mage. 'You have to.'

'Yes,' Nihal said stiffly. 'It would be unfortunate if anything fatal happened to Owain, wouldn't it?'

Even from the other side of the dragon hall, Inghean could hear the note of scathing sarcasm in the mage's tone. Caitrin was either oblivious to the sound or too wrapped up with her concern for Owain. She simply clutched at Nihal's arm and insisted that the magicks should be performed.

As cruel as it sounded, Inghean thought Owain looked in need of the help.

He had taken a bad fall and Robert of Moon Valley now stood above him ready to deliver a death blow. Even though time was stretched out to a crawl around them, Inghean did not think Owain had much longer than a few seconds remaining.

'Please,' Caitrin begged. 'Nihal. You have to intervene. You have to save him. I'll be yours for all eternity if you'll just intervene and save him.'

Inghean watched intently, desperate to know how the mage would respond. A hand clutched hers and she understood that Meghan was watching with an equal vested interest.

'Save him,' Inghean muttered.

Meghan squeezed her fingers tighter. 'Nihal?' she whispered. The wyvern fluttered to her shoulder and cawed, 'Lover?'

'*Transportum*,' called Nihal.

A line of sparkling silver light erupted from the tip of the mage's wand. It flashed against Owain's brow and then shot across the hall to touch Gethin's face. Inghean glanced from one to the other and realised that Owain and Gethin had swapped places.

The dragon handler now stood with the temple maids. The three women caressed him for a moment before realising he was not the man they had been embracing a moment earlier. Realisation came in the same moment as all three women stepped back in surprise.

Gethin ap Cadwallon lay beneath the death blow being threatened by Robert of Moon Valley. He stared up, blinking in surprise. His expression seemed remarkably accepting of the fact that he had been apparated. He acted with the speed of a dark mage unaffected by the slowed passage of time that held everyone else in the dragon hall.

'Nihal?' muttered the dragonmeister. 'Is that you?'

The mage glanced toward Meghan.

It was only a cursory glance but in that expression Inghean could see that the pair had a history. She didn't know what had gone on between Nihal and the dragonmeister but it was obviously something serious because Meghan was frowning and suddenly furious.

Inghean could see a pout of delight, despair and a flash of animosity.

The wyvern on Meghan's shoulder jumped free and flew to Inghean's arm. As it settled, Inghean was treated to a series of images that she knew had come directly from the dragonmeister's memory.

In the blink of an eye Inghean could picture Meghan and Nihal naked together, locked in a passionate embrace and both sighing with extremes of ecstasy.

'Lover?' croaked the wyvern.

Meghan and Nihal were kissing in the memory. Inghean got the impression that the pair had been lovers when they both lived at the southernmost borders of the North Ridings. Nihal was a young trainee mage; Meghan was a young trainee dragon handler. And, whilst representatives of those two vocations seldom saw eye-to-eye, this pair were clearly working hard to defy that convention.

Nihal's face was buried between Meghan's thighs. The trainee mage licked and lapped and devoured until Meghan exploded in a wet cry of euphoria.

The couple were outdoors and rolling naked in dewy spring grass that hugged their bare flesh. Meghan kissed Nihal, panting with satisfaction and clearly eager to take things further.

'Come back to the Bedgerid with me,' Meghan urged. 'Dragons give off this aura and when you pet them or stroke them it intensifies ...'

Her voice trailed off.

Nihal was frowning. 'No,' said Nihal. 'I'm a trainee mage. I can't be influenced by the aura from a dragon.'

'But,' Meghan began. She got no further.

'If you loved me, you'd give up your dragons,' Nihal said sharply.

'And if you loved me you'd give up your magicks,' Meghan responded with equal bitterness.

'Does that mean we don't love each other?' Nihal asked.

Meghan glared at the mage. 'It means I won't be seeing you again.'

With those words, the memory ended.

'Lover?' croaked the wyvern.

Inghean felt the air flow from her lungs as she sighed unhappily. Her stomach had folded into a knot of disquiet as she experienced Meghan's memory. Meghan and Nihal had been lovers and the parting had been painful. And Inghean knew, whatever Meghan now felt for her, it was not an emotion that had the intensity the dragonmeister had once had for Nihal.

'Fuck,' muttered the mage.

'Fuck,' agreed Meghan sadly.

Inghean said nothing, sure that the couple had said as much as needed to be spoken.

She glanced toward the battle that was now taking place between Robert and Gethin, fearful that the abbot might have accidentally struck a death blow. She did not care for Gethin ap Cadwallon but, whether he was a high laird or a dark mage, she did not think he deserved to die in a confused battle.

But it seemed that Gethin ap Cadwallon was going to triumph. Working within a different flow of time, moving with deceptive swiftness, Gethin had avoided Robert's death blow and started to attack the abbot. Admittedly, Robert was wielding a longsword but Gethin had the advantage of inhuman speed and blatant ruthlessness.

Inghean opened her mouth to scream a protest.

A red dragon flew into the hall.

The creature screeched. It spat a stream of flame into the room that instantly scorched the air. The dragon's cry was a loud and toneless call that sat flat against the walls. It swooped down, talons extended, and wrenched Gethin from the floor.

Robert's blade glanced against the creature's bared breast.

The creature cawed. The cry was a sound borne from momentary pain. But the injury must only have been small because the beast was lifting a struggling Gethin into the air and dragging him out through one of the higher windows.

Inghean swallowed as she realised the dragon was taking him to the easternmost catacombs. Goosebumps rippled over her bare flesh.

'Hostlers,' called Meghan.

Inghean had thought the world seemed to be moving slowly before. Now that Gethin ap Cadwallon was gone the speed of events around them seemed to have returned to its normal pace.

Caitrin had rushed to embrace Owain. She knelt by his side, smoothing concerned fingers through his hair and frowning with obvious worry. She told him that everything was going to be alright and she promised that they would remain together forever.

Nihal remained standing in the doorway of the dragon hall. The mage scowled toward Meghan.

And Meghan shouted for her hostlers.

'What's happened to Gethin?' Inghean asked.

Meghan studied her carefully. 'He was taken by the dragon. Didn't you see that?' She turned away and shouted again for her hostlers.

'I saw that he was taken by the dragon,' Inghean agreed. 'But what's happened to him? Is he safe?'

'I don't know what's happened to him,' Meghan admitted. 'But I know it will be for the best of the

Ridings if the dragons have killed him. He was going to start a war.' She called again for the hostlers and this time four of the men came rushing into the dragon hall.

'Robert of Moon Valley has injured one of our stock,' Meghan told the men. 'You know what to do with him. You know the penalties on Gatekeeper Island for anyone who injures a dragon.'

As Inghean watched, the hostlers began to grab at Robert.

He protested. He argued that the dragon had been injured by accident. He even tried to fight with one of the hostlers but it was all to no avail.

They disarmed him and knocked him unconscious and then hauled him out of the dragon hall.

'Where will they take him?' Inghean asked.

'We have a prison.' She spoke without looking at Inghean. Her gaze was locked on the mage. 'I'll make a decision on his fate in the days to come.'

Inghean nodded.

She watched Owain and Caitrin. The couple were kissing like reunited lovers at the end of a romance play. Inghean stared at them with jealous dismay. She slowly became aware that Nihal was watching the pair. Seeing the pained expression on Nihal's face, Inghean understood that Caitrin would not be held to her promise to remain with the mage for eternity.

'What are you doing on my island?' Meghan asked Nihal. 'I thought we'd agreed never to see one another ever again?'

Nihal continued to stare at Owain and Caitrin. 'I discovered Gethin was a dark mage after the birlinn left,' the mage explained. 'I came here to try and –'

The dragonmeister shook her head, cutting the mage off mid-sentence. 'You've been forbidden from visiting Gatekeeper Island.'

'These were exceptional circumstances.'

Meghan turned away and scowled.

Inghean could not recall ever desiring a person more than she wanted Meghan in that moment. The woman looked strong and vibrant and seemed to personify control. And Inghean also knew, in that moment, Meghan had no interest in her at all.

'Do you want me to leave?' Nihal asked.

'No,' Meghan said. 'I want you to rectify all my problems. Isn't that what a mage is supposed to do? You have the power of your all-important dark magicks, don't you?'

The haughty tone to her voice was a challenge.

'How can I rectify your problems?' Nihal asked stiffly.

'Cast a shape-changer spell on Owain,' she said quickly. 'Do that and he and Caitrin can return to the West Ridings in place of Gethin.'

Inghean saw that the words were like a slap across Nihal's face.

Grudgingly, the mage nodded. 'I can do that. That would be good for the kingdom. Anything else?'

'Cast a restoration spell so that the damage done to this hall is rectified.'

'Is that all?'

'I think that will be enough,' Meghan said dismissively.

'And what will you be doing?' asked the mage.

Meghan turned to Inghean and extended a hand. 'I'll be saying farewell to my lovely guest from Blackheath.'

'Farewell?' Inghean could not stop the surprise from colouring her voice.

Meghan nodded. 'I'm dragonmeister. I'm not allowed the pleasures of a permanent relationship whilst I'm in charge of the livestock on Gatekeeper Island.'

Inghean frowned but nodded, ready to accept this rule.

'I'm not allowed a permanent relationship,' Meghan said as she took Inghean's hand. 'But I guess you and I could stay together until your husband returns to Blackheath.'

The words made Inghean brighten until she felt the mage place a hand on her arm. She stared into the pained and solemn hurt of Nihal's bright almond eyes and had a premonition of what was going to come.

'My apologies, Lady Inghean of Blackheath,' the mage began.

Inghean closed her eyes against the threat of tears.

'Your husband's ship returned the night before I set off here,' Nihal explained. 'Captain Clement of the Blackheath Cavalry requests that you return home at your earliest convenience.'

Meghan's fingers tightened around Inghean's hand. The gesture implied security and compassion and understanding. 'She will return,' Meghan said. 'But I'm sure Inghean and I can have at least one more night before this has to end.

Epilogue

Inghean stood on the dock of Gatekeeper Island, watching the two birlinns depart. They looked to be travelling side-by-side but she knew they were headed for different destinations. The birlinn bearing a sail that showed the arms of the Order of the Dark Knights – crossed swords over a castle tower, picked out in silver on black – was taking Alvar and Tavia back to Blackheath. The birlinn sailing beneath the flag of *Y Ddraig Goch* was headed for the West Ridings.

Aboard each boat, Inghean could see a sister waving farewell to her. Tavia the fair stood aboard the vessel heading back to Blackheath. Caitrin the dark stood aboard the birlinn travelling to the West Ridings.

'I trust your sisters know they will be welcome at Gatekeeper Island whenever they choose to return?' the dragonmeister asked gently.

Inghean nodded.

She suspected it would be difficult to keep a dragon

lover like Owain away from Gatekeeper Island, and she didn't think Caitrin would want to let her new husband alone on Gatekeeper Island with someone as sexually voracious as the dragonmeister.

That was one couple who would almost certainly return.

The same could be said for Tavia and Alvar. Their birlinn sat heavier in the water than its sister vessel. Inghean didn't know how many casks of dragon horn they had loaded into the hold but she figured it was enough to weigh the birlinn deeper in the tide. Her sister and the seer would undoubtedly be able to build their own empire on sales of the legendary elixir now they had a source. And Inghean figured they would constantly return to Gatekeeper Island to update their supplies.

'I'm sure my sisters know you'd welcome them.'

Inghean wanted to ask the dragonmeister if she too would always be welcome on the island. For some reason the words refused to pass her lips.

She glanced at Nihal and realised the mage seemed inordinately distracted by the placement of the sun and the honking of the black-legged kittiwakes above. Occasionally the mage glanced to the roof of the dragon hall where the two red dragons perched and nuzzled one another.

'The mage will take you home via the tunnel beneath the Last Sea.' Meghan spoke as she stared out to the horizon and the towers of Blackheath. It seemed to Inghean that the woman could no longer bare to look at her. 'I know you didn't enjoy the sea travel before,' Meghan explained. 'I figured the tunnel might be better for your disposition.'

'I wish I could stay,' Inghean said quietly.

'You have duties at home.'

'That doesn't stop me from wishing for things,' Inghean insisted.

'No,' Meghan agreed. She cast a sour glance at Nihal and added, 'If only there was someone at Blackheath capable of granting wishes.' She looked set to say more and then stopped herself. A sly smile crept across her lips. 'Would you care to share a drink before you have to leave?'

'That would be pleasant,' Inghean admitted. 'I'd love that.'

Meghan turned to Nihal and said, 'You should start travelling through the tunnel on your way back to Blackheath. I'll send Inghean along after we've had a quick drink together.'

'I can wait for her,' Nihal insisted.

'No need,' Meghan said shaking her head. She took hold of Inghean's hand and squeezed. 'There's no need to wait for her at all.'

On Meghan's shoulder, her pet wyvern cawed cheerfully: 'Dragon horn.'

www.ingramcontent.com/pod-product-compliance
Ingram Content Group UK Ltd.
Pitfield, Milton Keynes, MK11 3LW, UK
UKHW022304180325
456436UK00003B/201

9 780007 553280